Bulletproof

a *Songbird* novel

MELISSA PEARL

ISBN: 1503161846
ISBN-13: 978-1503161849

NOTE FROM THE AUTHOR

I love to dance. As a child I never had the confidence to pursue it, and I will always regret that. There's nothing cooler than getting lost in a song, letting your limbs do the talking for you. I love feeling that beat move through my body.

Bulletproof is filled with music you can dance to. The playlist is a treasure trove of songs that get my hips moving. I love every song in this book, and I hope you can enjoy listening to the playlist as much as I do.

Have fun taking this journey with Morgan and Sean. They have some tough issues to deal with, but I love their romance...and, of course, I love the music

BULLETPROOF SOUNDTRACK

(Please note: The songs listed below are not always the original versions, but the ones I chose to listen to while constructing this book. The songs are listed in the order they appear.)

WE ARE NEVER GETTING BACK TOGETHER

SHAKE IT OFF

Performed by Taylor Swift

WE FOUND LOVE

Performed by Rihanna & Calvin Harris

CLARITY

Performed by Zedd & Foxes

DON'T STOP THE MUSIC

Performed by Rihanna

MMM YEAH

Performed by Austin Mahone & Pitbull

LADY MARMALADE

Performed by Christina Aguilera, Lil' Kim, Mýa & Pink

BULLETPROOF

Performed by La Roux

I GOTTA FEELING

Performed by Black Eyed Peas

GIVE ME EVERYTHING

Performed by Pitbull, Ne-Yo & Afrojack Nayer

ME & U

Performed by Cassie

TIK TOK

Performed by Ke$ha

FOREVER AIN'T ENOUGH

Performed by J. Holiday

GOT ME GOOD

Performed by Cody Simpson

BULLETPROOF

HALO

Performed by Beyoncé

ALL OF ME

Performed by John Legend

EVERY TIME I CLOSE MY EYES

Performed by Babyface

BURN

Performed by Usher

BREAK FREE

Performed by Ariana Grande & Zedd

RED

Performed by Taylor Swift

NOW YOU'RE GONE

Performed by Basshunter

WISH U WERE HERE

Performed by Cody Simpson

COME AWAY WITH ME

Performed by Norah Jones

TITANIUM

Performed by David Guetta & Sia

FIGHT FOR YOU

Performed by Jason Derulo

READY OR NOT

Performed by Britt Nicole & Lecrae

IS IT YOU

Performed by Cassie

ANGELIA

Performed by Richard Marx

For Taylor Swift -

A woman who writes in vibrant colors and sings the most amazing love stories.

Thanks for inspiring me with your music.

PROLOGUE

MORGAN

I cringed, scrunching my nose as the bald guy in the plaid shirt tried to negotiate the high note on "Wind Beneath My Wings". My shoulders were bunched tight as he came to the end, and all I could hope was that the guy would step away from the mic and let someone else have a turn.

He raised his arm with a final flourish, and the only sound in the karaoke bar was the enthusiastic clapping of his adoring wife.

"Encore!" she shouted with a giggle.

"Please, no," Jody whispered, gripping my wrist. "I don't think I can sit through another one."

Ella choked on her bottle of Sprite as she tried not to laugh. I leaned forward and patted her back as she scrambled for a napkin. Wiping her chin, she looked at us both and then started giggling. She'd been doing that a lot since she and Cole moved to LA a couple of weeks ago. It normally wouldn't bother me—Ella's laughter was music to anyone's ears—but tonight it was grating.

Who was I kidding? Tonight, *everything* was grating.

"Maybe we should just go, you guys."

"No way." Jody's blonde curls danced as her head spun away from the stage. "We came out tonight to cheer you up after Brad's suck-fest turd of a break-up text. You're not allowed to go home until you're feeling better."

I pointed at the stage as Baldy started up "Killing Me Softly". If only it would kill me.

"I don't think this is going to help cheer me up."

Jody rolled her eyes and groaned. She did everything with such dramatic flair, I couldn't help smiling. "It's because we need to get our butts up there and do some singing."

Ella made a little whine in her throat. It didn't matter that she sounded like a pure songbird; she and public singing were not friends.

"Yes." Jody looked at her. "Ella Simmons, you are getting up on that stage. We all are. It's time to man up. It's time to get Morgan out of her break-up funk."

"Jody." I frowned. "It's been two weeks. I'm allowed a little bluesy time."

"Oh come on, it's been more than two weeks. You guys have been breaking up and getting back together for months...and yes, in case you're wondering, it was painful."

"How was it painful for you?" I sniffed, pulling my shoulders back.

"Oh Jody, I don't know what to do." My kid sister impersonated me—badly, I might add. "He's so hot and sweet, but maybe we're not meant to be."

I glared at her, which only spurred her on.

"I miss him. We should get back together. We got back together. We broke up. We got back together, but now he's being kind of mean, I don't know if I should stay with him."

I crossed my arms and slumped back in my seat, wrinkling my nose at her. What did Jody know? She'd never had a serious relationship before. Hell, I didn't even think she'd done it yet, which I was quietly very relieved about. My soon-to-be nineteen-year-old sister was a bubble of sunshine, and I didn't want anyone to ever burst it. There was a pureness to her that just couldn't be beat.

Glancing across at her cheeky smirk, I could feel my traitorous lips twitching.

"I wasn't that bad." I squeezed my arms and lifted my chin.

"You were pretty bad." Ella patted my knee, her smile full of sweetness. "But we love you...and we just want to see you happy."

"And smiling," Jody added.

"And free." Ella's gaze turned serious for a minute.

I glanced away from it, not wanting to decipher the underlying meaning.

"Okay, fine." I slapped the table. "So how are we gonna make that happen?"

Ella sat up straighter, swiveling her petite frame to face me properly. "You need to swear off guys for a while."

"What? No, I don't. I need to find someone else. Someone who can treat me well and wash away all the Braddy badness."

"Since when has that ever helped you?" Ella's hazel eyes were tearing strips off me, so I turned to face Jody instead.

"You need to cleanse, sis." Her bright blue eyes danced, her rosebud lips quirking into that half-smile of hers. Damn it, I was going to miss her so much when she left for college.

"Cleanse? What does that even mean?"

"It means you need to rip up every photo of you and Brad. It means you need to clean out your closet and buy some new clothes."

"Jody, I haven't managed to find a job yet. In case you haven't noticed, my funds are like...zero."

"You'll get a job." She flicked her hand. "You're amazing and talented and brilliant at organizing people. You'll make the world's best PA to some rich CEO who'll treat you like a superstar."

I rolled my eyes. "I'd be happy to be a receptionist at a used car lot right now." That wasn't true at all, but I was getting desperate. I'd started applying for jobs months ago, hoping to walk into a job straight after graduation, but every application I sent out had been rejected. I'd even considered looking for work in Nebraska, until stupid-ass Brad broke up with me...for the final time. He made that very clear in his five-sentence text.

Asshole.

My lower lip started to tremble, so I nipped it with my top teeth and focused back on Jody.

"You know what we really need." Jody pointed at the stage with her thumb. "We need to get that squalling cat away from the mic and wow the crowd. Let's liven this place up."

"I don't know, Jo-Jo." Ella's soft defense would never stand up to an enthusiastic Jody.

"It's not an argument, Ella-Bella. We need to sing some Taylor, because that always gets Morgan's happy juices flowing."

"My happy juice? Ew, what is that exactly?"

Jody stood with a beaming smile and grabbed

my wrist. "It's that tingle you get inside your body when the music starts to flow through you. You know what I'm talking about."

I knew exactly what she was talking about. Jody understood better than anyone the power music had over me, especially when it came to dancing. She'd never know the whole truth, I wouldn't tell her that, but what she did know was that nine times out of ten, music could cheer me up like nothing else.

"Why didn't we go to a club instead?" I let Jody pull me toward the stage, pausing her long enough to grab Ella's hand and drag her up there with us.

"Because, there are two extremely important songs you need to sing tonight." Jody applauded with Baldy's wife as she ascended the stairs and nudged him out of the way. Turning to the karaoke touch-screen, she got busy punching in the songs she wanted before shuffling Ella next to her and giving me, the giant among us, the spare mic.

I cleared my throat, grimacing as it echoed through the room. My expression stayed in place as a familiar guitar riff started up, and I instantly recognized "We Are Never Getting Back Together" by Taylor Swift.

Jody grinned at me. "Go for it, Morgs. Pretend Brad the Bastard is in the back of the room and you're singing this just for him."

Taking a breath, I gazed toward the back of the bar and pictured my boyfriend of nearly two years standing there staring at me. His beefy arms were crossed over his chest, and the sweet smile I originally fell for melted away to the judgmental smirk he wore for the last few months of our relationship. Why I didn't break up with him first was beyond me.

As I opened my mouth to sing, I felt like a total fool. How'd I let him keep treating me like that for so long? I was stronger than that, damn it.

The words flowed out of me with a force I hadn't expected. It felt good, though. I directed each and every syllable at the guy who'd been messing me around for far too long.

SEAN

I stepped out of the private room my sister had booked for her birthday. She'd turned 30 today, not that you'd know it. Having a child-free night with her friends and family brought out the crazy in her. With a chuckle, I slid the door shut on the screeching giggles and headed to the bar.

"What can I get you, buddy?"

I held up three fingers to the bartender. "Corona with lime wedges, please."

He nodded and turned to get my order. I leaned against the bar, peering over my shoulder at the three women on stage. They sounded good together. They were harmonizing over a Taylor Swift song.

The tall blonde at the front was taking the lead, singing into the mic with an intensity that seemed out of place at a karaoke bar. It was like she meant every word coming out of her mouth, like singing this song was releasing something inside of her.

I couldn't take my eyes off her. She was stunning with her small, sharp nose and pointy chin. Everything else about her seemed long. Long neck, long arms...long legs. My eyes traveled down her tight, black pants and my brows rose with approval.

The song ended and the room erupted with applause. The two girls next to her giggled. The shorter blonde with big curls and a sparkling smile bowed low, while her petite counterpart tucked a lock of hair behind her ear and looked to the floor. The tall one...she just swallowed, a look of sadness sweeping over her features. She held out the mic to her blonde friend and looked ready to leave the stage.

"No, just one more." The blonde girl refused the mic with a shake of her head and began bopping on stage.

The tall girl pushed a smile over her lips and began swaying to the beat, laughing as they all broke into an enthusiastic rendition of "Shake It Off". Another Taylor number. They must have liked her. All three knew the lyrics by heart, barely looking at the karaoke screen as they clumped together and belted out the words.

It was so engaging, the bartender actually had to tap me on the shoulder to let me know my drinks had arrived. I passed him some cash with a smile and ignored the narrowing of his eyes, turning back to the singing before he could figure out who I was.

The song came to a triumphant end and even I applauded this time. I couldn't help smiling as I watched them descend the stage. They looked close...like sisters maybe. Part of me wanted to ditch my family and go and join them for the night. It'd no doubt be entertaining.

I reluctantly turned away from them and reached for the beers, ready to head back to the private room Helena had booked, but something stopped me.

She was coming this way. The long, sexy one. Her curvaceous hips swayed slightly as she approached the bar, and against every logical thought in my brain, I let go of the beers and gave her a smile.

Rhonda would kill me. After all the media hype I'd just endured, my manager would throw a fit if she thought I was trying to chat up some chick in a karaoke bar, but the smile just happened and once it did, I couldn't take it back.

Long Legs faltered and she glanced over her shoulder before looking back at me. My grin grew. Her brow furrowed slightly, her head tipping with a skeptical frown as she made the last few steps toward me. Placing her hands on the bar, she gave me a long stare, her eyes eventually warming with a smile.

"Okay, I know that I know you, but I'm pretty sure you don't know me. So, why are you smiling at me right now?"

I liked the sound of her voice; it had a confident definition I found attractive.

I stood there grinning like an idiot mute before finally nodding with a shrug. "Can you do me a solid and pretend I'm just this normal guy and I've seen a pretty girl I want to introduce myself to?"

She was taken aback, her large eyes narrowing before she finally nodded. "Sure, why not." She chuckled.

I stuck out my hand. "Hi, I'm Sean Jaxon."

She got that slightly awestruck look on her face that most people did when meeting a celebrity. For a second, I thought she was going to prove all my observations wrong by covering her mouth and running back to her friends with a titter, but thankfully she grasped my hand and gave it a firm shake.

"Morgan Pritchett."

"And what do you do, Morgan? Other than lighting up a karaoke stage, of course."

"Oh yes, I'm sure." She shook her head and looked to the countertop, her laughter dry. "I'm—um, actually looking for a job. I just graduated from UChicago."

I grabbed one of the beers and passed it to her, figuring she must be around twenty-two, just two years younger than me. I raised my own beer in a toast to her. "Congratulations."

"Thank you." She clinked bottles with me, and we both took a swig. "So, I have to admit I never expected to see someone like you in a place like this."

"Of all the gin joints, in all the towns..." I tipped my head, glad I managed to get a smile with my lame-ass Humphrey Bogart impersonation.

"I didn't think you'd be into singing. I thought you were an action man. Mr. Bulletproof. What was your character name in the Dominos series, again?"

"Clay Brockman."

She clicked her fingers. "That's right. You and Judas Domino made one hell of a team."

I chuckled. "You know, Bryant and I hardly got to do any of the really cool stuff. The stunt guys ended up doing most of it."

She rolled her eyes. "Don't shatter the illusion, Mr. Jaxon, please."

I laughed. "The truth is, I'm here for my sister's birthday party." I pointed toward the private room. "I grew up in a musical house. We were always singing and dancing, so of course Helena chose karaoke."

"And you don't like it?" She took another sip of Corona. I tried not to stare at the gloss of beer on her lips.

"No, it's okay. I like it. It's fun to let it out sometimes, you know."

She nodded.

Oh yeah, she knew. I'd just seen her let it all out.

I pressed my lips together, knowing I should get back with the beers but not wanting to leave either. Her smirk was captivating, and I wanted to know what it meant.

"What?" I grinned.

"I'm just so used to seeing you dodge bullets, and slide over hoods of cars and jump out of buildings. I was trying to picture you dancing and singing on a stage."

"Yeah." I rubbed my hand over my tight, black curls.

"I can see it, you know."

I met her gaze, noticing for the first time how pale her brown eyes were, just a hint of chocolate.

"I'm sure there's a role like that with your name on it somewhere."

My lips wanted to break into a grin, but I forced them to remain in a steady line. There was no way I could tell her I'd been offered a role like that. My manager had been talking me out of it, to the point where it was in the no-go pile.

"I'm sure people would freak out. Mr. Bulletproof doing ballet or some shit. It wouldn't fly. No one would pay to see that."

"I don't know." She shrugged. "You've seen the Step Up movies, right?"

I nodded, not wanting to admit how much I enjoyed them.

"Dancing's cool. It's sexy. It's intim—" She shrugged with a grin, her cheeks turning slightly red. "I don't know." She took another swig from her bottle, her eyes flicking to me. The tip of her tongue brushed over her lower lip. There was nothing suggestive in the movement at all, but the very idea of that tongue ever touching mine sent shockwaves through my system. I willed my breathing to remain normal. In my line of work, I was surrounded by beautiful women constantly, but none of them had this kind of effect on me. I didn't know what my problem was. After the Abigail incident, I thought I'd be put off women for life.

Morgan's eyes glimmered as her lips pulled into a lopsided smirk.

So maybe not put off for *life* then.

"I'd watch you dance. I think you'd be really great."

The urge to call my manager right then and tell her to yank that offer back onto the table was damn compelling. I absentmindedly touched the phone in my pocket.

"Jax, hurry up, brother." I glanced over at my older brother, Kip, his head poking out of the karaoke room. Strains of Rihanna's "We Found Love" filtered out the door. It sounded like my eldest sister, Florence, was giving it a shot...she was good.

Kip spotted Morgan and shook his head. "Don't you be thinking 'bout giving my beer away to a pretty white girl. I will whoop your ass."

Morgan's laughter sprinkled over me. I turned back to the sound, enchanted by it.

"Thanks for the beer, Mr. Jaxon." She tipped the bottle my way.

I wanted to tell her to call me Sean, but what was the point. The chances of ever seeing her again were zero. As much as I wanted to, I couldn't pursue this. My career was right on the edge. I was still coming out of the public Abigail-break-up firestorm, and I needed to keep a low profile. Rhonda warned me that I wasn't a big enough name to screw up and get away with it. I had to score myself a lead role in something. I had to move from sidekick to superstar...and this beautiful blonde might have unwittingly given me the answer.

"It was nice to meet you, Morgan."

"Likewise." Her smile and words were softer this time, showing me yet another dimension. Turning to the bar, I ordered another beer and let her walk back to her friends. Collecting the cold bottles, I headed toward Helena's birthday, refusing to look over my shoulder. I didn't need another glance anyway. I would never see her in person again, but Morgan Pritchett would remain in my memory forever.

ONE

MORGAN

2 months later...

I clung tight to my baby sister, ignoring the approaching departure time. I'd spent four years away from her when I went to UChicago, but this time was different. This time she was leaving me, and I wasn't sure I was ready to let her go.

"This is the final boarding call for all passengers flying US Airways 2980 to Tucson, Arizona. Please make your way to Gate 53 immediately."

Jody tightened her squeeze and then pulled away from me, blinking at tears as she hugged Ella once more and kissed Cole on the cheek. Finally, she turned to Dad and with a watery smile gave him another long hug. He patted her back the way he always did, never one for long farewells.

"You take care, Sunshine."

"I will, Daddy. I love you." She kissed his cheek and collected her carry-on.

I held it together, not wanting her to see me cry. With a brave smile I waved goodbye, my hand not dropping back to my side until she was out of sight.

"Do you think she'll be okay?" I rubbed my arms as if I was somehow cold.

"She's gonna be fine, Morgan. She's a big girl now." Ella wiped at her tears and snuggled against her towering boyfriend.

"She survived just fine when you were gone, Marshmallow." Dad hugged me, and I didn't have the heart to remind him how much I hated his nickname for me. He was feeling it, too.

I wrapped my arm around his waist, and we walked out of LAX as a foursome. After paying for parking, I watched Ella and Cole walk hand-in-hand toward their car, feeling that slight pang of longing. They were crazy about each other...and so incredibly happy together. She deserved it. They both did...but when was it my turn?

"You want me to drive?"

I glanced at my dad and nodded, tossing him the keys. "Sure."

Dad pointed the keys at my white Mazda6 sedan and it beeped open. We slammed ourselves inside and basically didn't talk the entire way home. Dad was a man's man, kept his cards close to his chest. I'd seen his eyes water a few times, but I'd never seen him actually cry. He was a sweet, gentle guy, but he would take small talk over in-depth conversation any day.

I didn't think I was capable of talking about the sunny weather, so I kept my lips sealed and my eyes out the window.

It took about 40 minutes to drive home to Pasadena. As soon as Dad parked the car, his phone started ringing.

"Pritchett Electrical, Marshall speaking." Dad's wrinkles creased as he listened to the caller. Since turning forty-five last year, I'd started to notice his aging skin and grey hairs. His head bobbed. "Uh-huh...yeah... No, I've handled problems like that before. It won't be an issue." He glanced at his watch. "Well, I can come right now, if you like... Sure. No problem. I'll just need your address." He scrambled for a piece of paper in the glove compartment of my car. Unlike his, my car was neat and orderly. He threw me a frown when all he could find were the car manuals and a packet of gum. I rolled my eyes and fished a pen and pad from my purse.

Dad scribbled down the address and hung up, his smile fading as he looked at me.

"Sorry, Marshy, I gotta go."

"No problem." I shrugged. It was mid-week; I expected him to be working anyway. It was sweet he took the morning off to say goodbye to Jo-Jo.

He ran inside and changed into his little company shirt before jumping into his van and zooming away. I lifted my face to the sun, hoping it would warm me, but my spirits were too deflated.

I slumped up the front steps and closed the glass door behind me. The house was quiet and it felt weird. We'd lived in this place since before I could remember. I was four when Jody came along, and since that day, the house had never been quiet. She filled it with light and sound. Even after Mom left, shattering our idyllic world, Jody still made noise. Admittedly for the first year it was tantrums and drama, but then in the sixth grade she scored the lead in the school musical, and it helped channel all her raging emotion into something constructive.

Pressing my lips together, I blinked at the rush of tears. My eyes stung as I tried to deny them, trudging up to my room and remembering how I'd braided Jody's hair and done her makeup each night she performed. Her excitement was contagious and my pride for her bloomed that day...and then kept growing. She wanted the bright lights of Broadway, and if anyone could get them, it'd be her. She had more talent in her pinky toe than I possessed in my entire body. For her, it wasn't a case of getting in somewhere after high school; it was a case of choosing where she wanted to go. I was secretly relieved she chose The School of Theatre, Film and Television at the University of Arizona where she would focus on Acting and Musical Theatre. It meant she was close. Heck, it wasn't even that much of a drive. Dad just shelled out for a flight because he couldn't afford the time off work. Even after twenty years of owning this place, Dad was still paying off the mortgage. I think he had about five years to go. What a relief that would be.

I plonked onto my desk chair with a heavy sigh. Money.

Man, I needed it. I didn't want to live here with Dad. I knew I should. Jody was gone, and it would be mean to leave him all by himself. Who would cook him dinner and clean the house? He worked like a Trojan, and the guy needed someone to take care of him...but did it have to be me?

Being in Chicago was the first time since I was fourteen years old that I hadn't had to look after anybody else. It had been refreshing. I'd needed it, and now that I'd had it, I wanted it again.

Opening my laptop, I swished my finger over

the pad to bring the screen to life. I could picture myself in a little studio apartment, somewhere not far from here so I could still check in on Dad.

My mailbox dinged and I scrolled through my new messages, my heart accelerating as I recognized the address for a job I'd applied for. I felt like my interview had gone well. It'd taken over an hour, and I'd answered everything quickly and precisely, showing my competence.

Dear Miss Pritchett,

Thank you so much for your interest in our company. We are sorry to inform you that, although a final candidate, we will not be offering you the job.

Your interview and application were impressive; we are confident that you will find work without a problem.

Best of luck to you.

They were confident? They didn't know jack-shit!

I covered my face with my hands and screamed. I'd lost count of how many rejection emails and phone calls I'd received. When I'd first started fishing for work, I'd been selective, but three months into it, I'd started applying for any job that vaguely interested me. Now I was applying for anything. I just needed a foot in the door, something to earn me a little cash while I looked for something else. I wasn't quite ready to fill out an application at a fast food joint yet, but it was getting close.

I slammed my hands on the desk, ready to push up, stomp down to the kitchen, and devour the box of donuts my dad had brought home last night. My fingers gripped the edge of the wood, stopping me. I couldn't. I wouldn't let myself get fat again. Going through high school as a chubster had never been my intention, but food was a comfort, and since I hadn't been able to dance anymore, chocolate and sex became my best friends.

Thankfully I'd given up the chocolate, but I wasn't willing to let go of the sex, and that only came when I watched my weight.

Sitting up straight, I smoothed a hand down my stomach and reminded myself I had a date the next night.

I'd met him at the grocery store. His name was Alec and he seemed nice. I hadn't told anyone we were going out. I'd kind of agreed to swear off men that night at karaoke, but I hadn't been able to do it. Why should I? Ella had Cole, Jody had her dreams; they just didn't get it. I had nothing. The only enjoyable aspect of my life was being taken out to dinner by good-looking guys. I didn't see that as a crime.

My index finger brushed over the keypad, taking the arrow to IMDb. I had it saved on my Bookmark Bar. As soon as the page loaded, I typed in Sean Jaxon, my lips curling into a smile as his photo and bio appeared. His blue eyes hit me first, the way they always did. Set into his chocolate skin, they were piercing. His tight curls, cut so short his head was practically shaved, and his perfectly-maintained goatee made my insides curl with desire. I traced his big lips wondering what they'd feel like on my skin.

Pulling in a breath through my nose, I sat back with a sigh. I'd read his bio a hundred times now. Knew he came from Santa Ana and was born into a poor family. He was the fifth son to Morris and Gloria Jackson. His first movie was *Final Score,* where he was an extra. Apparently he stood out to the director and ended up getting a speaking part on the film. Since meeting him eight weeks ago, I'd rented every single one of his movies from the DVD store. It was lame. I wasn't afraid to admit that, but I was kind of obsessed with the actor who'd given me his beer.

Why? Why had he done that?

I would never get over my shock at the fact he even noticed me.

Because of him, I'd actually applied for jobs in the TV and film industry, trawling the Internet for any work in Hollywood. I'd applied for five production assistant roles and been interviewed for three of them. I'd missed out on all counts. It was pretty crushing. The very idea of being on a TV or film set thrilled me. It could mean I'd capture a glimpse of Sean— the scruffy, down-and-out teenager who'd been noticed and turned into Sean Jaxon, supporting actor for *Domino Effect*.

I scoffed at my daydream of working alongside him, watching from the sidelines as he acted out a scene. As if that would ever happen.

I didn't bother scrolling down to see what he was working on. Last time I checked, he had nothing new on the board. His last movie had been the final in the Domino Series— *Domino's Demise*. It was actually kind of sad. He died at the end, in his friend's arms. Mr. Bulletproof had finally been beaten. I'd cried with Judas Domino as he'd held his bloodied partner in crime. I'd never been so affected by a movie before.

Hopefully things would pick up for him soon and he'd score a role in something new. According to my Internet stalking, Sean Jaxon had kind of gone underground after a few unfortunate photos with Abigail Tripoli. They'd been a pretty hot couple after *Domino Effect* came out. She was a big-time star, and she'd helped pull him into the limelight. But then she'd cheated on him, and their big break-up fight was caught on camera. One shot made it look as though he was about to hit her, but on closer inspection, you could see he was just raising his hand in frustration. Unfortunately, closer inspection didn't count in the media, and

Sean Jaxon had been torn to shreds for his behavior.

I felt sorry for him. The guy I met at karaoke didn't seem the kind to hurt a girl. Being cheated on and to then have it all go public must have been so humiliating. I leaned toward the screen, gazing into those bright-blue orbs of his. I couldn't imagine a mean streak existing in those kind eyes.

My insides turned mushy as I brushed my finger over his face, pretending he was real, when he really wasn't.

Well, he *was*, but not to me.

"Morgan, you are so pathetic. You have to get over this." I rolled my eyes and slammed my laptop shut. Checking my watch, I was disappointed to see I still had four hours before I needed to get ready for my date.

"Shit," I muttered, my mind wandering to those donuts in the refrigerator. I was about to give in when my phone started tinkling.

Snatching it up, I checked the number and felt that familiar spike of hope.

No way. Could it be?

"Morgan Pritchett speaking." I kept my voice precise and professional, trying to sound upbeat.

"Yeah, hi, Lisa Crampton here for Polychrome Studios. I'm first assistant to Travis McKinnon. You interviewed with us several weeks back."

"Yes." I sat up straight, snatching a pen so I'd have something to fidget with. "I was told the position had been filled. I didn't have enough experience."

"You didn't. I'm not ringing to offer you the job of production assistant."

"Okay. So, why are you calling me then?"

"Our current runner and second assistant to Mr. McKinnon had to leave, and we would like to offer you the job."

"Runner."

"Yes, runner, gofer. Mr. McKinnon or I ask you for something and you go and get it, basically. You'll be working for us first and foremost, but if we don't need you, you'll help the other runner with her stuff."

I pressed my lips together, resisting my sarcastic reply of *sounds great*.

Instead, I pushed a smile over my lips and put on my perky voice. "Thank you so much. I would be honored to accept."

"Great." The girl sounded relieved. "That makes my day so much easier, thank you. To be honest, I thought you were a long shot, with your degree and everything. I thought you would have been snatched up by now."

"Yeah, you'd be surprised how little a college education can sometimes mean. I know I am."

"Well, look, I'm sorry I'm not calling to offer you more, but at least this is a foot in the door, right?"

"Absolutely. I'm excited about the opportunity to work for a TV show."

The girl chuckled. "That's the spirit. You can start tomorrow, right?"

"Uh, yes. Of course. I will absolutely be there."

"Good. I'll have a security pass couriered to you this afternoon, and we'll see you at seven a.m. We'll be on set tomorrow, so I'll send directions with the pass. Just ask for me when you get here."

"Thank you, Lisa, I appreciate this opportunity."

"No problem. I'll transfer you to Mr. McKinnon's secretary so she can get your details."

I couldn't help a smile as I was transferred to the secretary to give her my address and social security number. She rattled off a bunch of instructions, which I scribbled down.

Hanging up the phone, I threw it onto my bed,

raised my hands in the air and let out a squeal.

I had a job.

I had a freaking job!

Not necessarily the job I'd been hoping for, but it was a job!

TWO

SEAN

The alarm wouldn't stop buzzing. With a groan, I reached out and slammed my palm over the clock. It blurped a couple of times and then went quiet. Sleep evaded me once more, draping over me like a warm blanket, until reality kicked in and I lurched out of bed.

Rubbing my eyes, I glanced at the clock and scrambled for my clothes. I was due at rehearsal in forty minutes. Damn snooze, why did they even invent that shit?

Throwing on a shirt, I grabbed my toothbrush and did a swift job of my teeth before buckling my belt, grabbing my unpacked bag from last night, and heading for my car. Sliding into the current love of my life, I tenderly ran my hands over the leather-clad steering wheel as the garage door ascended.

The engine of my red Camaro revved to life and I pulled onto the road, taking off toward Polychrome Studios. The set was about a twenty-minute drive away, but this was LA and traffic was at constant rush hour. Braking at the lights, I waited my turn, pumping up the volume so Pitbull's beat reverberated through the car.

I tapped my thumb on the steering wheel as I went over my schedule for the day. Dance rehearsal was mainly for Ashlee's benefit this morning. It was her character's number, but I was going to be joining in for the second part of it, which probably meant I'd be filming most of the day. Man, it was gonna be a long one...again.

The light turned green, and I sped through the intersection. It was Thursday and I was dog-tired. Fourteen-hour days on set near killed me. If I didn't love it so much, I'd beg Rhonda to find me an out. TV was so different than film. I was used to doing intense filming for shorter periods of time. Still long days, but long days week after week after week...they were hard. And this wasn't just filming, either; this show involved dance rehearsals, singing practice and recording tracks in the sound studio as well. It was all good, but I was a busy man.

I turned down my music as the phone started ringing. Quickly plugging it in, I pressed the screen with a smile.

"Hey, Mama."

"Morning, Sean baby. I just checking in with my boy."

"He's doing good."

"You workin' today?"

"Mama, I work every day."

"Not Sunday though, right?"

I rolled my eyes. "Not Sunday."

"Good, 'cause we getting together. It's Jackson Five time." I cringed the way all my siblings did when she referred to us that way. She thought it was cute. We all thought it was painful. Besides, it was hardly the Jackson Five anymore. With all the marriages and babies that had been happening in the past ten years, we were now a Jackson seventeen—my parents included. It was hardly a quiet get-together, but when was my family ever quiet? I grinned.

"I'll be there. What should I bring?"

"Yourself."

"Come on, let me bring something. That's a lot of people you'll be feeding."

"We'll be fine, don't you worry about us."

I rolled my eyes, irritated with this same argument. I was finally earning some decent cash and could actually afford to help them out, but they wouldn't take it...but they couldn't refuse if I just showed up with some sweetness, so I'd do that.

"Okay, fine. I'll see you Sunday then."

"Good boy. Now you go be my little superstar."

"Love you, Mama."

She hung up with her standard chuckle and I had to laugh too. She always thought her jokes were hilarious and the fact she did, made them so much funnier.

When I'd sat down and told my parents I'd signed on for the first season of *Superstar*, a musical TV series about a performing arts school, they had both jumped from their chairs and wrapped me in a hug. My dad had been a high school teacher for over thirty years, and my mama was the music in our house. The fact I was going to be playing the role of a dance teacher at a music school was like all their dreams for me coming true at the same time.

"I knew it. I knew one day you'd stop jumping out of windows and start using your real talents." Mama had beamed.

It'd made the whole signing on thing way less scary. Rhonda had tried to persuade me against it. Polychrome was a small-time studio run by some eccentric billionaire named Donald McKinnon. *Superstar* was his son's baby, and they were making it happen. Rhonda surmised that it was all to do with "who you know" and nothing to do with quality, but I held my ground. The pilot had been a big success, and the show had been picked up by CBS. Polychrome was hoping for a prime-time spot. I was confident they'd get it. The music, the script, the cast, the crew...they were all top-notch. We all felt like we were sitting on a goldmine. It was hard for Rhonda to argue that.

My phone began singing again and I raised my eyebrows.

"Speak of the devil." I touched my screen. "Hey, Rhonda."

"Are you nearly there?"

"Ten minutes away."

"Okay, good. Your day's pretty tight, but we need to schedule a meeting at some point. I've managed to score you a cologne ad and photo shoot."

"Cologne, huh."

"Yeah, it'll be good for your image. A sexy, nice-smelling man who can dance. It's a total turn-on...and continues to add to your clean, nice-guy image."

I stifled my groan and checked the road before taking the turn.

"Okay, whatever, Rhonda."

"So, according to your schedule, you can fit me

in for thirty minutes at 2:30. I'll come to the set so you're not wasting travel time or anything. I'll see you then."

She hung up before I could even say goodbye. I shook my head with a wry smile. She was a piece of work, that chick, but was good for me. She'd worked closely with my publicist, Andrew, and helped the world see me in a different light after the Abigail debacle. She'd scored me numerous interviews and photo shoots that all promoted me as Mr. Nice Guy. She'd instructed me every step of the way through that whole mess, and I owed my career to her. It had been hell, but she'd dragged me through it, and I was once again able to walk out of my house without being attacked by hungry press and yelling reporters.

People were still chasing Abigail. I saw her images splashed all over the magazines. According to the headlines, the guy she'd cheated on me with was now cheating on her. She didn't seem to care; she'd moved on to a rock star. I couldn't remember his name, but all the pictures seemed pretty loved up. I was so glad not to be a part of it anymore.

Pulling into the lot, I flashed my pass to security and parked in my designated spot, trying to clear my mind before heading inside. I couldn't bring any of that crap on set with me. I needed to focus. I needed to be Harley Barnes.

"Hey, Jax." I waved at Ashlee as she skipped ahead of me into the large warehouse that had become the Franklyn Performing Arts School. Harley was a first-year teacher and had come into the show in the second episode. He was falling madly in love with the lead, a nineteen-year-old freshman named Sasha...played by the lovely Ashlee Johnston.

My character would spend most of the first season resisting her sweet, country charm. I was guessing the writers would have us together by the end of the season, but I wasn't sure. Knowing them, they'd torture the audience until the last episode.

I grinned, relishing the anticipation that would build throughout the season.

So far, Harley and Sasha had stuck with flirty hellos and sweet conversation. Sasha's dance for this episode was pretty much an *I want you* proclamation for Harley, but he'd have to resist her. I could almost hear the audience groaning with the sweet agony of it all.

Walking out of the sunlight, I made my way down the corridor to my dressing room. I didn't need to change for another couple of hours; I wasn't due in makeup until nine. Pulling off my jeans, I yanked a pair of sweats from my bag and pulled them on for warm-ups and rehearsal, discarding my T-shirt for a plain black tank. Isabella ran a tight dance ship, and she made us work those routines hard. This week's episode had a big dance number at the end, which was kind of tricky. I was enjoying the challenge, in spite of the long rehearsal hours.

Stepping out of my room, I ambled down the corridor, noticing the crew setting up for filming.

"You think I give a shit it's your first day? This isn't rocket science. Figure it out and get moving," Travis barked from his chair.

His spindly finger pointed at a tall, blonde woman. There was something familiar about her, but I couldn't place it. She scuttled out of view before I could catch a proper look at her face. Poor thing. She must be the new runner. The last one had quit on Tuesday, slammed down her clipboard and stormed out in tears. Travis was a hard man to work for, I wouldn't deny that. He was pretty good with the cast, but the director and crew had the patience of saints. He'd gone through two runners already since filming began. I didn't know how Lisa handled him. I wondered how long this one would last.

She came back into view before I turned the corner, her head held high, her expression calm as she approached Travis. He glanced at the paperwork she held out to him before snatching it from her hand.

"Thank you," he mumbled.

"Welcome." There was a commanding strength to her voice that appealed to me and stirred the whisper of a memory in my brain.

I'd met that girl before.

But where?

And damn, did I want to meet her again.

"Hurry up, Jax, or we'll be late." Ashlee shuffled past me, grabbing my hand and yanking me toward the dance studio.

We scuttled down the hallway together and slipped in just as Isabella was starting her warm-ups. She grinned as I walked through the door and gave me a wink. I smiled back at my long-time friend and got ready to work.

This day would be huge, and I didn't really need the distraction of some leggy blonde. Although, I did have to admit that before the day was out, I was going to talk to the new runner, and no amount of workload would stop that from happening.

THREE

MORGAN

Frazzled. That was one word I could think of.

Inept was another.

Flustered. Out of my depth. Struggling to stay calm. Indignant.

Yes, those were all ways of describing how I felt as I hurried off set for my ten-minute break. It took me less than thirty minutes to figure out why the last runner quit. It was because she was working for the world's biggest asshole. People said Travis McKinnon had a brilliant mind, I really wasn't sure. All I knew for certain was that manners and respect were pretty damn low on his list of priorities.

I huffed as I pulled out my drink bottle,

suddenly wishing I was a smoker. Standing in the California sun and taking a sweet drag on a cigarette sounded like perfection right now. I shoved on my shades and leaned against the outside of the warehouse.

It was only ten o'clock. Ten! I still had at least seven hours, if not more, to go. Could I do it? Could I then come back tomorrow and the next day to be yelled at by some skinny guy with long, floppy hair and the reverence of most of the cast?

That was what I couldn't figure out. He was nice to them! Treated them like freaking royalty. Maybe he was one of those eccentric artsy types, constant angst perched on his shoulder...and he saved it all up for his poor little gofer.

Well you know what, there was nothing poor about me and damned if I was going to let him ruin the only job I'd managed to score. I could take it. He was just some weedy prick with a big mouth. I'd dated worse in high school. I could do this.

Glancing at my watch, I decided to return early from my break, to prove I wasn't scared of his sorry ass. With my chin high, I stepped back inside. Walking past the coffee machine, I closed my eyes and drew in a breath. Like the guy needed more caffeine, but it was a gesture.

I figured he probably took it black...you know, to match his soul. Walking back on set with as much confidence as I could, I approached him quietly and waited for him to finish chatting to Conway, the director, before handing him the mug.

"What's that?" He frowned.

"Coffee. Black. I don't know if you like it that way or not, but if you don't, you'll have to let me know."

He gave me a long, hard look, which I decided to meet head-on.

"I like my coffee black, so if you don't want it." I

drew the cup away from him, but he paused my action with a slight smirk.

"Hand it over." I gave it to him with a sickly sweet smile that he saw straight through. His smirk grew an inch before he turned back to Lisa and started barking out new instructions. He sipped his coffee and threw me one more glare.

"You're welcome." I tipped my head and looked over the schedule for the rest of the day.

Sasha would be dancing her scene in about five minutes and would be joined by Harley at the end of the song.

Harley as in Sean Jaxon. I had nearly died when I read that the night before. I'd stayed up until midnight, researching everything I could about the show. There really wasn't much. It didn't go to air for another three weeks and promos were only just starting, but IMDb had a cast list up already and Sean was on it. Sean. If McKinnon didn't yell me off the set to do some menial task in the next hour or so, I'd see Sean!

Not that he'd remember me or anything, but just seeing him in the flesh once more would be a trip.

I couldn't believe he took this role. Was it because of what I said to him?

I shook my head. As if!

But maybe...

From the glimpse I'd seen of the day's script, I knew that Sasha was in love with Harley, a young teacher at the school, and she was trying to woo the reluctant twenty-two-year-old into a relationship.

Ashlee walked into the room, looking gorgeous in dancing leggings, a baggy sweater, and bare feet. Her dark hair was pulled back into a loose messy bun, strands of hair flying free. She looked almost ethereal as she stepped under the lights. The makeup artist studied her and moved forward to pat some extra powder on her nose while the lighting guys moved around her.

Conway called out instructions, looking over the cameraman's shoulder.

"Yeah, yeah, that's good. Just like that." He held up his hands and stepped toward Ashlee and a redheaded woman who looked to be around my age. "Okay, my darling Ashlee, this is the dance of the episode. You get me?"

She nodded with a sweet smile.

"I need you to pour everything into it. Harley is watching Sasha through the glass and although she's pretending she doesn't know it, she actually does. You are wooing him with this number, and we need every move to be a sensual caress to the camera."

The lady beside her nodded and caught Ashlee's eye. "So those sweeping arm movements just before the bridge, make sure you really extend on those." The woman did the moves, looking like a pro. I couldn't take my eyes off her body as it twisted gracefully. "And make sure your eyes really smolder, when you cross for the crouch. You need to look at that glass. You're calling him to you, like a siren."

Ashlee crouched, following the well-practiced step, her lithe body stretching out across the floor before swiftly rising like a feline killer.

"But remember, you're still that sweet country girl at heart. We don't want your moves to be sexy like Violet's and Kristina's; they need to have a purity to them."

The girls both nodded and Ashlee drew in a breath. "Okay, do you want me singing with this take, or am I just mouthing the words this time?"

"Let's try you singing along with the recording to see what it looks like, and then we can drop it on extra takes if we need to."

"Sounds good."

Conway smiled at Ashlee, patting her shoulder before turning back for his chair. Travis nodded his approval at Conway before throwing his nearly-empty coffee mug at me as he passed. Thankfully I caught it without spilling any on myself. I pulled a Kleenex from my pocket and wiped the drips on the floor.

"Okay, ready on set! And action."

The song "Clarity" by Zedd began playing, the soft piano music quickly building as Ashlee's recorded voice boomed through the speakers. She sounded so good. Her head tipped back as she sung the lyrics with her recording, her body moving like flowing liquid over the dance space...and then the beat kicked in. Her body shifted from flowing water to pounding raindrops, her movements punchy and strong. I couldn't take my gaze off her. She was totally pulling off the smoky-eye effect and my insides surged with her. I could feel each move as if it were my own. The choreography was beautiful, the movements a stunning combination of sharp and fluid.

I looked past Ashlee and spotted her choreographer, her face beaming as she watched her dance come together. I made a mental note to find her later and tell her how impressed I was. I spent hours choreographing stuff as a kid. I dreamed of doing it for a job one day, but that dream died when Mom walked her selfish butt out the door. I became a mother then to a scared little ten-year-old who wouldn't have coped with my heavy dance schedule. I gave it all up in one fell swoop. The only time I choreographed after that was with Ella and Jody when we goofed around in the summer holidays, pretending we were professional dancers. Those times hurt, but I didn't want to let my sisters down, so I'd pretended the pain didn't ricochet through me each time I came up with a good move.

Squeezing the clipboard to my chest, I stood there until Conway yelled, "Cut!" and snuck away before anyone noticed me just standing there doing nothing.

*****

My feet were killing me by lunchtime. I had spent the last two hours running errands, making phone calls, and delivering all manner of things from Gatorade to a box of batteries. I shuffled to the cafeteria, grabbing a tired-looking sandwich off the tray and scoffing it down. I didn't really feel like it, but I had to keep my energy up; I still had half a day to go.

Reaching for a bottle of cold water, I spun around to find a seat and smacked into the redhead I wanted to congratulate.

"Oh, sorry." I smiled.

"No problem." She grinned up at me before stretching out her hand. "Isabella Fontaine."

"Hi, I'm Morgan."

"Welcome to the crazy house."

I chuckled.

"And good luck." Her eyebrows rose, sending me a message that was not hard to decode.

"I can make it."

"Let's hope so." She shook her head and went to step away, but I stopped her with my arm.

"I just wanted to compliment you on your amazing choreography for 'Clarity'. I only saw the first part, but it was brilliant; you really captured the song."

"Thank you." Her sparkling smile reminded me of Jody. "You a dancer too?"

I opened my mouth to say yes, but settled for a

shrug instead. "I did a little when I was a kid."

"Why'd you give it up?"

"Life got in the way."

Isabella's petite nose wrinkled. "I can't imagine life ever getting in the way of dancing. Life is one big dance."

"Yeah." I had to nod, because I used to believe that with every fiber of my being. "I mean, I still love it. I just...don't study it anymore."

She quietly considered me, obviously trying to decipher my answer. I looked away from her and cleared my throat. "Anyway, I should probably get back."

"You know, if you want, you're welcome to come to our rehearsals in the morning."

"Me?" I pointed at my chest.

"Yeah," she chuckled. "Some of the spare crew sometimes join in at the back, just for some exercise. You look like you could probably keep up."

I grinned. "That could be cool."

"Could be?" She pulled a face. "It's freaking awesome."

"Okay then." I grinned. "Sounds like fun. What time do you start?"

"Around seven-thirty."

I tipped my head with a resigned frown. "I start at seven."

"That's okay. I get here at six. We can do our own little pre-rehearsal before the cast gets here...if you're up for it."

"Okay." I nodded. "Yeah."

Why? Why was I saying yes to this?

Because I couldn't stop myself. Because the idea of starting my day with dancing was so damn appealing, refusal wasn't even an option. Nerves zinged through me as I unscrewed my water bottle. I was insane. I was exhausted after half a day of work, and now I wanted to start an hour earlier with a dance session?

The phone Lisa had handed me that morning beeped.

Get your butt back to set. I want a turkey sandwich on rye. Make sure it's fresh!

I held my sigh in check as I headed toward the catering area. "I gotta go. It was nice meeting you, Isabella."

"You too, and if you can sneak back on set soon, you might be able to catch the rest of 'Clarity'. They're doing close-ups after lunch."

"I'll try. If I can sneak away."

"Don't let that jackass boss you around too much. He might be brilliant, but he's still just a guy."

I grinned. "I knew I liked you for a reason."

"Oh we're gonna be good friends, I can already tell." She winked at me and for the first time since arriving on set, my smile actually felt genuine.

FOUR

SEAN

I listened to Isabella's instructions while watching the blonde over her head. Travis was talking her ear off as she handed him a fresh mug of coffee and a wrapped sandwich. She was taking it well, not cowering away from his strong demeanor. If anything, the louder he got, the higher she stood. She was actually taller than him when she pulled her shoulders back and extended her neck. It was damn appealing.

"Yo, Jax, you listening?"

"Yeah." My eyebrows rose in feigned innocence, but Isabella saw straight through it. She glanced over her shoulder, her left dimple appearing as she gazed back at me.

"Her name's Morgan. She's the new runner, and the quicker you get this right, the sooner you can meet her."

Morgan. Morgan. I tipped my head, the name conjuring up an image I'd laid to bed eight weeks ago. My karaoke girl.

I grinned.

"Would you put those pearls away, you're about to film a serious scene here."

"Sorry." I cleared my throat and drew my attention back to the petite dancer as Conway stepped toward us.

"Okay guys, we're doing close-up shots now, so Sean, when you walk in behind Ashlee as she's dancing and collect her up, make sure you're really feeling it."

"As the beat builds before the second chorus, it should be flowing through your whole body," Isabella interjected. "Make sure your frame is really strong when you hold that statue position."

"Then she'll sing her *why are you* line and you'll drop her forward, spinning her around so you guys are facing. We'll pull the camera in around you for those shots, so make sure you're aware of where it is. We don't want any collisions."

I nodded at Conway.

"Ashlee, don't forget to really rotate your hips on those shimmies and spins." Isabella moved her hips to demonstrate. "Then come back together, pull apart, then the heavy breathing, long stare."

Isabella crouched low in the position we'd rehearsed and I copied her movements.

Conway's eyes moved down the choreographer's body. I hid my smirk when he looked back at me. "Now, remember, that resistance needs to be there the whole time. It's a battle. When you collect her up, it's because you can't help yourself. When you drop her down, you're trying to let her go, but then you pull her back in, because you have to have her."

"Yeah, got it." My eyes flicked back to Morgan. She blew a stray wave of hair off her face as she jotted down Travis's instructions.

Isabella grabbed my chin and forced my eyes back to her. Her grin was all-knowing.

"Shut up."

Her laughter was like sprinkles on a cupcake. It was one of the first things I'd noticed about her when we met. She was on the set of *Domino Effect*, choreographing a pole-dancing scene. She worked pretty closely with Abigail. That's how I'd gotten to know the petite redhead so well. We hit it off and our friendship had stayed solid despite the mess. It was actually Isabella who'd pitched my name for *Superstar*. I still hadn't thanked her properly for that one. I'd have to take her and her husband, Dean, out for dinner one night. She'd been married about a year now and happier than ever.

"Okay, we good to go?" Conway beckoned us over, and I walked out of the shadows. My eyes were trained on Morgan as I did so and the pleasure that bloomed over her face when she saw me was almost comical. She swallowed, stepping behind Travis's chair.

I grinned at her. Once again, she looked over her shoulder to make sure no one was behind her before she turned back to me. Her smile was pure magic as she met my gaze head on.

Conway commanded my attention, breaking our little moment. I nodded at him and then Ashlee as he verbally walked us through the last few details.

I took my place off set and waited for my cue. I had to really concentrate. My eyes kept wanting to shift, to move to the other side of the room and catch another glimpse of magic. With a deep breath, I closed my eyes and forced Harley into my mind. Sean, the actor, took a backseat to the new dance teacher with a passion for music and a burning desire to inspire his students. The only thing hindering his first year in the workforce was the irresistible charms of a southern belle with the heart of an angel and the body of an enchantress. Snapping my eyes open, I gazed at the set, but this time it looked different. There were no cameras, no people, no lights. Ashlee was now Sasha and the only thing I could see was her beautiful body floating over an empty dance floor.

As the beat grew to a crescendo, the male voices in the background building, I scooped Ashlee into my arms and lifted her high. Her tight frame held her position as she sung her line, and then our bodies turned from stone to water as we flowed around each other, the battle of will against logic building with force. The final hiss sounded as we stared at each other, an invisible force locking us together. Slowly, as if coming to, I broke it, rising from my position.

"Sasha, we can't. I'm sorry." I was still out of breath, my puffing adding to the broken words.

Her dark gaze grew stormy as she fought the tears before covering her mouth and running from the room. I placed my hands on my hips and dropped my head, the lights fading to black.

"And cut! Okay good, let's run that again."

The lights came back up, and we shuffled into our start positions. I looked for Morgan as I moved to my spot, but she was gone.

*****

I rubbed my aching shoulder as I walked back toward my dressing room. Ashlee was light and all, but lifting her over my head for that many takes was exhausting. I couldn't wait for a hot bath. Scrubbing my hand over my face, I realized that was still hours away. Travis decided he wasn't happy with the lighting for the close-ups, so he wanted to run them again...and I had my meeting with Rhonda.

"Nice work, Mr. Jaxon." My hand dropped to my side, and I spun back to face Morgan.

Her pale brown eyes were still enchanting, and I moved toward them as if pulled by a magnet.

"Karaoke girl." I grinned. "How are you?"

"I'm good." She nodded.

"I see you have a job now."

"Yep." Her cringe made me laugh.

"Well, you may not like it, but I'm kinda glad."

Her cheeks warmed with a slight blush.

"I know Travis can be...forceful, but he's really talented, and there are great people on this set."

"Yeah, I've met most of them. The crew is so nice and..." She tipped her head. "The cast isn't bad either."

There was that cheeky smirk of hers again. Damn. She'd undo me in a second.

"So, um, I feel like I owe you a beer and a congratulations."

"For what?" I pushed up my shirtsleeve.

"For being brave...for stepping up." She winked.

"Thank you." I wanted to tell her I wouldn't have done it if she hadn't told me to, but I felt like it would kill our light flirting session, and I didn't want to do that. There'd be plenty of time for thank-yous later.

"Well, I guess I'll see you around then." Her face lit with a smile, which I tried to match but never could.

I watched her walk away, not even worried if she turned to see me doing it. She didn't turn back, so I let my eyes wander down her sleek body and wondered what the curve of her hip would feel like under my hand.

"You ready?" Rhonda's sharp voice jumped me out of my reverie.

I spun to face her. "Yep."

"Who's that?" She lifted her chin after Morgan and I shrugged.

"Just the new runner. No one special."

I didn't know why I said that. She *was* special. I could feel it in my core, and maybe that was why I wanted to protect it...protect her. I glanced over my shoulder one last time, catching a final glimpse of her long legs as they walked away from me.

A thrill ran through me at the idea of seeing her again and the fact I'd be able to before the day was out. I clicked my tongue and couldn't resist a goofy smile as I headed after Rhonda. I loved my job before, but hot damn, if I didn't love it even more now.

FIVE

MORGAN

I dragged my ass out of bed at five-thirty and made it to the studios by six-fifteen. Thank the stars I'd canceled my date with the grocery store guy. By the time I got home at eleven, I was so shattered, I could barely make it up to my room. Ella had been texting me all day, wondering how I was getting on. I'd managed to reply to her twice. I'd sent her a final message at eleven-thirty and fallen asleep with the phone still in my hand. I woke up in my rumpled clothing, scrambled my way through a shower, and left the house before Dad was even up. I fought off the *living dead* feeling the whole way to work, buying a double espresso on the way.

Once I pulled into the lot, I started to perk up.

Maybe it was the idea of doing a little early morning dancing that energized my limbs. Whatever it was, I ran up the stairs to find Isabella in the rehearsal studio, her long, auburn hair splashed over the floor. She was folded in half perfectly, stretching out her muscles. My bag slid from my shoulder, and I quietly walked toward her.

"Morning," she chirped. "How you feeling?"

I groaned. "I think I clocked up sixteen hours yesterday. Is it going to be like that all the time?"

"Be prepared. Some days are worse." She drew up from her stretch and grinned when she noticed my expression. "Let me guess: your feet are killing you, you feel sleep-deprived, frazzled, and in desperate need of strong coffee."

"The coffee's been taken care of."

"Perfect, let's work on the frazzled part then." She skipped over to her stereo and a thick beat pulsed through the room.

"Don't Stop The Music" by Rihanna.

A smile bloomed over my face as I ran to Isabella's side and copied her stance. I felt the beat move through me as I bent my knees and started tapping out the rhythm with my heel. Her hips swiveled and I followed, my arms and legs taking over as I let the music fill me.

Bella was a sharp mover, and I felt rusty as I tried to keep up with her, but the more my limbs moved, the looser they got. I was soon following each of her steps with relative ease.

Man, it felt good. The frazzle slipped off me as I lost myself in the song, the rhythm releasing all the tension in my muscles.

The dam inside me wanted to break, the place where I stored it all up, kept myself safe. This happened to me every time I danced, and every time I wanted to let go, but I couldn't. Things changed eight years ago, and I didn't think I'd ever be able to dance like I used to.

"Beautiful arabesque, Morgan." My dance teacher applauded. "Nice extension."

I grinned as I lowered my leg and spun into a double pirouette, feeling an explosion of energy run through me. My arms spread wide on my finishing position, breaths punching past my smile.

I felt like I had wings and could soar right off the stage.

Ms. Finnermore's voice brought me back to reality.

"Morgan, you are a delight. I can't believe you choreographed that whole piece on your own. You will do just fine at your exam on Saturday."

"Thank you." I tucked a curl behind my ear, biting my lip.

"Don't be nervous. There's something about the way you dance that moves people. It's like you let every emotion you feel flow out of you in a burst of energy. You're only thirteen. Imagine what you'll do as an adult."

I smiled, basking in her praise.

"I know it's still early days, but you should start thinking about where you want to study dance after high school...or if you're open to it, we could look into some performing arts high schools."

My stomach danced a crazy jig, excitement making me lightheaded.

"I'll talk to my parents."

Ms. Finnermore patted me on the shoulder. "Tell them they can call me to chat at any time."

I skipped home that day...actually, I think I flew.

But the week before my fourteenth birthday, my wings were clipped, those school applications were forgotten, and I'd built that dam as fast I could.

I blinked against the memory, focusing back on

Isabella's beaming smile as she finished the song with a series of chaînés.

I stood back and watched her, clapping loudly as Rihanna's voice faded away.

"Nice."

"You like it?"

"Definitely. Great moves," I puffed.

"I'm gonna finish with a canon."

"Oh, so this is a piece for the show?"

"Uh-huh." She nodded, running over to the stereo to pause the music blasting over our conversation. "It's our big, final number for this week's episode."

"Cool." I grinned. "I really like your style; it's an edgy blend of hip hop, contemporary...classical. I feel like it's got a taste of everything. Did you start with ballet?"

"When I was three years old." She chuckled. "My grandmother used to own a dance studio. I'd spend so much time there. She bought me my first pair of slippers for my third birthday, and I was the happiest kid on the planet." Her sparkling smile faded. "She passed away a few years ago and man, I just wanted to give up. She'd been my inspiration for everything I tried. She was the one who encouraged me to study a whole bunch of different styles. I just couldn't imagine dancing without her there to watch, but my husband, Dean, told me if I quit, I'd regret it for the rest of my life." She shrugged. "He was right."

My throat burned as I listened to her, hating how much the words resonated with me. Where was my Dean? Why hadn't anyone told me not to quit?

It was too late now. I couldn't.

I'd never dance like I did before. It hurt too much.

Isabella twirled back to the stereo and pressed

play again, running to the center of the room and resetting her stance as "Mmm Yeah" by Adam Mahone and Pitbull began playing. I clicked my fingers in time with her and watched in the mirror as she slunk across the room. Once again, I followed each of her moves, slipping up every now and then, but catching on easily.

I couldn't believe how quickly it all came back to me. My hips swayed, my feet moved, and I grinned as I dipped to the floor and back up again, sliding into a set of robotic moves that were tight and sharp.

The song came to a finish and I clapped.

"I love that one."

Isabella nodded. "Thank you. It's actually a piece for the show. The guys are doing a response dance to the girls."

"And 'Please Don't Stop the Music' is the girls' dance?"

"No, actually, for the first time ever I've been given a bit of free rein." She looked to the ceiling. "My instructions are a number that's sensual, tight, and explosive."

"Wow, okay. What songs do you have to choose from?"

"I have to give them a list by tomorrow so they can check out rights to see if we can use the song. To be honest, I've been so busy with the big final number for the current episode, I haven't even had a chance to think about it. It's on my list."

My brain began spinning the way it used to when I studied dance. There was always a move or two playing in my mind back then.

"What's your setting for the song?"

"The cafeteria. Basically the girls come in with this sexy little number. Violet is trying to prove to Nixon that she's the better dancer, and Sasha's still upset by Harley's rejection from the episode before, so she wants to do something wild and shocking."

I raised my eyebrows. "Does it work?"

"Well, the students are fully into it, and Nixon and his crew respond with 'Mmm Yeah,' because Nixon's actually hot for Violet, and he kind of wants to let it show. Harley only catches the end of the number and he's not impressed. He likes his sweet little country girl, you know."

"Something sexy and shocking enough that the teachers won't approve."

Isabella nodded. "I was initially thinking of 'Break Free' by Ariana Grande and Zedd, because it's kind of like a *well if you don't want me then fine* type number for Sasha, but this is actually Violet's song, and I think it's the wrong message. And I really want that shock value to be strong."

I tapped my lip and then clicked my fingers, my lips quirking with a smile. "Do you think you could get away with 'Lady Marmalade'?"

Isabella's eyes rounded, her face starting to shine. "OMG, that would be freaking perfect!"

"I can just kind of picture them, you know, slinking into the lunch room." I moved my shoulders and body, cruising across the floor. "And then somehow incorporating the tables or something."

"Yes! Yes, yes, yes! I'm loving it!" Isabella ran to her iPod and quickly found the version done by Christina Aguilera, Lil' Kim, Mya, and Pink.

She turned and with the moves of a professional, traveled toward me just like I'd described. I laughed, nodding my head. Damn, she looked hot. The girls doing that in the cafeteria would send the crowd wild.

As the song played, Isabella came up with a run of smooth steps. I couldn't believe how quickly she put it all together. By the end of our session, she'd basically choreographed the entire song, using me in different positions to make sure the spacing worked.

"Yes, I'm loving this." She clapped her hands and then checked her watch. "Sweet. The girls should be here shortly for rehearsal. I need to get me a table and chairs in here so I know it can work."

"Don't you need to get the song approved first?" I felt bad for being the cold water on this super-hot idea.

"Hey, even if it doesn't get approved, I want to see these girls do this dance. Don't you?"

"Ah, yeah! But I don't want to get you in trouble for wasting rehearsal time."

"We'll call it warm-up." She winked.

"Okay, then I'll go find you that table and chairs."

"Perfecto!" She spun away from me, snatching up her phone as I left the room. "Yeah, Lisa, hi. I was wondering if you could please check with Travis and the writers to see if I can use 'Lady Marmalade' for the cafeteria number.... Yeah, for the next episode."

I skipped down the stairs feeling light and energetic. I'd helped Isabella come up with an idea...a really good one.

This was going to be a good day. I could feel it.

SIX

SEAN

The dance studio was buzzing by the time I got there. Strains of "Lady Marmalade" filtered down the stairwell as I made my way up for rehearsal.

"Yes, and contract then rise slowly, pushing your hips out. Nice!" Isabella's enthusiasm was effervescent. "And the pirouettes!"

I looked over at Ashlee. She was standing on the table with the other girls, her body spinning quickly. She came out of the move and stepped back so Trudy (aka Violet) could take center stage again. The song came to a sizzling finish and a swift cheer rose from the dancers.

The girls stood, puffing and elated, on the table. They looked smoking hot, even in their sweats.

That song, in full costume, was going to be amazing.

"You girls think you can do it for Travis and Con?"

They nodded. "Let us run through it one more time." Ashlee raised her finger, and they jumped down from the table to reset.

I dropped my bag and leaned against the wall next to Quinn.

"Hey, man. What's this dance for?"

"The next episode."

"I thought we were working on the big final number today."

"We're supposed to be. Isabella got distracted."

"She's gonna get in trouble," I sing-songed and we both chuckled.

"Lady Marmalade" cut off our laughter, and I studied the girls as they shimmied through the number again. It was a really good dance; everybody felt it.

I loved that buzz running through all of us as we got excited about future scenes. The song ended and we all clapped again, Quinn whooping extra loudly.

"You're happy." I grinned.

"Yeah, well, if you read the script for next week, I get to make out with that hot young thing in the next scene."

I shook my head. When fiction became reality. I knew Quinn liked Trudy. Lucky for them their characters were into each other, too. I glanced at Ashlee, struggling to imagine feeling that way about her. She was cute and pretty, plus a real sweetheart. It wasn't hard for Harley to be in love with her, but she definitely wasn't my type.

A firm throat-clearing grabbed everyone's attention, and we looked over at Travis McKinnon as he stepped into the room. Conway stood beside him and Lisa hovered behind. The girl who I was pretty sure was exactly my type slipped into the room and leaned against the wall. She had her clipboard at the ready and was lightly tapping her pen on the wood.

"Okay, show me." Travis nodded at Isabella.

A hush of anticipation spread across the room as the girls took their positions.

"Now, it's still a little rough." Isabella raised her hands at the men. "We'll obviously shine it up, but this will give you an idea of what I have in mind."

They both nodded, their eyes narrowing critically as the opening clicks of the song echoed through the room.

Having seen the dance twice, I actually kept my eyes on Travis, Con, and—I couldn't help myself—Morgan. The edge of her lip kept rising into that lopsided smirk. Her eyes were glued to the dancers; I could feel the energy flowing out of her as if her body wanted to move with them.

I turned back to the girls and pictured Morgan up there. The image was so damn sexy my groin started twitching. I stood up straight and crossed my arms, deciding it was best not to look over at the tall blonde again.

The girls clustered together for their end position as the song finished, and once again a roar went up. We obviously weren't sick of seeing it yet. All eyes turned to Travis and Con. The director was grinning, his head bobbing with approval. Travis remained staunch for a few agonizing beats before finally giving a stiff nod.

"I like it. Sexy as hell. It'll be perfect for that scene. Lisa, can we get the rights?"

"I'm working on it."

"Good job." He nodded at Isabella.

"Actually, it wasn't just me." She pointed toward Morgan with a smile.

The showrunner's face turned hard as he looked over at his new gofer. "Her?"

"Yes, sir. She had some really great ideas. She was actually the one who suggested the song."

I could see what Isabella was trying to do. Travis had been such an ass the day before, any points for Morgan would be helpful...although it really wasn't having the desired effect.

"What the hell were you doing up in the dance studio?" He glared at Morgan.

"I got here early."

You could tell she was embarrassed and obviously wanted this to happen someplace else, or not at all, but she stood her ground. She wasn't blinking at tears; she kept her chin up, and her beautiful gaze didn't waver.

"It's not your place to come up with dance moves. You're a runner, my *second* assistant. You've been in this industry for a day. You don't have the right to an opinion. You shut up and you do your job. That's it."

"I understand." She nodded without a flinch, acting as though the words were just bouncing right off her.

Isabella rolled her eyes, crossing her arms and firing a few angry glares at our boss.

"Okay." He turned back to his choreographer with a sigh. Her glare disappeared, replaced with a forced smile. "So, I still want to use it. Keep working on it, but not today. The big final number needs to be perfect before we start filming in two hours. Run through a few rehearsals and get your asses to makeup."

He gave the actors a broad smile and then spun out the door, but not before giving Morgan a few sharp words I couldn't hear. She kept her dignity, even waiting until Travis left the room before wiping a drop of his angry spittle off her face.

I wanted her to turn and catch my gaze before she left. I wanted to flash her a sympathetic smile, but she never looked my way. As soon as Travis left, her eyes dropped to the floor and stayed there.

Isabella gave me an exasperated look before clapping her hands.

"Okay, people, 'Don't Stop the Music', let's go."

We ran into our positions, ready to start. My eyes traveled to the door one more time, but it was empty. Although Morgan wasn't there anymore, it was nice to know I'd end up bumping into her again...and when I did, I was asking her out. Anyone who could withstand that kind of humiliating put-down in front of basically the entire cast was worth my time.

SEVEN

MORGAN

So my super-awesome start to the day had been completely shat on by the lovely Travis McKinnon. I thought I was going to die when he gave me worm status up in that dance studio. It was so humiliating, I wanted the floor to open up and swallow me. Thankfully, I'd managed to maintain my dignity. I knew how to switch off my emotions when I needed to; it was an art I'd begun practicing at fourteen. Jody was such a mess, I didn't want her to see me cry as well, so I learned to just switch it off, pretend it didn't hurt. Life was too short for tears.

I spent the rest of the day in robot mode, completing every order with a quiet calm. No smiles, no tears; that was the way to get through. I avoided everyone I could, keeping myself busy. I could sense Sean's eyes on me this morning, in the dance studio, but I couldn't look at him. His smiles were enough to turn my knees to putty, and after what Travis said to me, I didn't want to face anyone.

Clearing my throat, I dug out my car keys and clipped out of the building. It was just on nine p.m. My brain was fried, my feet were killing me...again...and all I wanted was a hot bath and bed.

"Hey, Morgan."

I froze at the sound of Sean's voice. Glancing over my shoulder, I watched him run after me.

"Are you okay?" I strove for my quiet calm, but it was damn hard with him standing that close. If I stretched out my hand, I could touch his face, run the pads of my fingers over his goatee. I clenched my bag strap and smiled. "Did I forget something?"

"No." He shook his head, his white teeth shining. "I was just wondering if you were hungry...or thirsty. I mean, do you drink...or do you...eat?" He winced.

I couldn't help a snicker.

"That was meant to sound way smoother than that, by the way. I even rehearsed it before chasing after you."

My stomach rumbled with mirth, and I pressed my lips together, trying to control it. Sean Jaxon, aka Mr. Cool, was struggling to talk to me?

I was still trying to get over the shock that he was standing out here in the lot, having chased me down.

The keys jingled in my hand as I spun them around my finger. "Actually, I do both of those things."

"I was hoping you'd say that." A smooth smile eased over his face. "I'm also kind of hoping you'll say you're hungry and thirsty right now, because I could remedy that for you."

Holy shit. He was asking me out. This wasn't real.

I swallowed, trying to mask my astonishment. I should have been telling him I was really tired and needed to head home. It might have been Friday, but I still had a full day of work tomorrow. But...

"Yeah, you know what, that'd be great."

"Okay." His dark lips stretched into a smile. "Well, do you want to follow my car and we'll go find us some chow?"

"Sounds good."

I watched him walk a few cars down and get into a very lush Camaro. Feeling like the poor cousin, I started up my sedan and followed Sean. I pulled to the side of the road as he ran into a Subway, loving how real that small gesture made him. Celebrities ate sandwiches, just like we did. I shook my head with a grin and followed him to Griffith Park. We parked on Crystal Springs Drive and walked to a nearby picnic spot.

Taking a seat at the table, he handed me a twelve-inch sub. "Hope you like ham and cheese."

"I'll eat anything." I took the drink with a smile and sipped from the straw. "Mmm, good."

"I figured you could do with some sweetness after your day."

I slowly unwrapped my sandwich and let out a half-laugh, half-sigh.

"Travis is a dick. He shouldn't have treated you that way."

I shrugged. "He just wants people to know who's in charge."

"He should treat his assistants better though."

"He treats Lisa okay."

"She's been with him for a couple of years now."

"Yeah, she probably earned her way into his good books, I guess." I took a bite of the sub and let out a happy sigh.

"Good, right?" Sean took a mammoth bite of his roll and wiggled his eyebrows.

I smiled around my mouthful.

"So, Miss Pritchett, do you think you'll be able to survive the throes of a TV assistant's job?"

"I better be able to. It's the only job I could find." I shook my head, still baffled and embarrassed by this fact.

"It'll be okay. You just have to work your way up the ranks. Who knows, soon you might be a showrunner yourself."

I smirked. "Yeah, right."

"Come on, now. You were amazing today."

"How?"

"Your idea, for the 'Lady Marmalade' song. It was good."

I made a little scoffing noise in my throat.

"Hey." Sean's voice was stern. "It was good. It was sexy. Damn, woman, the show needs ideas just like that."

I tried to hide how much his compliment meant to me by taking another bite of food.

"You used to dance?"

"When I was a kid."

"I could see it today, when you were watching; you looked like you wanted to be up there with them."

"What can I say; music does something to my body."

"Makes it want to move. Makes it want to groove."

I chuckled. "Pretty much."

"So, why you being a runner then? Why you not

dancin'?"

I had to bite back my smile at the way he was talking. It was like a part of his old self was breaking through his cool exterior. I had no idea what he was like as a kid, but it definitely made me curious about his upbringing.

"I had to give it up." I played with the edge of my Subway wrapper, my throat thickening with regret. This was why I never spoke about it...the thickening in my throat. It came on every time I relived that awful day when I stood in front of my dance teacher and told her I had to quit.

"You have to what?" Ms. Finnermore's lips parted.

"I'm sorry, but I just can't fit it in anymore."

"Morgan, you can't just quit; you're one of my best dancers."

I ignored the compliment, knowing I had to stay strong. Jody needed me to.

"It's not that I don't love it, and I might pick it up again one day, but right now, I have other responsibilities."

"Like what? You're fourteen?"

Her incredulous tone was like a whip across my cheek.

I knew how old I was!

"Life's just gotten a little complicated, and I have to be home straight after school now."

"What about the high school applications?"

"It's not—" I shook my head. "Dad can't afford it, and it'll still be busier than normal school. Plus it's not in Pasadena, and I really need to be near home."

"What's going on, Morgan? Is there anything I can help you with?" Her long fingers rested gently on my shoulder.

My eyes burned, but I refused to them glisten with tears.

"No." I cleared my throat, trying to eradicate that

thickening in my windpipe.

"Morgan, what's happened?" I wanted to open up to her right then, to let all my tears fall and tell her my tragic news, but I couldn't. If I fell apart in that dance studio, I'd never be able to pick up the pieces.

"Look, it's kind of private, Ms. Finnermore. I appreciate you wanting to help and everything, but you can't. Things have changed, and I have to be there for my family. Dancing will just have to wait."

And it did.

"Why'd you give it up?" Sean studied me carefully in the dusky light.

My bottom lip stuck out and I shrugged, not sure why I felt like telling him. I rarely mentioned this to anyone. "My mom left and I had to look after my little sister. There just wasn't time to fit in dance rehearsals around grocery shopping and cooking and cleaning and helping a ten-year-old with homework." My voice hitched. I sniffed and took a large bite of my sandwich, hoping to avoid talking for a minute.

"Where was your dad?"

I brushed the crumbs from my bottom lip and swallowed. "Working. Mom took her part-time wage with her and things got a little tight."

"Where'd she go?"

My chest restricted, the muscles pulling so tight I thought they might ping straight off my rib cage.

"I don't know where she went then, but last I heard, she sings at this little lounge in a Las Vegas casino." I placed my sandwich on the table, a bitter taste filling my mouth.

"You ever see her?"

"Nope." I accentuated the P.

"How old were you when it happened?"

"Fourteen."

"Whoa, that's kinda harsh."

I shrugged. "It made me strong, I guess. Bulletproof." I smirked, needing this conversation to be over.

"Bulletproof?"

"Yeah, it's a good way to live. It's helped me get over numerous breakups and whenever life gets particularly shitty, I can just give it the finger and start singing." I immediately launched into "Bulletproof" by La Roux.

Sean's laughter rose as I worked my way through the verse, bobbing my head and lifting my finger. When I got to the chorus, he joined me, even harmonizing on the long notes. Man, he had a good voice. I stopped singing and let him finish the chorus by himself.

"What?" He grinned at me.

"You're just..." I shrugged. "Really talented."

"So are you." His quiet voice was silky, making my skin tingle.

Words filled my mouth, but none of them could break free. I was paralyzed by his soft blue gaze, unable to look away from it, desperate for it to never end.

Loud laughter from across the grass made me jump.

Glancing at my watch, I realized it was already ten-thirty, probably not the best time to be out in a park.

"I guess we should head off."

"Yeah, I guess so." Sean started gathering up the trash. I went to help him, but he raised his hands. "No, ma'am. Let me do the dishes, please."

Laughter shot out of my belly and I raised my hands, stepping away from the table. I fished out my keys as I waited for him to finish cleaning up and then stepped in beside him as we walked to our cars via the trash can.

Our arms kept brushing, our hands occasionally

hitting each other's. I felt like I was in middle school again, that giddy feeling flickering through my stomach as I wondered if he was going to take my hand.

He never did.

We got to my car, and he stood a pace away from me, his hands in his pockets, his eyes gently caressing me.

"Thanks for joining me for a late-night snack."

"Anytime." I smiled. "You owe me anyway."

"I owe you?"

"Yeah, you somehow managed to wrangle a little family history out of me, and you now owe me some history of your own."

"I'm surprised you don't know it all already." He frowned, scratching behind his ear.

"I only know what the Internet tells me, and that's not always true."

His lips pursed to the side before breaking into a smile. "I knew I liked you for a reason, Morgan Pritchett."

I could feel my insides glowing as he winked at me, reaching past me to open my door. I slid into the seat, buckling my seatbelt and waving goodbye as he turned for his car. He followed me out, honking farewell as I turned off toward Pasadena.

I guess it couldn't really qualify as a date or anything. He didn't kiss me goodbye, didn't even try to hold my hand. In fact, there was nothing date-like about our evening. It was just two people having a bite together.

As I slowed to a stop at the intersection, it occurred to me that I hadn't done that with a guy in years. I had basically been dating since I was fifteen. Guys were never friends with me, because they always knew they could get more.

I couldn't decide whether to be happy or sad.

On the one hand, being friends with Sean would

be amazing, but man, I wanted so much more.

"Who the hell are you kidding?" I looked at my eyes in the rearview mirror. "Sean Jaxon! Take whatever you can get, Morgan."

I rested my head back against my seat as I waited for the light to turn green, a smile slowly stretching my lips wide.

Sean Jaxon.

Unreal.

EIGHT

SEAN

"And that's a wrap for today. Sean, you can go whenever."

"Thanks, Con." I gave him a quick salute and headed straight for my dressing room. I was so ready to be gone. This week had been huge, but thankfully I didn't have any more shoots. I had a recording session in the studio for one song the next morning, and then I was free until Monday. Man, that felt good.

I moved sideways to let a harried runner through. In contrast to Morgan, she wore her heart all over her sleeve, and everyone knew when she was having a bad day. For some reason, Travis didn't seem to notice her as much. I didn't know what it was about Morgan, but he really seemed to have it in for her.

I hadn't seen her around much throughout the week. She'd been in and out a lot more. The two times she pulled a full day here, I managed to catch up with her after work. The first time, I saw her leaving as I was unlocking my car. She came over and we ended up talking in my car for nearly two hours, just shooting the breeze, mainly about my family that time around. It wasn't until my watch beeped eleven that we even noticed the time.

Then on Wednesday, I managed to stop her before she drove out the gate. I was really stopping her to say goodnight, but she asked if I wanted to follow her for some chow. She took me to a little Mexican restaurant in Pasadena. We sat in a back booth and once again time disappeared until, at midnight, the proprietor kicked our laughing butts out the door. I was so drunk on tiredness and my one beer, I don't even know how I made it home.

Working long days took its toll, but it was also energizing, and ending my day with a fix of Morgan was never a bad thing.

She fascinated me, she enchanted me, and the days I didn't get to see her were always disappointing. I still couldn't believe I hadn't gotten her phone number yet. What a damn fool.

I was tempted to ask Lisa but didn't want her nosing around or jumping to any conclusions. It didn't matter that they were the right ones; on-set gossip was a pain in the ass, and I didn't want to fuel it. What I wanted was to find Morgan in a quiet little corner and ask her out on a date. A real date.

I had planned on asking her that day, but the one time I spotted her, she'd been rushing out the door while I'd been heading into makeup. I hadn't seen her since.

With a heavy sigh, I glanced at my watch and figured there was no point sticking around for three hours on the off-chance she might come back. I might as well just head home and kick my feet up.

Running a hand over my head, I glanced up and noticed Rhonda leaning against my doorframe.

"Hey." I smiled. "What are you doing here?"

"I was driving past."

"Everything cool?"

"Yeah, just wanted to book you in for a couple of things." She flipped open her iPad Mini case and punched in her code. "So, the cologne ad is set up for two weeks from today. I've checked your filming schedule and you're free. It'll just be a one-day shoot, probably nine 'til three, something like that. Nothing too taxing."

I couldn't think of anything worse, but I nodded and forced a grin.

"And things here seem to be going pretty well. You have a lighter filming schedule next week, so I thought we could actually catch up for a meal or something; there are some dates coming up that I want to plan for. I also checked in with your talent agent, and she has a couple of things in the pipeline I think we should discuss."

"Sure. Whatever. You look after my calendar, so go ahead and book me in."

"Will do."

I pulled off my shirt and hung it in the closet before rummaging in my bag for a fresh T-shirt. Collecting my stuff, I threw Rhonda another smile and headed for the exit. She followed me, her clipping heels sounding like gunshots on the hard floor.

"Are you free tomorrow night?" she asked over my shoulder. "Maybe we could catch up then."

I shrugged, about to say yes, when I saw her. It was only a flash of blonde, but I knew that stride anywhere. "Actually, no."

I paused, my eyes traveling to where Morgan might be going.

"What's the matter?" Rhonda frowned, her small glasses sliding down her nose.

"Nothing. I just saw someone I need to talk to."

Her eyes narrowed, her big lips pulling into a half-pout.

"What?"

"You dating someone?"

I rolled my eyes, not really wanting to get into it. "No."

"Who was that girl who just came in?"

"Huh?"

Her left eyebrow arched. "That girl. The one who made you stop walking, the one who made you suddenly change your mind about our meeting tomorrow."

"Oh her; that's, um..."

"Don't tell me it's no one."

I sighed. "Her name's Morgan and it's no big deal."

"Your face tells me otherwise." Rhonda huffed, flipping open her iPad again. "Who is she?"

"No one you need to know about."

"Actress? What role does she play?"

I licked my bottom lip. "Not an actress."

"Hmph, so why are you interested in her then?"

"It's—Rhonda, you don't need to know this."

"I don't need to know this?" She pointed at her chest. "Two words for you, Sean— Abigail Tripoli."

I bit the inside of my cheek and cleared my throat.

"Do I need to say more?"

"This is different. She's not famous; no one's interested in her."

"They're interested in you, and if you like her,

they're gonna want to know about it." She tutted. "It's too soon for another Abigail situation."

"We're not going to get another Abigail situation."

"Look, you know as well as I do that they're freaking vultures. They'll jump on anything, and now that Abigail's been cheated on, she could be coming after you again."

"Isn't she dating some rock star?"

"They broke up last night."

"Huh." I shrugged, feeling very nonplussed about the whole thing. I couldn't give two shits who Abigail was seeing, and if she ever showed up on my door again, I'd tell her exactly where to go.

Rhonda tipped her head, giving me an exasperated look. "You're not going to drop this, are you?"

"One date, that's all."

"Okay, fine. I'm not your booty boss, but make sure you take her somewhere nice and quiet...somewhere private where the press can't find you."

I forced a smile and gave her a nod. "I'll watch my back, Rhonda. Don't worry."

She gave me a motherly grin. "I just want to look after ya."

"I know, and you do a great job." I wrapped my arms around her small frame and gave her a squeeze. She let me go with a little laugh and then her phone started chirping.

I took my chance to walk the other way. I didn't want to let Rhonda down. I knew she had my best interests at heart, but I also didn't want to have to hide in the shadows, either. I wanted to take Morgan dancing, and there was a hot little club in town I knew she'd love. I was pretty sure the press weren't allowed in, so if we could sneak in the door, we'd have a private evening; there just wouldn't be anything quiet about it.

I grinned, heading the way Morgan had gone. I saw her standing next to Travis, nodding at something he was saying. Not wanting to cause any more trouble for her, I hung back, watching the exchange.

"I did everything you asked me to," Morgan said calmly. "I can't control the traffic in Los Angeles, so the thirty-minute delay was not my doing. Now, is there anything else you need before I leave for the night?"

He looked his watch. "You've still got three hours before I let you go, so don't think you can skip out early."

"I wasn't asking to skip out early. I was asking if there was a job you would like me to do; otherwise, I'm happy to go and take a coffee break."

He glared at her. I couldn't see her face, but I bet she was smirking back. That seemed to be her best defense against him.

After a long pause, Travis grunted. "I'm sure there's some studio that needs cleaning or something. Lisa." He tipped his head toward Morgan.

Lisa gave her co-worker a sympathetic smile before mumbling something.

Morgan pulled her shoulders back and gave a stiff nod before leaving the room. I let her walk straight past me and quietly followed her down to the lunch room. She strode up to the counter and placed her hands on the cool metal, gripping the edge and letting out a long sigh. Then her back went straight. She flicked her head and opened the cupboard, yanking mugs down one by one and slapping them onto the counter.

"Hey."

She jumped and spun to face me. "Oh, hi."

"I didn't think you were in today."

"Yeah, I've been in and out. The dry cleaning/car wash run took longer than I thought."

"Was Travis giving you a hard time?"

Her jaw worked to the side. "Nothing I can't handle."

She spun back to the coffee machine and loaded up a fresh filter.

"Job getting to you, huh?"

"No." She shook her head. "It's not the job. I'm grateful to even have one, I just...look, it's immature."

I perched my butt on the nearest table to her. "I'm sure it's not."

"I just..." Dumping a healthy spoonful of coffee into the machine, she slammed the lid shut. "I just hate the way he talks to me, like I'm some worm. I mean, a thank-you would be nice, sure, but I don't even expect that. I know this is a busy place. I know everyone plays an important role in making this happen, I just— I don't— Why does he have to make my role feel worthless? Why the fuck did he even hire me, if he doesn't want me here!" She threw her hands in the air.

I wanted to reach for them, rub my thumbs over her knuckles as I pulled her into my arms.

"He needs you here. We all do. You're right; we're all part of this big machine and every single person is important to making it run smoothly." I stood and carefully approached her, sliding my hand across her lower back. "Even the coffee maker," I whispered in her ear.

She drew in a breath through her nose, turning to look at me. Our faces were an inch apart, our eyes dancing as we breathed each other's air.

A slow smile worked across her lips and I took my chance.

"You busy tomorrow night?"

"I'm working until eight...supposedly." She

rolled her eyes.

"Do you think you'll have enough energy to go home, shower up, and let some guy take you out dancing?"

Her brown gaze surged with surprise. Pleasure followed swiftly in its wake.

"You asking me on a date, Mr. Jaxon?"

"Yeah, I am."

Her lips parted, her eyes rounding as she looked away from me. Her finger tapped on the countertop as the coffee started filling the pot. My hand dropped from her back, and I stepped away from her, eyeing her carefully. Crossing my arms, I decided to go for cocky and see how she'd take it.

"Come on, you know you want to say yes."

Her eyebrows arched, a smirk cresting over her lips. I moved back toward her, sliding my hand along the countertop until it rested against her pinky finger.

"It's dancing. I know you can't resist."

Her tongue brushed across her bottom lip as she looked across at me.

"You're right; it's the dancing I can't resist." Her smoldering brown eyes said something else entirely. Electricity fired through my muscles like a shock wave.

I hissed in a breath. "Damn, girl, you're gonna do me in."

She grinned. "Wait 'til you get me on the dance floor."

I thought I was going to combust. She pulled off cocky a hell of a lot better than I did.

"Morgan, where the hell are those coffees!"

I jumped away from Morgan before Lisa appeared.

"Hey, Lisa." I grabbed my stuff and headed out the door as she burst into the room.

"Oh, hey, Sean." She barely noticed me, her eyes

going straight for Morgan. "Travis is going to have a fit. You've already been late today."

"I can't make water boil any faster, Lisa."

"I know." The first assistant sighed. "He just told me to come down here and give you hell."

I paused outside the door, peeking my head around the corner to see Morgan's reaction.

She spun to face Lisa with a tired frown. "That guy is such a—"

I caught her eye and did a quick shimmy in the doorway. The last thing she needed to do was insult him. If Lisa ever let it slip, Morgan would be fired...and selfishly, I wanted her to stay.

Her lips quirked with a smile, and I ducked out of the way before Lisa turned to see me.

"Tell Travis I'm pouring the coffee now and will bring him the very first cup."

Lisa sighed. "You're doing a really great job, Morgan, way better than your predecessors. I know it's hell to start with, but if you can hang in there, it'll get better. I promise."

"Yeah, I'll try."

"Just make sure when you're away from this place you have as much fun as possible. Find whatever it is you love and do that thing. It helps release the tension."

A smile crested over my lips as I heard Lisa's words and Morgan's amused reply.

"Good idea. I'll make sure I do that."

I'd make sure of it, too.

NINE

MORGAN

"So, you're enjoying it then?" I glanced at the iPad perched on my desk as I wiggled into my maroon dress.

"Yes. It's amazing!" Jody squealed from the screen. "I love all my classes, my roommate's a peach, my teachers are so incredible, and my dance teacher...holy deliciousness."

I grinned at my little sister, her sparkling demeanor making everything better.

"What's the workload like?"

"Pretty intense. We've already started rehearsals for a freshman performance in December, but it'll be okay. It doesn't feel like hard work when you enjoy it, you know what I mean?"

"Yep." I clipped the word short, hoping she wouldn't notice. I didn't want to tell her about the epic fail my job had become. I did the side-zip up on the dress and smoothed it down over my hips. "How do I look?"

"Freaking amazing. I can't believe you are going on a date with Mr. Bulletproof. Sean Jaxon! Holy crap, Morgan!"

"I know. I know. It's insane, but he's a really nice guy. Normal." I perched on the edge of my chair and looked at the screen. "When I'm at work with all these people, you can forget they're celebrities; most of them are just easy-going talented people. The fame hasn't gone to their heads."

"That's cool. That's what I want to be like. You know, when I get famous."

We grinned at each other.

"It'll happen for you, Jo-Jo. You're such a mega-talent."

"Oh, stop." She flicked her hand at me, but I could tell she loved it. She'd wanted to be on stage since Mom took us to the stage show, *Annie*. I was nine, she was five, and since then she'd had stars in her eyes.

I went back to my closet and pulled out my silver pumps, holding them up so Jody could see them.

"Yes, definitely, and then you could wear those silver drop earrings and that bracelet that matches."

"Oh yeah, good idea." I moved to my jewelry box and pulled out the different pieces. "These ones?" I held them up to my ears.

"Yep, perfect." She beamed and then did another squeal.

"Jody, stop, you're gonna make me nervous."

"Well, I'm sorry, but I'm happy for you."

My insides buzzed as I slipped the earrings in. I suppressed the urge to jump up and do a happy dance. I was so excited, I nearly felt ill. When he'd touched my back and asked me out, I thought my heart would stop beating. I hadn't felt this way about a guy since high school. Even Brad hadn't sent my mind into a giddy spin. Maybe it was because we'd ended up in bed together on our first date. With Sean it seemed different; we were getting to know each other in this slow, old-fashioned way, and I actually kind of liked it.

I bet his father was a gentleman; he totally had those qualities about him. I wondered if I'd ever get to meet his family. Would our relationship go that far?

Sick nerves bubbled in my belly. When it came to Sean, I didn't have butterflies—I had bumblebees. The lightheaded rush made me smile.

Jody giggled as she watched my face.

"Shut up." I laughed. "How about you? Anyone sweeping you off your feet?"

"Maybe." She looked coy, her gaze dropping away from me as her lips grew with a smile.

"Ooooooo, nice! What's he like?"

"He's sweet and funny and so incredibly talented. We love all the same things."

"That's a good sign."

"Yeah, I know. I..." She let out a breathy laugh. "I've never felt this way, Morgan. It's..." She wrung her hands.

"I'm happy for you, sweetie. What's his name?"

"Um..."

The doorbell rang. I jerked in my seat. "Oh my gosh, that's him."

"Yay!" She gave me a thumbs-up. "Go, dance your ass off and have fun."

"Okay." We both grinned at each other and blew a kiss. I pressed the screen and shot out of my chair, feeling bad that I hadn't gotten to ask more about Jody's man. I'd have to do that next time.

The doorbell rang again. I grabbed the clutch off my desk and headed down the stairs. When I opened the door, Sean was standing there in dark jeans and a turquoise button-down shirt that matched his eyes perfectly. He smelled like heaven and looked even more divine.

It helped that his eyes were on fire as they trailed down my body and back up again. His forehead wrinkled as a look of awe crossed his face.

"Wow."

One word and it was enough to send my insides twirling.

"Way to make a girl feel pretty, Mr. Jaxon."

"Well, you are. You should wear this to work." He held out his hand, and I took it with a chuckle.

"I'm sure Travis would love that."

"Who cares about Travis. I'm talking about me."

"Now, now. I wouldn't want to be a distraction." I winked and turned to lock the door. Dad was out bowling with his friends. It was a relief to be able to slip from the house without making introductions. I was nervous enough as it was, and I didn't tend to get nervous very easily. It was obvious that when it came to guys, Sean was in a league of his own.

He opened the car door for me and I slipped inside, smoothing down my dress and picking at a piece of fluff.

Sean slid in and started up the engine.

It rumbled to life and I nodded. "This is a really nice car."

He made a clicking sound with his tongue. He did that a lot and I really liked it. It was cute.

Checking the road, he pulled out and then glanced over at me.

"I've wanted a nice car since I was a kid. I didn't

grow up with much money, and we always had these falling-apart family wagons. I dreamed of owning something fast, something new...and I finally got it."

He ran his fingers over the steering wheel as if the car was his baby.

"What'd your parents think?"

"Oh, you know. Mom thought it was a waste of well-earned money. Dad said that, but later asked if he could take it for a little drive." Sean chuckled. "He loved it."

"You close to your dad?"

"Yeah, I mean, I'm close to both my parents. We're a pretty tight family."

"That's cool. You're lucky. Not everyone gets that."

"I know." He gave me a soft smile.

I swallowed and looked out the window, wishing I hadn't made the conversation all serious. Tonight was supposed to be about fun, about forgetting a grueling day at work and relishing the fact I could sleep in tomorrow.

"So, where are we going?" I clutched the purse in my lap.

"Well, with you lookin' so fine, I figure I should take you dancin'."

I grinned.

"There's a little club I know. Great DJ, great dance floor. I used to go there all the time."

"You haven't been in a while?"

"Nah." His big lips turned down. "Kind of been laying low for the last few months."

I wanted to ask him if it was to do with the Abigail thing but didn't want to admit that I'd been stalking him online. I pressed my lips together. He'd tell me about that when he was ready.

"Are you sure you don't mind taking me out? We could do something quiet if you wanted to."

"Hell no. Girl, we're going dancin' tonight."

I grinned, loving the way he talked. He was so different from Brad, Mr. Nebraska. Sean had a street cool that was so incredibly sexy. I'd never dated a guy like him before.

We spent the rest of the trip chatting about work. I didn't really want to, but it inevitably came up. Thankfully, most of the conversation was about Harley and Sasha's love story and where we thought the writers should take it. We came up with some very comical scenarios, and by the time we got to the club we were both fighting hysterics.

Sean pulled up outside and handed his keys to the valet. As soon as I was around his side of the car, he put his hand on my lower back and practically pushed me through the door. He gave a short nod to the bouncer, who let us pass quickly, and then we were standing at the top of the stairs leading down to the club.

"You okay?" I turned to him when we got inside.

"Yeah." He nodded.

I touched his arm.

"Just wanted to avoid the cameras."

"I didn't even see them." I glanced back to the door.

"They're always lurking." He shook his head. "Come on, let's go have some fun."

The DJ must have read Sean's mind, because as we descended the stairs, a new song started pumping - "I Gotta Feeling" by Black Eyed Peas.

"I love this song!" I yelled in Sean's ear.

"Let's go, baby."

We dumped our stuff on a free table and jiggled toward the dance floor. Sean's hand rested lightly on my hip and I spun to face him, lifting my arms in the air and swaying my hips to the beat. He stepped into my space and started moving in time with me.

We both shouted, "Mazel Tov!" and laughed, building up a quick sweat as we boogied with the crowd. The beat pulsed through me, making me forget about work, Travis, my aching feet, and my tired body.

In that moment, I was alive.

"I Gotta Feeling" faded and was replaced with "Give Me Everything" by Pitbull. I let out a whoop and changed my rhythm to match the music. Sean grinned at me, placing his hands on my hips and sliding them up to my waist. Electric currents flowed through my body, sparking every place his hands touched me.

Our eyes connected as we swayed together, his laughing eyes turning serious. The strobe lights started and with each flash, I caught a glimpse of his vibrant blue orbs. The beat thumping around us went fuzzy in my ears as he touched a hand to my face, his long, black thumb gently running over my lip. The chorus kicked in, talking about giving everything and making the most of the night. I slid my hand up his arm, my fingers resting on his shoulder, willing him to move toward me, to touch his luscious lips to mine.

I watched them quirk with a little smile. The strobe lights stopped flashing, and there he was, leaning into me, ready to...

"Hey, holy shit, man. It's Sean Jaxon!" Someone grabbed his arm, pulling him away.

Disappointment marred his expression, mingled with a flash of anger. He pressed a smile over his lips and looked down at the enthusiastic guy who'd pulled us apart.

"I loved you in *Domino Effect*."

"Thanks." He nodded.

"Can I get your picture?"

He cleared his throat. It was so obvious he

wanted to say no, but instead gave a little nod and let the guy put his arm around him and snap a selfie.

"Thanks so much, bro."

Sean shook the guy's hand and turned back to me. I went to step into his space but was shoved aside by a waif of a girl who reeked of alcohol. My heel turned, and I fell into the person behind us.

The guy caught my elbow to stop me from falling.

"Sorry." I gave him a weak smile. He brushed it off and went back to dancing while I turned to the little spitfire who was now going off at Sean.

"What you did to Abigail was unforgivable. So she cheated on you, get over it, it's not like you can't score yourself another girl!" Her words slurred over each other as she pointed a finger in Sean's face. Her small body only came up to his shoulder, but her words were like cannonballs.

Sean stood back from her, his hands in his pockets, just taking it all. He looked over her head at me and indicated for me to go and get our stuff.

I hated to leave him but knew our night was pretty much over thanks to that inebriated little bitch. I quickly retrieved our stuff and made it back to Sean's side in less than a minute.

"Didn't your mother ever teach you not to hit girls!"

That was it. There was no way in hell she was getting away with that one.

I gripped her shoulder and spun her around to face me.

"He never hit her, you little psycho."

Her head jerked at my insult before her face bunched into an angry snarl.

"As if it's any of your business anyway. Who the hell do you think you are? You don't even know this man." I pointed over her head at Sean. "So back off!"

I'd said my piece, far less elegantly than I meant to, but I was pissed. Just because he was a celebrity didn't mean people could come up and openly slander him.

I went to move past the drunken little tart, but she side-stepped and got in my way again.

"No one talks to me like that."

I didn't even see her fist coming. It landed straight in my belly, and for a chick that small, she was surprisingly strong. I doubled over, letting out a breath, my hand curling into a fist.

I wasn't a fighter normally, but this girl needed putting into her place.

"Hey!" Sean grabbed her arm before I could do anything, spinning her away from me.

And that's when the flashes started. Unfortunately, it wasn't strobe lights this time; the click of the camera was right in his face.

"How the hell did they get in here?" Sean muttered as he shifted his body and tried to block me from the lens.

Taking my arm, he shuffled me across the dance floor, using the crowd to shield us. I had gotten over the initial blow to my stomach and went to straighten up.

"Keep your head down." Sean placed his hand on my head and made me crouch again.

The clicking still followed us, along with repetitive shouts. "Mr. Jaxon! Mr. Jaxon!"

"Sean! A minute of your time!"

"Sean! Sean Jaxon!"

He ignored the calls and kept moving, pulling over to the far corner of the room. As soon as we were beneath the exit sign, he pushed it open with his shoulder and guided me outside. Stopping in the doorway, he scrambled in his pocket for some bills and handed me a small wad of cash.

"Take the stairs, they'll lead you up to the main street and you can catch a taxi."

"You're not coming with me?"

"I don't want them to see you. You shouldn't have to put up with this shit."

"But—"

"I'm sorry." Regret washed over his expression. "Text me when you get home, so I know you're safe."

"But, what about—" He was gone before I could even finish my sentence, back into the shark pit. I glimpsed a couple of bright flashes before the door slammed shut.

I had no idea what Sean was about to do; I was guessing smile at a few photographers and slowly make his way out the front door...leave like a gentleman.

Letting out a short sigh, I headed up the stairs. I knew Sean wanted me to stay out of sight and catch a taxi home, but I wanted to make sure he was okay. Sneaking around the edge of the building, I kept my eyes on the door of the club. It took thirty minutes, but eventually Sean popped out of the club door, surrounded by photographers. He kept a pleasant smile in place and waved to everyone as he got into his car.

I wondered what happened to Little Miss Punchy.

Sean pulled away from the curb, and I moved, heading around the block to hail a taxi. I caught one easily and was home thirty minutes later. Feeling pretty dejected, I paid my fare and then slumped up the front steps.

My phone buzzed and I pulled it out.

You home safe? Sorry about tonight.

With a glum smile, I texted back.

Home safe. Don't worry about it. Maybe another time?

He never replied.

TEN

SEAN

I stayed in bed until two in the afternoon. I'd turned my phone off as soon as Morgan had replied. I didn't have the heart to send her a text back. What could I say? I'm surprised she even wanted a next time.

I still couldn't believe that drunk little bitch had punched her in the stomach. Hearing Morgan stand up for me was pure gold. I mean, yeah, I wished she hadn't said anything, but it was also pretty sweet to watch her go for it with that firecracker.

I loved her fearless strength. No one really got to see it at work, but man, I wished they could. I wished she could stand up to Travis like that, but she'd be fired in a microsecond.

With a groan, I checked my clock, glad I didn't have a family thing on today. Kip was away on business and Florence's kids were all sick. No one wanted the germs passed on, so Mama had canceled the weekly lunch. I had been relieved; it meant I could have spent as long a night as I'd wanted to with Morgan and slept my Sunday away.

Unfortunately, thanks to the frickin' paparazzi and a psycho fan, my night had been cut short. Damn, I'd been so close to kissing Morgan; I'd felt her breath on my skin. Squeezing my eyes shut, I tried not to imagine how good she would have tasted. It was probably better not to know what I was missing.

I couldn't date her again. It wasn't fair to inflict my fame on her. She deserved to date a normal guy who could take her anywhere and she'd be safe.

Punched in the stomach!

Shit!

That had to be the lousiest date in the history of man.

Picking up my phone, I ran my thumb over the black screen, wishing I could leave it that way for the rest of the weekend, but I'd never get away with it.

I held down the button and tapped in my code when the screen came to life. I had ten text messages and three missed calls.

I hadn't even cleared two texts when the phone started singing.

With a sigh, I touched the screen.

"Hey, Rhonda." I winced, rubbing my eyes.

"What the hell, Sean! I told you to take her somewhere quiet. Did I not say that to you?"

"We wanted to go dancing." My voice sounded flat and hollow.

"So, choose some celebrity-less dive."

"That club has the best DJ in town. I wanted her to have a good night."

"Well, yeah, she obviously did. I mean, I think. The reports say you arrived with some blonde girl and left on your own. What did you do with her?"

"I snuck her out the back." I propped myself up on my elbow and rolled onto my side. "Did they get any photos of her?"

"No, just you man-handling some little drunk bird."

"That bitch punched Morgan in the gut."

Rhonda sighed. "That's why I told you quiet."

"Look, I got her out and went back in and did some damage control, okay."

"Yeah, I guess I have to admit there's some great shots of you here."

I grimaced. "What does it say?"

"After a minor altercation with a drunken Abigail fan, Sean Jaxon made the most of his night, dancing with his fans and flashing his stunning smile at the camera. He remained tight-lipped about his current work, but told us that something would be brewing in September. We all wait with eager anticipation to see what Mr. Bulletproof has in store for us next."

"Well, that doesn't sound so bad."

"I haven't read the other one yet."

I groaned.

"Who is Sean Jaxon dating now? Arriving at Club Hybrid last night with a tall blonde, Sean ended up leaving the venue alone after an altercation inside. No one knows the mystery woman's name, but I'm sure we'd all like to know what Abigail Tripoli thinks about it. Having just broken up with her rock star lover, rumors are floating that the pole-dancing actress is hoping for reconciliation with her ex-boyfriend."

"That is such bullshit!"

"I know, I know, but this will blow over. Just don't talk about your love life. You know, I really think, for your sake, that you should refrain from dating...or at least public dating, for a little longer. If you like this girl, you really don't want to pull her into anything."

"Yeah, I know. She doesn't deserve this shit."

"The trials of being a celebrity, huh? Well done for working it to your advantage."

"Yeah, thanks," I mumbled.

"Oh, and expect a call from Andrew today. You know he'll want every detail."

I cringed thinking about my publicist and how long that call would take. He liked to analyze everything, making sure all the angles were worked to the best advantage.

I hung up the phone with a heavy sigh, not wanting to check the rest of my messages.

Throwing it onto the covers, I rolled to my stomach and buried my face in my pillow. I wanted the world to stop moving for a couple of days. I wanted to sink into my mattress and not exist.

How the hell was I supposed to face Morgan tomorrow?

What the hell was I going to say to her?

*****

I took the chicken's way out and spent most of the next day buried in work. I saw Morgan flash past me a couple of times, but I didn't chase after her. Thankfully, Travis was keeping her so busy she didn't have a chance to corner me, either.

It ended up being a really shitty day. There was a problem with the lighting, and we had to re-shoot all our morning's work in the afternoon. I was so over watching the "Lady Marmalade" dance and giving Ashlee a disappointed glare at the end of it.

For such a show-stopper, I think everyone was hating the song by the time we left at the end of the day. It was nine thirty when I finally started heading for my car. I was tired, flat, and wanted to crawl into bed. Sleep would be a sweet respite.

"Sean."

I placed my hand on the roof of my car, tempted to open the door and drive off before she could reach me. But my pop had taught me better, so I slowly turned to watch Morgan approach me.

She paused her step, waiting for a car to drive past us before closing the gap. I leaned against the car and crossed my arms, glancing across the lot. It looked like there weren't many left. I was glad I had ignored my designated spot and parked in the back corner this morning. I had felt like being in the shadows today and my hunch was right. I didn't want people seeing me and Morgan together. If any of them had seen the headlines, they'd be able to piece things together too easily.

"Are you okay?" She sounded so concerned it made my chest restrict.

"Yeah." I rubbed my hand over my head. "Yeah, how about you? Your stomach okay?"

"All good." She rubbed it with a short smile. "I'm really sorry about the weekend. I didn't mean to make it worse for you."

"Hey, you didn't."

She shook her head. "I should have kept my mouth shut with that chick, but I just hated the way she was talking to you. You don't deserve that. She doesn't know anything."

"Some fans are...a little over the top."

"A little." She scoffed. "That bitch was insane."

"Drunk." I shrugged.

Morgan pressed her lips together,

disappointment flashing over her face as she read my expression.

She tipped her head to the side and nodded, reaching into her bag and pulling out some money.

"Here, this is for the cab ride." She held out a small wad of cash.

I lifted my hand. "Don't be insane. I wanted to pay."

"No, it's the change. I appreciated you paying for it. Thank you for getting me home."

"Keep it." I flicked my hand.

"Sean, it's your money; I don't want it." She stepped toward me, holding the cash.

"Neither do I." I closed my palm around her hand, my breath catching in my throat. The current traveling up my arm was intense. I wanted to pull her to my chest and finish what I started on that dance floor.

She swallowed, her eyes sad. "I know you don't want to date me anymore. I like to think it's because you're trying to protect me, rather than not wanting to spend any time with me."

"Of course that's the reason. Damn, Morgan, you...you're gold."

Her lips rose with a little half-smile. "I'm not afraid, you know, of the cameras...and the fans. I can do it."

"You deserve better than that."

"I don't want better. I want you. I'll take whatever risks come with that."

Her words stumped me. I wanted to argue with her, to tell her she was wrong and she'd regret it later, but... she wanted me and dammit, I wanted her, too.

I squeezed her money-filled fist and tugged her toward me. She landed against my chest, her soft breasts pressing into my shirt. I held her against me, spreading my hands over her lower back and loving the way her spine curved. I loved her shape. She wasn't a skinny arrow; she was an hourglass. I ran my free hand over her shoulder, gliding my fingers up her long neck, my thumb skimming her sharp chin.

Damn, she was beautiful. Her breath whistled over me as she closed the distance between us.

The pressure of her lips on mine sent my senses to a new planet. My fingers gripped the nape of her neck as her tongue brushed my lower lip. We opened our mouths together, our tongues dancing a smooth tango. She tasted like peppermint. I gently sucked her bottom lip into my mouth before pulling away from her.

"Girl, you must have some kind of magical powers or something. I ain't never gonna be able to resist you now."

Her breathy laugh kissed my skin and she looked me in the eye, her brown gaze dancing with pleasure. "So don't."

With a grin, I pressed my palm into her back, melding us together and diving into another kiss that held a new level of intensity and passion.

Yes, there were risks, but we could face them. We'd just keep things quiet like Rhonda suggested. No one had to know we were dating. That way I could keep Morgan safe and we could be together, because after this taste, I didn't think I had the power to let her go.

ELEVEN

SEAN

I was right. I couldn't let her go. Everything about Morgan drew me in. Like a moth to a flame, I was done.

I watched her from the corner of my eye as she spoke to Lisa, my conversation with Isabella from only an hour before skirting through my head.

"You're smiling again."

I ran my fingers over my lips, my mouth making a big O as I tried to eradicate my constant grin. It was damn hard. Morgan had been on set all morning, and every time I got a glimpse of her smoky hotness...damn, it was getting hard to control myself, especially since I hadn't seen her in nearly a week.

We'd been secretly dating for just over a month. We hadn't openly said we should keep it hidden on set, but we both did it. Maybe it was a sixth sense or something, but when we saw each other, we acted as if everything was normal. At least I thought that was what we were doing.

The whole secrecy gig, combined with the long hours at work and the fact Travis had Morgan driving from one side of LA to the other running meaningless errands, made it really hard to see her. We snatched moments when we could, but I needed to make an effort to snatch moments that mattered. Travis had poor Morgan working like a dog. I'd been leaving most nights before her, and so far our relationship consisted of more late-night phone calls than anything else.

Part of me wanted to be waiting on her doorstep when she got home from work, but I didn't want to freak her dad out, and I definitely didn't want anyone spotting me, or my car, near her place. I knew she said she could handle the media, but did she really know what she was talking about?

In saying that, brushing her arm as I passed her in the hallway was no longer cutting it. I needed to take things to the next level. There was no point denying it; I wanted Morgan Pritchett...all of her.

My lips grew with a grin as I pictured various scenarios, my mind ticking over with ways I could make it happen.

"There you go again." Isabella shook her head, reaching past me to snatch a sandwich off the tray. I threw her a dry look and headed to the round table in the back corner of the lunchroom.

The petite dancer followed me, her impish grin making it impossible to be mad at her.

"So." She sat down, resting her chin on her palm, and winked at me, her eyes sparkling with mischief. "Who is she?"

I dropped my gaze, picking at the top of my crusty

bread roll. "Like I'm gonna tell you."

"Oh, whatever, I know it's Morgan."

My eyes popped up. "She told you?"

"No." *Isabella chuckled.* "It's just so obvious. The way your face lights up when she walks into a room. The way she takes in that slow breath when she sees you and then kind of nips at her lower lip. It's like the rest of the world doesn't exist when you two share the same space."

I winced, rubbing at my forehead. "I thought we'd been doing a good job at hiding it."

"To be honest, I think everyone else is too busy to really notice, but I love the idea of you guys together." *She squeezed my forearm.* "So, when are we going on a double with Dean?"

"Bells, come on. It's still new. We don't want anyone to know."

"Why?"

I shrugged. "I guess I just want to protect her from the limelight. I don't want anyone screwing this up. She's important, you know."

"Wow." *Isabella lightly bit down on her thumbnail.* "You got it bad, dude. Like way worse than Abigail. I mean, she enchanted you, but this..." *She wagged her index finger at me.* "This is different."

"Maybe it is," *I mumbled, a thrill racing through me.*

"Well, I think you should claim it. You want her. She wants you. Just do it."

My eyes popped up, heat rushing across my face as my crotch did a happy dance at the words "do it." What was I, sixteen now? I shifted in my seat.

"There are already too many secrets in this world and most of them are bad. I don't see why you should have to hide something like this." *Isabella grinned.* "I know work hours are long and your one day off is usually filled with family commitments. What's so wrong about making her part of those? At least you'd be together." *She tucked a thick curl behind her ear and shrugged.* "This is all just my opinion, of course, but Morgan's a strong chick. She* *can handle whatever you throw at her; I'm confident of that."*

I knew she could, so why was I playing coy? I wanted to jump across the sound stage right then and glide my arm across her lower back as she talked work with Lisa. On the days I finished filming before her and left for the night, I wanted to kiss her goodbye on the way. I wanted to whisper in her ear that I'd wait for her outside and we could drive to my place together. Why the hell was I stalling on this?

Morgan nodded at Lisa again and turned for the door. I took my chance, pushing off the wall and following my girl into the corridor. The phone in her pocket buzzed and she paused to extract it. With a grin, I stepped up behind her, snatching her arm and opening the door to our right.

I flicked it shut with my foot, spinning her in my arms and planting my lips on hers before she could protest. She let out a soft moan, dropping the phone on the counter behind her before opening her mouth to me. Her tongue was warm and sweet. I ran my hands down her smooth curves, lightly squeezing her butt and pushing myself against her. She responded with a nudge of her hips, and I wanted to lift her onto the countertop and take her right there.

I pulled back before I could, knowing I'd regret my first time with this gorgeous woman being a quickie in a storage room. Although the idea was kind of thrilling.

"Well, hello to you." Morgan panted, reaching for my lips again.

I gave her a light peck and rested my forehead against hers, squeezing her hips.

"I couldn't stand it. I had to taste you before the end of the day."

She grinned. "Thank you for your impatience. I, for one, really appreciate it."

We chuckled together, our breaths mingling. I wanted to swoop in and kiss her again, the dancing light in her eyes tearing at my resolve.

"I gotta have you," I whispered.

She brushed her teeth over her bottom lip, pulling in an electric breath that told me she was in.

"I know we're busy and work is making it impossible to see each other, and as much as I love talking to you on the phone, I want more, baby. I've missed you this week." I glided my hands up her back. "I need you. I need your skin. I need your touch. I need your lips." I dove for hers again, cupping the back of her head and pouring all my pent-up passion into the kiss. I wanted her to know I wasn't kidding. This had to happen...and soon, even if it meant the world finding out.

Her arms wrapped around my waist, her fingers lightly dragging up my back.

"So come over tonight," she murmured against my lips.

I swallowed. For some stupid reason, I still felt nervous about the idea of anyone seeing us together. It was the weirdest sensation, and I couldn't figure out why the hell I was hesitating. Isabella was right; I should be claiming this girl.

I opened my mouth to invite her to my place when the door handle jiggled. We jumped apart, Morgan pulling her shirt straight and flicking the loose wave of hair off her face. She reached for her phone, clearing her throat as the door flew open.

Travis McKinnon jerked to a stop when he saw us.

"What the hell are you doing in here?" He pointed at Morgan.

"I was just helping Mr. Jaxon find..."

"That's not your job! I texted you five minutes

ago. Why haven't you responded yet?"

"Sorry, I just got distracted helping—" She pointed at me.

"You don't get distracted on my watch." He stepped toward her, getting in her face.

I resisted the urge to push him away, my muscles straining as I stood my ground. I hated the way he spoke to her.

"You do what I say, when I say it. You respond to my texts immediately...not when the hell you're ready, but when *I'm* ready! And I was ready five fucking minutes ago!"

Morgan flinched as some flyaway spittle landed on her cheek. Her finger was shaking as she nipped it off her face, but her voice remained calm. "What is it you need me to do?"

"Read your damn text messages!" He flicked his hand at her, indicating she head for the door.

With a small nod, she slunk past him, lifting her phone and clearing the text as she exited the room.

My fingers curled into a fist as he turned to face me, shaking his head with an eye roll as if I should somehow sympathize with his plight.

Grinding my teeth together, I forced a tight-lipped smile. "Do you have to talk to her that way? She was just helping me out."

Travis froze, his easy grin disappearing. His beady eyes narrowed a touch further as he studied me.

I felt like a kid in the principal's office, beads of sweat breaking out on the back of my neck as I stood tall against his glare.

Straightening my shoulders, I lifted my chin to the door. "She works so hard for you. She's probably the best gofer I've ever seen on a set. She uses her initiative, she goes the extra mile, she's intelligent. Everyone thinks she's great." I crossed my arms, still unnerved by his unflinching expression. "I just don't understand why you have to treat her so bad all the time. You don't talk to Lisa like that."

"I used to." He crossed his arms, his eyes sparking. "Sean, are you questioning my methods?"

Rubbing a hand over my head, I rested my hand on my hip, hoping the stance looked casual. "I mean no disrespect, but yeah, I guess I am."

"I wouldn't." His voice was sharp and metallic.

"Excuse me?"

His face exploded with a broad smile as he chuckled and shook his finger at me. "You know the best thing about being showrunner, Sean?"

I shook my head, an edge of warning creeping up my spine.

"This is *my* show, and I can do whatever I want with it. In fact, just the other day, I was chatting to a fellow producer and we were talking about what makes good television. You know what we both decided?" He spread his hands in the air, as if selling me the world's best idea. "Drama. Shocking, unexpected drama. People say they hate it, but in truth, the audience lives for those surprises. Take for example *Superstar*. Can you imagine the reaction we'd get if, say, Harley disappeared off the show?"

I swallowed, my stomach twisting into a tight knot.

"Maybe he's contacted by a European dance troupe and leaves to follow that dream. Or maybe he dies in a car accident."

The cheeriness of his voice was like acid in my ears. I held my head high, keeping my expression bland in spite of the scowl I wanted to throw at him.

"Wow, Sasha's story would take on a whole new twist, don't you think? The impact of his death would be huge for her storyline. Now let's think about the impact Harley's departure would have on *your* story, Sean."

There was that damn finger again. I wanted to grab it and snap it right off his hand.

"I'm the son of one of the richest men in Hollywood. I have connections *everywhere*. You, on the other hand, are a B-grade actor, desperately trying to make your mark in the entertainment business, and so far the only thing people really remember you for is a shocking incident with Abigail Tripoli. Yikes. Wouldn't want that to rear its ugly head again, would we?"

My lips pressed into a tight line, anger pulsing from my gaze.

The emotion ricocheted right off his triumphant smirk.

"Now, now. Let's not get our panties in a twist. I'm just giving you a friendly reminder of how our little eco-system here at Polychrome Studios works. You want a future in this business, you do as I say and you don't question me. Are we clear on that, Mr. Jaxon?"

I swallowed, my jaw working to the side.

"Unless of course, there's something going on between you and my gofer. Now, that would be unfortunate. You see, I know for a fact it would definitely make her life much harder, if you catch my drift."

The stone in my throat dropped into my gullet, pressing down on me. It took every ounce of willpower I possessed to give a casual shrug and shake my head.

"There's nothing going on between me and that girl. She was just helping me out." I clicked my tongue. "I guess I like to see people treated fairly."

Travis chuckled, stepping toward me and patting my shoulder. "How about you let me be captain on this ship."

I gave him a tight nod, his threat still ringing in my ears.

He squeezed my shoulder and beamed me another smile that I wanted to punch right off his face.

"You're a good man, Sean Jaxon. Love having you on the show."

Catching the look in my eye, he tipped his head and gave me a glare. "But always remember, the show will go on whether you're here or not. Can you say that about your career?" He gave me a mocking wince. "Once I'm done with you? I don't think so." Slapping my shoulder, he stepped back and looked around the small room. "Now, if there's anything you need help with, why don't you let Lisa know; I'm sure she can find it for you."

"I'll go see her now." I punched out the words, scrambling to think of something I might need as I shuffled past him.

Breaking into the corridor, I headed back to the set in shell-shocked silence.

What the hell just happened in there?

Travis McKinnon was definitely not the man I thought he was, but that didn't matter now. All I knew for sure was that I believed every damn word that came out of his mouth...and it made me scared. Not just for my career, but also for Morgan.

TWELVE

MORGAN

I was twitchy for the rest of the day. Travis had me scuttling around the studio all afternoon. Although I hadn't really done anything wrong in that storage room, aside from not replying to his text in two microseconds, I still felt like I'd been caught doing something really bad.

Heat rose on my cheeks as I stepped out of the bathroom stall and gazed into the mirror. Sean's hands on my body, his whispered words of longing electrified me. I'd been desperate for this since our first kiss in the parking lot five weeks ago. He was so hot and sweet and funny and...I was falling in love with him.

I rested my hands against the cool countertop

and smiled into the mirror. Although we'd only managed two quick dates since we'd officially started dating, we'd spoken on the phone every night. I'd never had a relationship like that before...gotten to know a guy so thoroughly before sleeping with him. I thought it'd drive me insane, but all it did was tantalize me. My muscles vibrated as I imagined our night together. Giddy bubbles shot through my body, most of them bursting as I tried to work out the logistics of my evening. Travis had been in a really foul mood since catching me "helping" Sean, and I had a sinking feeling he'd keep me late.

Damn that man.

I didn't want Sean to be too tired for work the next day. Maybe I should tell him we could wait until Sunday. I'm sure we could find a quiet, little corner to spend an afternoon.

Glancing at my watch, I figured I had five minutes before Travis expected me back from my break. Surely I could sneak in a quick convo with Sean or at least pass him a note. Skipping out of the bathroom, I tugged my skirt down and headed for his dressing room. He wasn't due for his last session of filming until four, so he was no doubt getting changed and would be heading for makeup. If I hurried, I'd be able to catch him.

I turned sideways to shuffle past Ashlee, returning her friendly smile with one of my own. She reminded me so much of Jody, such a bubbly sweetie-pie. I made a mental note to call my little sister tomorrow. I hadn't spoken to her in a couple of weeks. We were both so caught up with our hectic lives. At least I'd get to see her in a month or so. She was flying home for Thanksgiving. I couldn't wait.

My steps slowed as I neared Sean's room. I was lifting my hand to knock on his door when I caught a female voice inside.

"Travis McKinnon is a powerful man, Sean. You don't say stuff like that to him."

Rhonda. I recognized her voice immediately. I glanced behind me to make sure no one else was around and then pressed my ear to the door.

"...okay? I've lost all respect for the guy."

"It's not about respect. It's about protecting your career. If he does what he says, I won't be able to resurrect you from that. You got me? If he decides to destroy you, he will."

What? Fear coiled around my spine as I wondered what exactly Travis the Jackass had said to my boyfriend.

"What was I supposed to do? He treated her like shit right in front of me. I'm just expected to stand by and let it happen?"

"Yes! That's exactly what you should have done. She's a big girl; she can stand up for herself."

Sean let out a scoff that only made me love him more. He stood up for me after I left the storage room! My lips quivered into a shaky smile.

"Look, if you don't like it, tell her to find another job."

"I don't want to. I hardly get to see her as it is. Besides, I love working with her."

"Then be more careful, okay? Your career is more important than some girl."

"She's not just some girl."

"Oh don't get all romantic on me now. If you really don't want to give her up, keep her hidden. No more dragging her into closets for make-out sessions. This isn't high school. This is your life...your future."

His silent beat after her sharp statement had me worried. Whatever Travis said must have been a very believable threat.

"You can't have anyone here finding out about

your little affair, and keep her out of the public eye, as well. Travis cannot get wind of you two together...and I'm not just saying that for your sake. You know he wasn't bullshitting. He may be brilliant and talented, but he's a first-class asshole. If you care about that little gofer, you'll keep her a secret."

I heard movement in the room and jumped back from the door before it opened.

"I'll check in with you again next week. Have a think about that movie. It'd be a three-week shoot in May next year. Definitely worth considering. I'll send you the script as soon as I get it."

Rhonda bustled out of the room. I pressed myself against the wall, but she saw me anyway.

"Hi, Rhonda," I greet her softly.

She eyed me up with a stone-cold glare. I raised my chin, pulling up to my full height. Like hell I was going to let her intimidate me. Her look of warning didn't bounce off me the way it usually would. I absorbed it like a punch to the face. When she finally turned and clipped away, a shaky breath whistled out between my teeth.

Sean's door flew back, and I jumped as he appeared in the hallway.

"Oh, hey." His smile was sad. His gaze brushed over me before landing on the floor.

"I just wanted to come by and check...about tonight, but I take it that's not happening anymore?" I crossed my arms, holding in the hurt.

"I want it to, but..." His jaw worked to the side. "It was bad, baby."

"Can you tell me about it?"

"Not here." He shook his head. "I got to get to makeup."

"Yeah, I know. I need to go, too."

His blue gaze caught me, traveling over my face. His sad smile dropped away as he drank me in.

"Call me as soon as you get off tonight. Promise?"

I grinned and mouthed, "Promise."

He walked past me, lightly brushing my arm with his long fingers. I would have stood there watching his fine body until it disappeared from sight, but my phone buzzed. I couldn't help a groan as I pulled it from my pocket and cleared the text. With a huff, I replied *immediately* and took off down the hallway to do Travis's bidding.

*****

My feet were killing me by the time I made it to the car. These new flats were a bad purchase. I should have stuck with my usual attire and worn jeans and sneakers to work, but I'd felt like wearing something a little nicer. I smoothed down my fitted skirt as I slid into my car, reminding myself that unless I was greeting someone important for Travis, I just had to wear clothes that were one hundred percent comfy. It didn't matter what I looked like. It didn't matter that I'd wanted to look pretty for my boyfriend.

I relived our moment in the storage room. Too bad it'd had such a terrible ending. I frowned, reaching for my phone and sending Sean a quick text before starting the car and pulling out of the lot. It was ten o'clock. He usually waited up to say goodnight to me before going to sleep. I loved that about him.

I got a reply before I'd even made it to the security gate. I braked to check it.

Waiting down the road for you. Take your second right off the main street.

A thrill raced through me. I pushed on the gas and sped down the road, squinting to see Sean's car in the darkness. He flashed his lights at me as soon as I took the turn and I stopped beside him, lowering my window.

He leaned out and called across the road. "Follow me."

I nodded and did a U-turn, following him out of the street and winding our way up into the Hollywood Hills. Twenty minutes later, we were pulling to a stop in a very secluded lookout. I switched off the engine and drank in the sparkling lights of LA.

Sean opened my door for me. He looked tired and agitated. I ran my hand down his face and his expression softened a little. Taking my hand, he led me to his car and we leaned against the hood, gazing out across the city. Strains of music played from his car stereo. He'd left the window low so we could hear it.

I smiled, my body responding to the soft beat. I forced my hips not to sway as I took in Sean's serious expression. He crossed his arms and let out a heavy sigh.

"What did he say to you?"

Sean clicked his tongue. "Basically told me if I tried to stand up for you again or question his authority, he'd kick me off the show and make sure I never got another job in Hollywood again."

My mouth dropped open. "Can he do that?"

He glanced at me and shrugged. "I believed him, baby. Rhonda thinks he can."

I swallowed, anger and worry battling for top position within me.

"Travis is such a—" I pressed my lips together, not wanting to ruin my minutes with Sean cursing a boss who didn't deserve the time of day. Like hell he was going to stomp on the only alone time I'd had with my man in over a week.

"I thought he was better than that. I know he treats you like shit, but I kind of thought it was some sort of initiation or something. The guy's sick."

"What are you going to do?"

"I love my job. I mean, I love the show and I love acting. I don't want to give it up."

I squeezed his arm. "I'm not asking you to."

"And I know I should be asking you to quit. You shouldn't be expected to work for him, but—"

"I'm not quitting. It took me so long to get this job, and I've nearly got enough saved to get my own place. I think I've found a little studio apartment near work. I'm checking it out on Sunday. I need this job, Sean, and besides...if I left, I'd never get to see you."

He turned to me, his white teeth shining against his dark skin. The moonlight captured the edge of his face, bathing him in a soft light that highlighted his handsome features. I reached for him, brushing my thumb over his thin goatee before squeezing the back of his neck with my fingers.

"I'm falling in love with you, Mr. Jaxon...and I can handle Travis if it means getting to see you."

Sean turned to smile at me, his mouth tipping up at the side, his blue gaze intense. His finger fluttered down my arm before he lightly kissed my shoulder.

"He can't find out about us, baby. No one can. I told him there was nothing between us." His eyes filled with anguish as he muttered the words. "He said he'd make your life hell if there was."

"I can handle him."

"I can't handle him treating you like that."

"I'm not quitting."

He stepped in front of me, resting his hands on my hips. "I want to protect this...us."

"I know." I smiled.

"Me & U" by Cassie started playing. How appropriate. We both snickered, but the sound died out as Sean's expression shifted. I matched his gaze of longing, brushing my teeth over my lower lip and giving him a cheeky smirk.

His muscles flexed as he gently lifted me onto the car. His warm fingers pushed my skirt up my thighs until I could spread my legs wide enough for him to stand between them. My smirk grew to a grin, my inner thighs sparking as his jeans pressed against my soft flesh.

His thumb brushed my cheekbone, his blue gaze unraveling my center. "I love you," he whispered. "I don't want to lose you."

"You won't."

"So we keep this hidden...from everyone. I won't risk it. No one can know."

I wrapped my legs around his waist, pressing him into me. "No one will."

His grin was delicious as his hand skimmed up my thighs until my skirt was around my waist. The cool breeze kissed my exposed skin. Goosebumps rippled over my flesh, but Sean's warm hands shooed them away before traveling up my body and untucking my shirt. My nerves sizzled as his fingers glided up my back.

I captured his lips, relishing the heat of his tongue as it dove into my mouth. Gripping his shoulders, I pulled myself against him. My soft center pressed into his hard core, making me want to melt. His hands flew to my butt, his hips thrusting against me.

"Oh, baby," he murmured into my mouth.

I grinned, pulling his shirt free and lifting it over his head. I dropped it behind me and leaned back to take in the glory of his chiseled body.

"Damn, boy, you fine." I mimicked his voice, running my fingers over the ridges of his hard frame. We both chuckled, but he swallowed his grin as I reached the button on his jeans, his blue gaze penetrating me with a look so pure, I felt lightheaded.

I was about to make love to Sean Jaxon.

Fame aside, that was epic.

Licking his bottom lip, he slowly peeled the shirt off my body, brushing his lips over my shoulder as he pulled my bra strap aside. His tongue traveled up my neck, setting off rockets within me. Every nerve in my body was like a firework and his touch set each one off.

My insides whistled and crackled as I slowly undid his jeans. His hands were feather-light on my thighs until his thumbs gently dug into the soft flesh just below my core. I'm sure his look of yearning matched mine as he leaned toward me, our panting breaths mixing together before our lips locked.

The cool breeze continued to caress us as our long-awaited desires were finally met. The night air captured our moans of ecstasy, and my body was sent to a higher plane as Sean took me on the hood of his Camaro.

It was the best first time I'd ever had.

THIRTEEN

MORGAN

I glanced across the car and smiled at Sean. He winked back, making my insides sizzle. It'd been two months since the Travis warning, and we'd managed to keep our relationship under wraps. I thought it would bug me, but there was actually something kind of tantalizing about it all. We'd turned Travis's threat into something sexy and romantic. No one but Jody, Ella, and Cole knew I was dating the gorgeous actor, and I'd let Isabella in on the secret, too, but she already knew anyway. She was livid with Travis and had sworn not to breathe a word to anyone.

I was happy with my decision to stay at Polychrome Studios. It meant I got to see Sean. He didn't pull me into any more closets, but he had gotten into the habit of meeting me at my studio apartment after work some nights and on Sunday afternoons. Yes, my own little apartment.

It took me a while to convince him it would be safe enough. *Superstar* aired on TV in mid-September and so far the show was a huge success, which meant the media were hot for Sean. People couldn't believe Mr. Bulletproof was capable of pulling off song and dance, but he was now making it onto The Sexiest Most... lists all over the place. Fans liked him in this role, and the buzz over whether Harley Barnes and the nineteen-year-old Sasha would eventually get together was hot. Reviews for the show were fantastic, and the ratings were going strong. Even Travis was in a slightly better mood, which made work a little less painful.

For me, life was great.

Peering over my shoulder, I glimpsed my sister in the back seat and felt a pinch of worry. She was home for Thanksgiving. We'd had a quiet family dinner together. I'd wanted to go to Sean's, but he wasn't ready to share me with his family yet. I couldn't hide my disappointment over that one, but he told me to be patient. He wasn't planning on going anywhere, so what was the hurry. It was hard to argue with that.

Instead, my dad, Jody, Grandma Deb, and I had had a sedate celebration. Cole and Ella had been busy with his foster parents, Mal and Nina, who had popped over to LA for a visit. They flew back to Chicago this morning. Thank goodness Ella and Cole were coming out with us tonight. I was hoping their bright company would get my little sister smiling. She was usually a ray of sunshine, but something was obviously bothering her this weekend.

"Hey." I reached into the back seat and tapped her knee, trying once again to get her to open up.

She forced a smile.

"You looking forward to tonight?"

"Of course." Her sunbeam smile seemed dim to me.

"Are you sure you're okay?"

She raised her head to the ceiling. "Morgan, would you please stop asking? I'm fine!" She pushed my hand off her knee. "Seriously, I'm about to go dancing with my best friend, my sister, and Mr. Superstar. Trust me when I tell you, I'm great."

I didn't buy it.

Something was off, but I didn't want to ruin the night by being my overprotective self, so instead I grinned and sat back in my seat.

Sean reached over the gear stick and gently squeezed my knee. I ran my fingers over his hand, loving that I could openly touch him. Tonight would be fun. His brother, Kip, had pulled a few strings for us and managed to hire a private club tonight. Sean had then asked the DJ from Hybrid if he'd come play for us. So the party was going to be me and my friends, with Sean and his. It was the first time we were getting to meet each other's trusted friends, and I think we were both a little nervous.

Sean slowed and pulled into an underground parking garage. Jumping out of the car, he opened the door for Jody and helped her out. She sparkled him a smile, making me wonder if I was wrong and there was absolutely nothing wrong with her.

I hated when I got like this, but I'd practically been her mother since I was a young teen, and I could somehow sense when something was off. I found it really hard to just let her go. The guilt I'd felt while living in Chicago had been pretty epic, and I probably wouldn't have been able to handle it if I hadn't spoken to Jody on a weekly basis. I knew she was a big girl now and could handle things on her own, but I really wanted her to be okay. *Happy* and okay.

Sean took my hand as we walked across the garage and through the black door. We ascended the stairs, the crescendo of music hitting us the higher we got. I squeezed Sean's hand in excitement and laughed as we came through the door and were met with the excited greeting of Sean's friends. He let me go and stepped into their embraces before pulling me against him and introducing me. I shook about ten different hands then stepped aside so Jody could meet everyone. A few minutes later, Ella and Cole arrived. I wrapped them each in a hug and then tried not to be bothered with the length of hug Jody gave Ella. Her arms were practically trembling from squeezing her so hard.

Ella pulled back and gave her a sweet smile, her head tipping with concern, but Jody brushed her off, jumping back with a squeal as "Tik Tok" by Ke$ha started playing. She mouthed the words, making Ella laugh, and then the beat kicked in. I jumped over to them and started dancing, our bodies going into a slow-mo move on the word *tip-sy*. The beat kicked in again, and we danced and sang our way through the number, our bodies gyrating together, a smooth flow of water moving through our muscles.

I raised my arms and grinned as Sean's hands snaked around my waist, his body moving in behind mine. We swayed to the beat, his hands wandering to my hips; my legs crackled as if the energy was flowing straight from his fingertips and filling me. His touch was like magic.

I was hoping he'd stay the night at my place.

The little studio apartment was in Burbank, only ten minutes from work. It wasn't anything flash, but it was mine. I hardly had any furniture, but all Sean and I seemed to need on our days off was a bed anyway.

With the whole clandestine relationship going on, Sean insisted we spend all our time at my place or tucked into booths of unknown restaurants. He often parked in different spots in my neighborhood, hoping people wouldn't recognize his car. Talk about extreme, but he said it was to protect me more than anything, which was why he'd never spent the night—something I was hoping to change.

I grinned as the song came to an end, spinning to face Sean and draping my arms across his shoulders. I wasn't sure if he'd mind me kissing him in such a public arena, but he obviously felt safe here, because he planted his big lips on mine and the world disappeared for a second.

The hours ticked by with one dance song after another broken up with the flow of drinks and boisterous chatter. My voice was getting hoarse as I yelled a conversation with Sean's older brother Kip. He was telling me stories about Sean being the baby of the family and as a kid, how he really was a big baby. I grinned as Kip described Sean crying over a stubbed toe.

"He was the biggest drama queen; you'd think he'd had it amputated." Kip rolled his eyes. "And you know the funny part? He didn't even know he'd done it until Helena pointed it out. He saw the blood and started bawling."

I threw back my head and laughed.

"What lie's he telling you now?" Sean's arm wove around my back and he leaned against me. I let Kip take over, the brothers' banter making me smile. They were obviously close. My eyes skirted the room as they chatted. Cole and Ella were all snugged up on the dance floor. They'd outlasted everyone. "Forever Ain't Enough" by J. Holiday was playing, and they were dancing to the slow number. Cole dipped Ella, her body swooping down before being pulled back against him. They were so in love it wasn't even funny.

My insides swelled; Ella deserved this, and I was so grateful she'd found the strength to fight for what she wanted. She and Cole were perfect together. I squeezed Sean's shoulder, hoping the same for us. It was impossible to deny that I was way past falling for him.

I'd fallen, hard and fast. It had been brilliant and amazing and I wanted it to last forever.

I rested my chin on his shoulder, my eyes moving away from my best friend and landing on my sister. She was watching them too, her face awash with sadness. That pinch of worry nibbled on my insides again, and I slipped out of Sean's grasp.

"Back in a minute." I brushed Sean's cheek with my lips and wove through the party people to get to Jody.

"Hey." I slipped onto the stool beside her.

She glanced at me but didn't say anything.

It was a little quieter in this corner, and I didn't have to shout so loud. I leaned my head against hers.

"You ready to talk about it yet?"

"Talk about what?" she mumbled, running her finger around the glass in front of her.

I frowned. She wasn't old enough to drink yet. Not to be a Nana about it, but I didn't like the idea of my sister sitting in a bar drowning her sorrows, especially with straight spirits.

"Whatever it is that's bugging you." I reached for the glass, but she shifted it out of my way.

Giving me a defiant look, she downed the clear liquid and slammed the empty glass back onto the table. "I told you I'm fine, Morgan. Please, just drop it."

"I can't. You're my sister and I care about you." I snatched the glass and moved it to the other side of the table.

Her eyes narrowed. "Yes, my sister, not my mother. You don't have a right to pry."

I frowned at her snappy tone. I'd had to put up with a little lip when she was going through her early teens, but after moving to Chicago things became infinitely better. She seemed happy to have me as a mother-figure most of the time, so why the sudden change?

I swallowed, forcing a calm I didn't feel. After all I'd sacrificed for Jody, I really hated it when she got snarky like this.

"It's the guy, isn't it? Did he dump you?"

Jody whipped around to face me, her skin draining of color. "No."

"Okay, so, what's the problem? Did you dump him? Are you feeling guilty or something?"

"No!"

My eyes narrowed as I studied her face. "You slept with him, didn't you?"

Her lips pinched tight, her face blanching as she blinked at tears.

"It was your first time, wasn't it?"

"Would you shut up?" Jody whispered between clenched teeth.

"Come on, Jo-Jo. You can talk to me about anything. I know first times can be difficult; it doesn't always go well. I told you about mine."

"Which doesn't mean I have to share every detail of mine."

"He didn't hurt you, did he? I mean, intentionally."

"No, it was fine. It was great. It was perfection." Her sarcastic reply told me it was anything but. Her head dropped into her hand. Damn it, she was drunk!

I gently touched her arm. "It gets better...with time and practice."

Jody's shoulder tensed. "I know. I'm sure it will."

"Are you sure..." I licked my lips, wanting to word things correctly. "Do you care about him enough to keep trying?"

"I love him," she whispered.

"And he loves you?"

Jody's gaze locked onto the table, her eyes large.

"Jody?" I touched her shoulder.

"I don't feel very well." She slapped her hand over her mouth and stumbled away from the table. I chased after her, cursing myself for not watching how much she'd been drinking. This was a private function; no one would be checking IDs, and Jody would've definitely taken advantage.

I pushed the restroom door open as the stall at the end banged shut. Jody's retching filled the air. I wrinkled my nose and gingerly walked further into the bathroom.

"I'll go get you some water, Jo-Jo."

She replied with another heaving retch into the toilet. Closing my eyes, I pushed the door back open and made my way to the bar, feeling like the world's worst sister. I was so caught up with Sean; I should have kept a better eye on her. As I placed my water order, I realized that I didn't really know much about her boyfriend. I couldn't even remember his name. How bad was that? I'd been so busy at work and living in my little love bubble that I hadn't pressed for more details.

I knew he was a dancer and came from New York, but that was about it. They had dance class

117

together every day, and she had seemed so blissfully happy. They must have tried sleeping together before she came here and it'd gone really badly. Poor thing.

All I could hope was that she was telling me the truth and that she hadn't given it away to some selfish asshole like I had. That familiar wave of regret shuddered down my spine as I briefly relived my first experience with Jordy Lehman. I'd only been fifteen, hardly the best example for Jody. I should have lied and never told her, but on the night before I left for college, we'd stayed up with Ella talking until dawn and everything had come out.

"Thank you." I took the water bottle and uncapped it as I walked back to the bathroom. Jody was standing at the sink looking wrung out. The bags under her eyes were dark, making her look a decade older than her tender nineteen years.

"Here you go."

She grabbed it off me with a shaky hand and took a few sips.

"I'll take you home."

Spitting the water into the sink, she shook her head. "No, you should stay."

"I don't mind, Jo-Jo."

"Morgan, I want you to stay. All I'm going to do is crawl into bed and sleep this off." Her eyes skimmed the floor.

I resisted the urge to tell her off for drinking too much.

"Hey, is everything okay in here?" Ella's head appeared in the doorway.

"Yeah, Jody's just had a little too much to drink."

"Jo-Jo," Ella chided. "You naughty girl."

Ella's sweet grin made Jody laugh; it was a punchy one that sounded almost like a sob. I rubbed her back and guided her toward the door.

"I think I'll take her home."

"No, Morgan..." Jody started to argue.

"We can." Ella shook her head. "Cole and I have an early start tomorrow anyway; I was just coming in to say goodbye."

"Are you sure?" Guilt sat heavy on my shoulders. I was Jody's sister; I should be the one taking her home.

"Yeah, of course. Cole's saying goodbye to everyone now."

Ella stepped around to Jody's other side and gave her middle a squeeze. "Come on, you drunk squirt. Let's get you home."

Jody gave us both a tired smile. We guided her out of the bathroom, and I collected her stuff, handing it to Cole. He kissed me on the cheek and promised to take care of her. Crossing my arms, I watched them leave, worry making my face tight.

Sean approached me with a concerned smile, and I forced myself to relax.

"You okay?" He rubbed my arm.

"Yeah, a little worried about Jo-Jo, though. She got so drunk tonight, she actually threw up."

"Really?" He turned as they disappeared through the doorway.

"Yeah, I know. I always thought a drunk Jody would be wild, but she's obviously one of those tired, sedate ones." I frowned. "She just sat in the corner quietly downing straight vodka."

"You want to go, make sure she's okay?"

"No, Ella said she'll take her home."

Sean pulled me against him and kissed my cheek. "She'll be okay, baby. Why don't you come and forget your troubles on the dance floor with me."

I grinned as he pulled me back into the open space, letting his arms drift around me. I laid my head on his shoulder, and the slow music swirled around us. His soft touch soothed me, and I closed my eyes, trying to let go of my worries for Jody.

If only I could.

FOURTEEN

SEAN

"I said turkey on rye, not chicken; are you fucking deaf!"

I cringed as I watched a small glob of spittle fly from Travis's mouth. He was once again going off at Morgan. I hated the way he spoke to her, and I really wished I hadn't just walked past the door and heard it.

"There was no turkey available today, so I made you the next best thing." Morgan's voice remained calm, as usual.

"It's not the next best thing. If I want turkey, I expect you to get me TURKEY!"

I heard the splatter of food and assumed Travis had thrown his plate onto the floor. Why did he have to treat her like this? She was brilliant at her job. Everyone on set thought so. She was more organized than Lisa, anticipating people's needs before they'd even asked her to.

Everyone loved her.

Everyone except Travis.

Morgan pulled in a slow breath. "You told me I had to urgently send three emails and before I can do that, I need to make two phone calls, so which is more important, the turkey or the emails?"

"Don't give me lip, princess, okay? Clean this shit up, get me the right sandwich, and then go do your fucking job."

"Okay, thank you for helping me prioritize."

"Smart ass," Travis mumbled as he flew out the door, Lisa hot on his heels.

I jumped-to, pretending I was walking down the hall toward them and missed his big hissy fit. He slowed his pace to let me pass.

"Hey, Sean." He greeted me with a friendly smile, and I had to force my lips north. "Great job today."

"Thanks." I nodded and waited until he was around the corner before ducking into the onsite office.

"Hey."

Morgan glanced up from the floor, flicking a piece of chicken from her finger to the plate. "What's up?"

"Just checkin' in. You good?"

"I'm always good." Her reply was sharp, like staccato.

I cringed, closing the door and crouching down beside her. I reached for a piece of bread to help her with the clean.

"It's okay, I've got it. Your filming's up for the day. You should get going."

"I'm gonna wait for ya."

"You don't have to do that, Sean."

"I know, but I want to." I kept my voice light and soothing, trying to ease the tension radiating off her. Ever since Thanksgiving she'd been wound tight. I knew she was worried about her sister. Jody had flown back to school a few days ago, just left for the airport. She'd asked her father to take her, not even giving Morgan the chance to say goodbye. It had really hurt, not that Morgan would admit that to me.

I wanted to make it up to her, make her feel better, but Travis had been on a rampage today and I had barely had a chance to see her.

Morgan stood from the floor, picking a piece of grated carrot off her knee. "I better go make another sandwich for His Highness. Seriously, Sean, you don't have to stay; I can just see you later...or tomorrow."

I moved into her space before she could storm from the room. "I'm stayin'."

"Okay, fine." She stared at the floor.

Resting my fingers under her chin, I gave it a gentle nudge, compelling her to look at me.

"What can I do to make it better?"

"You can tell Travis to stop treating me like shit."

I swallowed; it sounded noisy in the still room. Morgan's tension was palpable, and I knew my answer wouldn't dissipate it.

"You know I can't, baby. If I speak up again, Travis will make your life a thousand times worse. I have to stay quiet. No one can find out about us, remember?"

She tutted and glanced away from me, her jaw working to the side. "I appreciate the fact that you're trying to protect me...and your career. I get it. But it also makes me feel like you're ashamed to claim me. I know it's dumb, and I know I'm probably just saying this because I'm feeling wrung out and beat up right now, but come on, Sean. This whole secrecy thing is starting to wear thin. I want to be your girlfriend, not your secret lover."

Her statement surprised me. I had no idea things were wearing thin. I thought she was happy keeping this a clandestine operation.

Her face crested with sadness before she stepped out of my reach. Her shoulders pinged tight and she moved around me, pausing at the door to give me one final look.

"Don't stay. Go home and get some rest. You've got a huge day tomorrow."

She walked out the door before I could tell her I wasn't going anywhere. With a heavy sigh, I ambled back to my room.

Morgan had it wrong. It had nothing to do with shame. She was gorgeous. I'd be proud to wear her on my arm, but I couldn't put Travis in his place again. I hated that this argument had reared its ugly head once more. I thought we'd dealt with it. I couldn't jeopardize this job. It was doing wonders for my career. This was the shot Rhonda and I had been looking for. This was my big break. Ratings were increasing with each episode. People liked me as Harley. They liked seeing my softer, emotional side and to be honest, I liked playing it.

I didn't miss the guns and the bullets. I loved the dancing. Travis had been sweet as pie to me since his little threat speech, and although I despised the way he spoke to Morgan and some of the other crew, it was hard to deny his creative brilliance. This show was his baby, and it was thriving.

I slumped onto the couch in the dressing room and rested my head back against the wall. Although Morgan and I didn't get to see each other as much as we wanted to, we were making it work.

Late-night phone calls were still a regular, and now that Morgan had her apartment, I was able to stop there a few nights a week for a little quality time before dragging myself back home. My answer for always declining her invitation to spend the night was, "I don't want to get caught leaving in the morning." But that obviously wasn't cutting it anymore.

I *did* want to spend the night. There'd be nothing sweeter than falling asleep with her wrapped in my arms. I was just trying to be careful. That was why I hadn't taken her to my place; I didn't want anyone seeing her car or watching her come and go.

I scrubbed a hand over my face. Was I just being paranoid? It suddenly felt like it. I grimaced. I couldn't believe she thought I didn't want to claim her. I had to make this right. Sitting forward, I pinched my chin as an idea lit the corners of my brain. It wasn't high risk, but it would still make a statement. Grabbing my jacket, I snatched my bag off the floor and headed for the parking lot.

*****

Three hours later, I sat in my car watching the exit Morgan usually left from. I kept my eyes on the door, feeling like a stalker as I waited for my girl to finish work. The parking lot was basically empty. There was only her car and two others. I saw Lisa walk out, a big yawn stretching her mouth wide. About ten minutes after she had driven off, I watched Con leave the building. The only car left in the lot was Morgan's.

With a frown, I jumped out of my car and ran across the empty space.

"Hey, Sean, you forget something?" Stan, the security guard, made me jump as he stepped under the light.

"Uh, yeah, am I too late to collect?"

"No, man, just remember to lock up when you leave. I'll be patrolling the grounds all night." His eyes wandered over to Morgan's car, and he gave me a knowing smile.

I winced.

"Don't worry. We haven't said a word."

"Thank you," I mumbled, tapping his shoulder as I walked past, suddenly hyper-aware of how much the guards probably saw.

I walked into the empty studio, heading straight for the office. It was empty. With a frown, I made my way to the main studio, but that was dark for the night too. I continued down the hallway, checking each room until I finally ran upstairs to the dance rehearsal studio. Morgan was sitting crossed-legged in the middle of the floor. Her back was straight, her eyes closed. To anyone else, it would have appeared as though she was meditating, but I knew better.

It hurt to watch her looking so strung out, her sad face taut with stress. I wanted to comfort her, to make it better.

"Hey."

Her eyes popped open. "What are you doing here?"

"I told you I was staying."

"I thought you left."

I shrugged. "I came back."

She glanced at her watch and whispered brokenly. "Why?"

"Because I love you, and I want to make you feel better."

Her sigh was heavy.

My faced bunched with a frown as she rubbed at her temples.

"There's nothing you can do, Sean. Things are

just the way they are." She sounded resigned, like she'd had to give herself the same speech multiple times before.

I swallowed, wondering how to play this. My eyes grazed the dance studio and a smile lifted the corner of my mouth. "Nothing I can do, huh?"

She shot me a dry glare, but I could see her lips fighting a smile as she took in my expression.

With a low chuckle, I headed for the stereo and pressed play. Yeah, I knew it was a sly move. When it came to Morgan, her best aphrodisiacs were music and dancing. And I also knew that if anything was going to make her forget the world for a few minutes... sex worked like a charm.

I didn't know what sound would come out of the speakers and was relieved when Cody Simpson started singing "You Got Me Good".

Morgan's eyes stayed on me, her brown orbs sparking with desire. I walked toward her, losing my jacket before stretching out my hand. She gazed at it for a few reluctant beats before placing her fingers on my palm. I pulled her off the floor and against my chest, running my hands down her body and lightly kissing her nose. Spinning her away from me, I lifted my arm over her head and wound her back to my side. I could feel her muscles loosening as she gave into the music...and me.

We swayed against one another, my hands trailing down her sides. Her back arched, her ponytail skimming the floor as I swung her around. As she lifted her head, I pulled the band, letting her blonde locks run free over her shoulders. Damn, she was beautiful.

I ran my fingers, feather-light, over the soft skin of her neck, hooking my thumb beneath the fabric of her tank top and sliding it off her shoulder. My lips followed, skimming over her smooth flesh.

The light beat of the song rained over us, Cody's easy voice casting a spell on the room. Morgan's hips kept swaying as she lifted her hands to the soft pulse of sound. With one swift move, I lifted her shirt, pulling it over her long arms. The fabric fell from her fingertips, my hands trailing back down her arms. I bent my knees and flowed with her, gliding over her curves.

My dark skin against her silky white torso made me smile. She was like milk, her supple skin practically glowing in the soft light. My hands ran over her hips, taking her pants with me. She stepped out of the wide leggings, her leg stretching over my shoulder. I stood, capturing her thigh against me and leaning back to the music. Her eyes were closed, her head falling back, being led by the potent sound. My lips found the pulse in her neck. It thrummed with the soft rhythm. I licked the beat, energy sparking inside my mouth as I trailed my tongue between her perfect breasts. Her nails scraped up my back, pulling my shirt off. Our naked torsos melded together, still gyrating to the velvety cadence floating around us.

I spun her around so she was facing away from me and pulled her back against my stomach, running my hand between her legs. A sweet moan reverberated in her throat, the sound always making me feel triumphant. She slid her panties to the floor, flicking them off her toe as Cody Simpson's voice faded and Beyoncé took over. The ethereal strains of "Halo" echoed off the walls as my hands traveled the plains of Morgan's skin. Each curve sent my insides into hyper-drive, the liquid sway of her hips turning my blood to boiling.

Morgan dipped to the floor, her hair sliding down my torso before she spun, and with painstaking slowness, rid me of my trousers. Her smile was wicked as she pulled them off and threw them across the room. They slid toward the mirrors, my belt buckle clicking on the hard, wood frame.

My eyes stayed on Morgan, mesmerized by the magic of her naked body. Her fingers skimmed up the backs of my legs, tickling me, enticing me, driving me to the edge of sanity...but I couldn't give in. This wasn't about my pleasure; it was about hers.

I stopped her lips before they took me, and I lost all power to think straight. She read my gaze and moved back with a smirk, her hands making a wide circle over the polished floor as she shifted away from me. I dropped to my knees and crawled toward her, my lips touching her pointed toes and working their way up the terrain of her shapely legs. I took my time, letting the song wash over us as I reached her center.

I lingered there, kissing, caressing, thriving in the mounting energy building inside of her.

Morgan's soft panting increased in tempo, her fingers scraping over my head as an orgasm rocketed through her. She arched her back and I supported her weight as she cried out, her legs trembling. Slowly she lowered herself back to the floor and with a smile, I kissed her stomach, my tongue spinning around her belly button.

"Please, Sean," she whispered, her hips rising from the floor and hitting my torso.

"All of Me" by John Legend played over us. It was the perfect song, because it was true. This beauty beneath me could have every part of me. My world made sense when she was in it.

With a luxurious smile I slid up her body, thinking about the gift I had tucked in my jacket pocket as I held myself over her and lightly kissed her chin.

"Oh, now you're just being mean." Her brown eyes hit me, demanding more from this dance.

With a soft chuckle, I entered her. A sweet sigh escaped her lips, landing on my cheek and once again confirming everything I felt for her.

I kept the rhythm slow to match the music, a luxurious ride of pleasure that still sent us soaring. Our rhythm changed as we created our own crescendo, fire shooting through me as Morgan's satin center sent me over the edge.

With a low moan I shuddered inside her, resting my lips against her silky neck and wishing time would stop.

"Every Time I Close My Eyes" by Babyface clicked on. I leaned away from my lover, gazing down at her beautiful face and tucking away a loose lock of hair. Her smile was languid, her eyes glowing.

"I love you," she mouthed.

I kissed those luscious lips that made me whole.

"I love you too...and I'm not ashamed of that."

She broke eye contact, ready to wriggle away from me, but I pinned her to the floor, the gentle pressure from my hips locking her into place.

"I'm sorry I'm not ready to flaunt the fact you're my girl, baby, but you have to believe that you are. You are the only one."

She stopped struggling and looked at me. "I know. I just..." She shook her head with a sad smile. "I love that you want to protect me." She squeezed my shoulders.

"I do." I licked my bottom lip. "But I also want you to be happy and I never, ever want you to doubt how I feel about you."

A soft blush lit her cheeks.

"I got you somethin'." Not wanting to move away from her, I stretched my arm as far as it would go, nabbing my jacket with my fingertips and pulling it toward us. Her giggles cut short as she saw me pull a small box from the pocket.

"Now, don't freak out; it's not an engagement ring."

"O-kay." Her eyes narrowed.

I flicked the box open to reveal a white-gold band with three sapphires inlaid. "It's a promise ring. I'm claiming you, girl, and I may not want to shout it from the rooftops yet, but every time you look at your hand, I want you to know that I love you and that ain't changin'."

Her lips trembled with a smile and relief flooded through me.

Putting my weight on my elbows, I pulled the ring free and gently slid it onto the middle finger of her right hand. It fit snugly over her knuckle, and I raised her hand to my lips.

"Thank you." Her fingers glided down my face.

"Come on." I finally slid out of her, rising to my knees and pulling her up beside me. "Let's spend the night at your place."

"Spend the night." Her eyebrows rose.

"Means I can sleep in for an extra thirty minutes." I shrugged.

She chuckled, looking at the ring on her finger and then back up at me. "And who says I'm gonna let you sleep?"

The mischievous twinkle in her eye made me growl, and I captured her in my arms, nibbling her neck and making her burst with laughter.

We did eventually make it back to her place, but she was right. Sleeping with Morgan's luscious form beside me was near impossible.

FIFTEEN

MORGAN

"He spent the whole night?"

"Uh-huh." I grinned, gulping back the childish squeal I wanted to set free. My mood was so good I felt like I could sprout wings and fly.

It helped that Jody was actually sounding upbeat for a change.

"Well, good for you, sis. I take it this isn't a one-time thing."

"Nope, he's come over about six times in the last two weeks, and he'll be here after his family lunch today...and now that we're on winter break, he can stay here for as long as he likes."

My smile was indulgent, I could tell. Sean Jaxon for an entire night had been perfection. We'd hardly gotten any sleep and dragged our butts through work the next two days, but then he'd come back again on the Saturday night...and spent most of Sunday here as well...and then the next Tuesday and Thursday... I twirled the sapphire ring on my finger and let out a giddy sigh.

"Okay, well, I guess I'll let you go primp and shave," Jody giggled.

"No, wait. I want to talk Christmas. I still can't decide what to get Dad, and it's only five days away. I thought we could go shopping when you get here. What day are you arriving?"

"Uh...Christmas Eve."

"Not until Christmas Eve? Didn't school finish for you on Friday?" My eyes shot to my phone on the counter. I leaned toward it as I waited for her reply to come through the speaker.

"Yeah, but you're not the only people in my life. Some of my friends are doing a few party things, and I don't want to miss them."

My good mood scuttled into hiding as I crossed my arms and glared at the screen. "Partying things? What's going on with you at the moment? You get drunk off your face at Thanksgiving, you leave for Tucson the next day without even saying goodbye to me—"

She groaned. "Would you let that go already. I've said sorry like a hundred times."

I squeezed my eyes shut. "I know, I just...it was so out of character. I'm worried about you, Jo-Jo."

"Stop! Please! I'm fine! Is it so wrong that I'd like to have a little fun with my new friends before dragging my butt home for some boring little Christmas dinner with Dad and Grandma?"

"What the hell, Jody! We're your family."

"Look, don't get all pissy with me, okay. I've already made my decision. Dad's fine with it. One of the girls here lives in LA; she's dropping me home on her way back. It's all worked out perfectly."

I humphed.

She let out an exasperated sigh. "What do you want from me?"

I nibbled at my lip, glaring at my phone. "Nothing, I just can't help feeling like you're hiding something."

Her pause told me everything.

I rolled my eyes. "Look, I know I'm not your mother, but I'm here for you, always. I just want to make sure you're safe and happy."

My fingers tapped on the counter as I waited for her to respond.

After another long pause she muttered, "I am. My life here is great... just let me live it, okay?"

"I love you, Jo-Jo."

"Love you too," her voice wavered. "I gotta go. See you in a few— See ya."

Her phone clicked off and the worries I'd managed to push aside surged forward like a bullet train.

What kind of trouble was my little sister getting herself into? Getting drunk enough to throw up? Partying? Maybe I should be popping down there to surprise her. Find out a little more about this boyfriend and meet some of her friends.

I snatched the phone off the counter, ready to dial Ella and find out if Jody had told her more than she was willing to tell me, but the doorbell rang.

I glanced at my watch. Sean wasn't due for another half hour. Maybe he was early. Thank God! I needed distracting from these issues with my evasive kid sister.

Honestly!

I threw back the door, ready to leap into his arms, but was stopped short by a very unexpected sight.

"Rhonda?" I gripped the door handle. "Um, hi."

"Hello, Morgan."

I forced a smile. "How do you...know where I live?"

"I can find out anything I need to." She stepped into my apartment, forcing me to shuffle back and open the door wider.

With a frown, I closed the door and followed her into my place.

"So, what can I do for you?" I should have been offering her a drink, but we hadn't exactly warmed to each other yet, and I wanted her gone before Sean arrived.

She spun to face me, holding out a wrapped gift. I took it from her, admiring the green and red paper.

"Just a little Christmas present for you."

"You came to give me a Christmas present?"

"And to have a chat." She placed her purse on my coffee table and sat in the single-seater opposite me. I lowered myself to the sofa, keeping a careful eye on her as I undid the bow. Inside was a box of decadent chocolate truffles. I smiled at her.

"Thank you." I slid them onto the table.

She flicked her fingers. "Don't worry about it. Just me looking after my client's interests." She winked.

I forced a laugh. For some reason, I couldn't shake my disquiet.

Rhonda smoothed down her straight, knee-length skirt and swiveled to face me head on. "I'll get to the point. I'm concerned about Sean."

"O-kay." My forehead wrinkled. "To be honest, I'm surprised by that. Things seem to be going very well for him at the moment."

Rhonda pulled in a breath and held it for a beat too long before letting it go and pasting on a smile I didn't buy for a microsecond.

"Listen, Sean and I have a really positive working relationship, and I don't want to do anything to upset that."

"That's good." Nerves skittered through my belly. Where the hell was she going with this?

"My main concern is making sure Sean's career is a success."

"Well, that *is* your job." I would normally be much more open and friendly with a visitor, but the underlying hostility oozing off this woman was making it impossible.

"Listen, sugar, I get that he's infatuated with you. I think that's really sweet and all, but I'd ask you to be cautious. Sean doesn't need any bad publicity."

My eyebrows rose and I forced a smile, swallowing back the flurry of words I wanted to unleash. She thought I was bad publicity for him? Hello blatant insult!

I swallowed, lifting my chin and forcing a serene smile. "Sean wants to keep things quiet, so you don't need to worry about that."

"Yes, I know, but he has been spending quite a few nights here recently. How's that keeping things quiet?" She eyed the ring on my finger, her brow arching as she reached for my hand and studied the sapphires.

"He parks around the block." I snatched my hand back and tucked it under my leg.

"Oh, well then." Her chuckle was hard. "I'm glad he's taking my advice. I just hope you will too."

"And what advice do you have for me?" It was hard to get the words out.

She gave me a patronizing smile, her head tipping to the side. "Sean's career is just taking off. This show is sending him in a new direction, giving him a new face, if you will. It's his chance to put the whole Abigail debacle behind him and really surge forward...become an A-lister, like he deserves to be."

"If that's what he wants, I hope he makes it."

"Oh he *will* make it...as long as nothing gets in his way. He really doesn't need any distractions right now."

I felt the snap inside me; it turned my gaze hard. I sent a silent warning firing across the coffee table.

"If you think I'm going to break up with Sean because you want me to, you can think again. He's a big boy; he can make his own decisions. If he doesn't want to be with me anymore, then so be it, but like hell I'm gonna let you come into my house and manipulate this situation to work in your favor. He's not a puppet, and he's allowed to love whoever he wants."

Her back pinged straight, her hard gaze matching mine head-on. "He doesn't need some prissy little girlfriend complaining about his life behind the scenes, putting demands on him and forcing him into a corner."

Is that what she thought I was doing? I pulled in a sharp breath through my nose.

"There are certain things we need to push to give him the best chance at public success."

"What kinds of things?" My eyes narrowed.

She pursed her lips and ran a finger over her left eyebrow. "All I'm asking, Miss Pritchett, is that you don't get in the way of Sean's career. He's a very talented man, and he deserves all the positive exposure he can get...and he certainly doesn't need some *nobody* whispering in his ear, demanding that he flaunt her to the world. I know he told you what Travis said to him, and if I'm honest, I'm highly annoyed that you would try to pressure him to say anything on your behalf. Fight your own damn battles, Miss Pritchett, but leave my client out of it."

My eyes bulged, my mouth dropping open at her harsh tone.

"It'd be a different story if I was dealing with a hot celebrity, but Morgan, you're a nobody...and how is that going to move Sean into the elite? We don't want Married to Who-the-hell-is-that-chick on his IMDb page. You get me?"

An arctic breeze rushed up my throat, drying out all my fiery words. Before I could even form a rebuttal, she stood and walked for the door.

"I want you to have a careful think about Sean's future. It's Christmas break now." She waved her hand around the apartment. "Hide away in here if you need to, spend every day in bed together if that's what it takes to get him out of your system, but come the New Year, I really expect you to pull back. I have plans for this talented man, and they don't include you. Don't jeopardize his entire future out of selfish desire, please. If you love him, you'll walk away."

The door clicked shut behind her, and I sat frozen on the couch.

What the fuck just happened?

I felt like I was waking up from a nightmare.

Who the hell did she think she was? Did Sean even know she'd come?

The doorbell rang.

What? Had she not finished?

I lurched from my seat, charging toward the door and ripping it open.

"What!"

Sean flinched, his dark eyebrows bunching into a frown.

My shoulders sagged. "Sorry, I thought you were someone else."

"Who?" His blue eyes rounded.

I tsked and walked back to the couch, letting

him close the door behind us. I was surprised he hadn't seen her leaving. She must have scuttled away pretty damn fast.

"Baby, what's wrong?"

Slumping down, I leaned my elbows onto my knees and flicked the box of chocolates toward him. "Rhonda came to give me a gift."

"Really?" He sat down beside me, running his large hand up my back. His touch made everything instantly better. "That was nice of her."

"Yeah, really nice." My eyebrows rose to match my sharp sarcasm.

He gave me a sidelong glance, accompanied with a funny smirk.

I sighed. "She came by to tell me to stop pressuring you."

"Pressuring me?"

"Yeah, I think she's annoyed by how much time we're spending together and that we're not being careful enough. Did you tell her what I said to you in the office the other week...about standing up to Travis?"

He shrugged. "I tell her everything."

"I wish you wouldn't."

He frowned.

"Now she's treating me like the bad guy. Like I'm somehow trying to ruin your career."

"She's just stressin'. She does that."

"She doesn't want us together, Sean." I swiveled to face him, my knee pressing into his.

"That's not her decision."

"I know that! Do you?"

He frowned at me, looking slightly pissed that I was questioning him.

I dropped my gaze, running a finger up the bridge of my nose and pressing it into my forehead.

"Look, Rhonda and I have always worked closely together and I trust her. She saved my career after the Abigail thing."

I pressed my lips together and gave a stiff nod. I was so sick of hearing about the Abigail thing. I hated the way he made his manager out to be some superhero savior. So she'd done a good job. That's great! Let's move on now!

"Hey." He gently squeezed the back of my neck. "I'm not letting her, or Travis, dictate who I spend my time with. Yes, we have to keep this under wraps. I'm not saying I love it, but we're making it work, right?" He kissed my shoulder. "Right?"

I sniffed out a snicker. "Yeah." I nodded.

"The most important thing is that we're together. That's all that matters."

"But she...she was pretty clear that I'm not the girl for you." I swallowed, daring to look at him. I knew how much she meant to Sean.

"I'll talk to her, okay? I'm sure she didn't mean to come across the way she did."

"Sean—"

He stopped me with an index finger on my lips. "Hey, it'll be okay. I'll make it clear that you're my girl. She's just trying to look out for me. That's all. She's never let me down before."

"But—"

"And she's not stopping me from inviting my girl to Christmas dinner."

"Christmas dinner?" I perked up.

"Yeah, Mama wants to meet you."

"You told her about me?"

"Kip kind of let slip and now she's doggin' me about it."

I threw him a droll look, which he laughed off easily.

"Come on, baby, you know the truth is I really want her to meet my girl."

I tipped my head, unable to help my cynical tone. "Are you sure?"

"One hundred percent."

My eyes narrowed. He matched my expression before pulling a funny face. It was an effort not to break into a smile. I fought my traitorous lips.

"When is it? I'll have to fit it around my family thing."

"Bring your family with you."

"Really?"

"Of course." He nodded. "The more the merrier. It'll just add to the chaos." He winked.

My lips lifted with a little grin that quickly faded. "Are you sure Rhonda won't mind?"

"I trust my family. They won't breathe a word to anyone. Rhonda has nothing to worry about."

I wanted to say more. I wanted to give him a word-for-word recount of my conversation with his bitchy manager, but the soft look in his eyes shut me up.

This was the one afternoon we had together this week, and I didn't want to screw it up with fighting. I just wanted to wrap myself in his arms and pretend the outside world didn't exist.

Things were what they were. I had to accept them and take what I could get. I was a pro at doing that.

Sean ran the back of his finger gently down my face. "You know it breaks my heart when you look so sad. Come on, baby, where's my smile?"

I gave in and his pearly-white teeth appeared, making my smile grow.

His big lips came for me, sucking on my bottom lip before trailing over my chin and down my neck. I wriggled my hand under his shirt, closing my eyes and relishing that "getting lost" feeling I lived for.

SIXTEEN

SEAN

I waited for the shower to click on before reaching for my phone. Tucking the sheet around my waist, I sat up in bed and pressed Rhonda's name on my contact list.

"Hey, Sean, what's up?"

I glanced at the bathroom door and swallowed. "Did you pop by Morgan's place today?"

"I certainly did." She sounded bright and chipper. "I wanted to drop off a little present for her."

I grinned. "That was nice of you."

"I thought you'd appreciate it."

Pulling in a breath, I hesitated over my wording, but Morgan had been so upset when I first arrived,

I needed to get this straight. "Hey, did you say anything to her?"

"We had a little chat."

"About what?"

"You know, your career. We talked about how important it was that you guys are really careful over this winter break. We don't want any paparazzi seeing you together."

"You didn't tell her that she wasn't the girl for me, did you?"

"What? No! Of course not. I'd never say that to her."

I scratched my collarbone. "She kind of got the impression you did."

"Look, I'm not going to say I wasn't firm with my warning. I'm still annoyed with her that she tried to get you to stand up to Travis. She knows what's at stake."

"I've already told you, she was just mad. She didn't actually mean it."

"Yes, but still, you shouldn't have to feel that pressure."

"I love her, Rhonda. She's my girl, and she's allowed to be herself around me."

Rhonda paused. I could picture her licking her lips and pushing her glasses up her nose. "Of course she's your girl, and you are an amazing boyfriend. I know how much you care about each other. You just have to be careful. I'm trying to protect your relationship."

"By telling her we shouldn't be together?"

"I didn't say that! Sean, I think she misinterpreted what I was trying to tell her. You know I would never go behind your back like that."

"Yeah." I sighed, rubbing a hand over my face. "Yeah, I know. But listen, can you do me a favor? Next time you want a serious talk with her, include me in it."

"Of course, I'm sorry I didn't this time. I honestly didn't think she'd take my warning in such a negative light. I was just trying to be helpful."

"I know, I know; you're just trying to look out for me."

"That I am, Mr. Jaxon."

I grinned. "Well, you have a good Christmas."

"You too. Say hi to your family for me."

I touched the screen, glad I'd called, and popped the phone back onto the nightstand. I'd been feeling uneasy since I'd arrived, wondering what Rhonda could have said to get Morgan so riled up. I knew she could be quite forceful sometimes, and what's the bet my girl rose to meet her warnings head-on. I grinned at Morgan's feistiness. It was damn sexy.

The bathroom door opened, and Morgan appeared in nothing but a towel. Her wet hair was brushed straight, but I could see the wide curls forming as it dried. Water dripped off the ends and landed on the curve of her breasts, disappearing beneath her towel. My gaze skimmed down her curvy form.

She caught my appreciative smile, her cheeks rising with color.

"So, what do you want to do for dinner?" She moved to her underwear drawer and pulled out a pair of black panties.

I tipped my head, my body responding in an instant. Throwing off the sheet, I stood so she could see the effect she had on me.

Her gaze traveled over me, a sexy smirk forming on her lips as I moved toward her.

"I was thinkin' we should eat in tonight." I hooked my finger into her towel and yanked it free before gently pulling her against me. Our bodies slapped together, and I relished her smooth skin against mine. I bent down to nibble her earlobe as my hands danced over her curves. "In fact, I was thinking we should probably stay right here until Christmas." With a grin, I lightly pushed her onto the bed.

She fell with a giggle, propping her chin onto her hand and nipping her lower lip. Her brown eyes smoldered with longing as I hovered over her, my tongue trailing up from her navel and curving over her silky breast.

Her sigh was sweet and euphoric, her head tipping back as she whispered, "Sounds good to me."

*****

"Okay." Morgan nodded. "So we'll just meet you there then. Do you know where it is?" She nodded again.

I stood at the door watching her jiggle into her black pumps and smooth down her fitted dress. She looked damn fine. Too damn fine to be taking to a Jackson Christmas dinner, that was for sure. She ran her hand down the back of her hair, which she'd straightened. The bracelet I'd given her when she woke up this morning slid down her forearm. I grinned, recapturing her reaction to it.

I stretched my neck, adjusting the collar of the shirt she'd bought me. She said it'd been near impossible to find me a gift, but in the end she'd done pretty well. A shirt, my favorite bottle of wine, and a jar of chocolate sauce...which she said we could use tonight. My insides stirred just thinking about it. I adjusted my pants and reached for my keys.

Morgan heard the keys jingle and gave me a

nod.

"Okay, Dad, I'll see you guys there." Her fast clips toward me stopped. "She what? When! I don't believe it... No, Dad, it's not okay." She closed her eyes and sighed. "Yeah, yeah, I know... Okay." She frowned. "You too. 'Bye."

She hung up the phone with a short curse.

"Everything all right?"

"Jody bailed," she snapped, touching her screen and lifting the phone to her ear. She took three paces across the room before spinning and walking back toward me. "Yeah, hi, it's me. Can you please call me and tell me what the hell is going on? You don't just bail on your family last minute. Dad's really disappointed, not that he'd ever let you see that. How could you be so selfish, Jody? You better have a good explanation for this. And if you don't call me back before the end of the day, so help me I am driving down there to yell at you in person."

I pressed my lips together, hampering my chuckle as she hung up the phone.

She spun to face me. "What!"

My shoulders shook in spite of my efforts. "You sound like my mama."

Her narrow-eyed glare shut me up. "Don't even." She pointed at me, but I could see the gleam in her eye. She was fighting a smile.

I gave her a wink and pulled the door open. "We'll talk about it in the car. I'll see you in a minute."

Five minutes later, she slammed into my Camaro and buckled her seatbelt. Her moves were fast and efficient accompanied with huffs and sighs. I pulled away from the curb of the empty street just a block from Morgan's place. I hadn't parked in that spot before, but it was a good one. I'd have to use it again sometime.

With caution, I slowly reached for my girl,

running my hand over her thigh. "You want to talk about it?"

"I just don't get why she's pulling away. She's always let me in before. It hurts. I really hate it."

"I know." I gave her a glum smile. "Do you want to drive to Arizona?"

"No! I want to spend my time with you. I finally have you without work getting in the way. The last thing I want to do is a road trip out of state to check up on my petulant little sister."

I grinned, glad she didn't want to leave me, but my smile didn't last. Her face was tense, her shoulders tight. I wanted to make it better, take away her stress. At least we were heading into the Jackson tornado. She wouldn't have a spare second to dwell on her sister with that force swirling around her.

"Listen, are you sure you're up for this?"

She glanced at me. "Of course. I can't wait to meet your family."

"You know it's gonna be loud and chaotic and..."

"I know." She touched my arm with a sweet smile.

"My parents don't have a whole lot of money. Their place is kind of small and it gets stuffy and..."

"Sean." Her voice was soft. "I know I'm going to love it. Don't worry."

"Yeah." I grinned, squeezing her leg.

About an hour later, we pulled up to my family home. I watched Morgan as she took it in. I couldn't help that familiar touch of embarrassment when I looked at the tiny box house.

A high-pitched scream came from the front door. Morgan flinched when she saw two little girls racing down the stairs, being chased by three boys roaring like lions. Their screams continued as they shot around the side of the house.

I winced. She laughed.

"Don't say I didn't warn you." I reached for the door handle. "Christmas Day here is like surviving an atomic bomb."

We got out of the car, pulling out the dessert Morgan had prepared the night before, along with a few bottles of wine and a hoard of gifts. It would have taken me several trips if Kip and Morris hadn't rushed out of the house to help me. Morgan smiled as Kip kissed her cheek. He wiggled his eyebrows at me after she'd walked past.

I threw him a dry glare and passed him a box of gifts. He just laughed at me, whistling as he turned back for the house.

"Uncle Sean! Uncle Sean's here!" The announcement from Helena's twin girls sent a ripple effect through the house, and as soon as I stepped in the front door, Morgan and I were engulfed. Her father and grandmother arriving a few minutes after us didn't help. We must have been trapped in the tiny front entrance for nearly twenty minutes, saying hellos and giving introductions. Finally we made it to the Christmas tree in the corner of the crowded living room and placed our presents down. Morgan was quickly whipped away from me and it took me nearly forty minutes to search through the house and find her again.

She was in the kitchen, one of Mama's frilly aprons wrapped around her waist. It was just the two of them, which seemed like some miracle. Usually the kitchen was bustling, but by the serious tone of the conversation, I was guessing Mama had kicked everybody else out.

"I think she's lying." Morgan shook her head sadly as she placed her phone back into her purse. "And I really don't know what to do."

"Now, child, don't you worry. She just breakin'

free, is all."

I leaned against the doorframe, smiling, as my mother rubbed her wrinkled hand down Morgan's back.

"But Jody didn't even sound sick. I don't think she has the flu. If she did, she'd be begging me to come down and take care of her."

"Hey, she called you back, didn't she? That has to count for somethin'."

Morgan frowned, reaching for the carrots Mama was holding out to her. She took the peeler in the other hand and sat down on the high kitchen stool, getting to work. "Yeah, I guess so. I just hate that her friends have become more important than family. We only have each other."

"Her friends will never replace you. She just stretchin' out those wings of hers. Believe me, I've had five babies, and they all done it to me. Going through some dumb, wild phase. It's like a rite of passage or somethin'. The worst was Sean and that stupid Abigail girl. Lord, help me! I lost too much sleep over that one. You see this grey right here?" She tipped her head. "That's Sean's doin'."

I rolled my eyes while Morgan snickered. She caught me standing there, her eyes softening with a smile.

"Are you okay?" I mouthed.

She nodded.

"Hopefully the ride won't last too long and then she be back. You don't have to worry, now." Mama patted my girlfriend's shoulder and walked to the refrigerator.

"Jody going wild scares me." Morgan cringed.

"You have to trust her. She's a big girl; she's just testin' the limits. You said she's got some new boyfriend. What's the bet she just wanted to spend a little *quality time* with him, but didn't want to hurt your feelings?"

"I don't like that I haven't met him."

Her eyes bulged as she turned to face my girlfriend, her hand planted on her hip. "Girl, I only just meetin' you and you been with my boy for near four months now. This just payback, is what it is." She flicked her hand in the air, her nose rising with that indignant sniff of hers.

Morgan chuckled. "I'm sorry. We just have to keep things quiet."

"Not from me, you don't." Mama pointed a finger at her.

"Come on, Mama, leave her be." I stepped into the room.

"Oh don't you get me started on you." She threw a dishtowel at me. "Dry those dishes." Her head flicked in the direction of the sink, and I moved toward it with a sigh, running my fingers down Morgan's arm as I passed her.

"Sorry," I whispered in her ear.

She grinned and shook her head.

"You keepin' this golden beauty from me," Mama muttered. "Not trustin' me to protect my babies. Like I would say anything to anybody."

I rolled my eyes, snickering at Mama's diatribe. She did this all the time. Muttered out her complaints until she was done. You had to go with it. If she didn't get it all out of her system now, she'd just bring it up again later.

Morgan and I worked in silence, throwing each other winks and smiles until Mama was good and done. Florence and Kip flounced in at one point but were barked straight back out again. They giggled their way into the living room as I collected up the last dish and ran the towel around it.

"But you here now." Mama's voice finally perked up. She turned and slid her arm across Morgan's shoulder, pressing her salt-and-pepper curls against her head. "And I'm lovin' you."

Morgan chuckled, while I breathed a sigh of relief, not realizing how much Mama's approval meant to me. She'd never warmed to Abigail, had actually been quite open about it. The one time we'd gone out to dinner with my folks, it'd ended with icy goodbyes and big eye bulges from my mother. I could only imagine the muttering poor Pop had endured on the ride home.

I knew she'd like Morgan, though. Who wouldn't?

I hung the dishtowel on its hook and leaned against the kitchen counter, smiling at the two most precious women in my life.

All the battles and angst Morgan and I were facing from work, and her sister, suddenly didn't seem important. I had her now and was going to cherish every moment we got together...even if I did have to share her with my family. I grinned, remembering the jar of chocolate sauce sitting next to her bed. Yeah, this was going to be the best Christmas Day I'd ever had.

SEVENTEEN

MORGAN

The alarm clock beeped incessantly, its cruel squeak making me wince. I knew the only way to get it to stop squawking at me was to reach over and hit *snooze*, but I couldn't make my body move.

A low groan from the other side of the bed made me smile, and a dark, muscly arm stretched over my body, solving all my problems with a simple tap. I ran my fingers over his chocolate complexion and captured his arm against my chest, turning to face him.

I loved his body—long, lean, hard muscles covered in cocoa skin that was good enough to eat.

Sean's eyes were still closed, his wide lips relaxed. I grinned before leaning forward and running my tongue over them. They twitched with a smile. Sean's broad nose wrinkled as he squeezed his eyes shut, and then I got a shot of blue, aimed right at me, turning my insides to mush.

"Good morning."

"The only good thing about this morning is the view." He lifted the sheet and scanned my naked body, a rumble of appreciation stirring in his throat.

I snickered and shuffled toward him, running my hands up his back and pressing our bodies together. Sean was practically living at my house now. The rest of December had been very low-key and consisted of sleeping, reading, playing board games, watching movies, and lots and lots of sex.

I grinned. Since the noisiest, happiest Christmas Day of my life, I'd been living in heaven, but now our break was over, and all the worries I'd hid myself away from were still there waiting for me, including my ongoing struggles with Jody.

I frowned. Our FaceTime calls had dwindled down to text messages and very quick hellos. Thankfully she got over her so-called flu but was now super busy with school and never really had time to chat. A spark had died in her eyes, and as hard as I'd tried, she would not tell me more about her boyfriend, or any of her friends for that matter. Part of me worried that she was in some kind of abusive relationship. If that were the case, I'd be flying to Arizona and killing him. I was tempted to fly to Tucson and just surprise her anyway, but with work once again crazy, I just didn't have the time.

The alarm started beeping again and we both groaned.

Sean's hands were gliding up my thighs, his large palm cupping my butt and giving it a little squeeze.

I wrapped my leg around him and pressed my lips into his neck.

"The things I'm gonna do to you tonight," I murmured.

"Hmmmm." His lips found mine, his warm tongue waking up every sense in my body. If only we had time now.

Sean rolled me onto my back, pressing himself against me as he slapped my clock quiet. I ground my hips against him...maybe we did have time...but then Sean jerked away from me, rising onto his elbows.

"Tonight."

"Yeah." I ran my nails lightly down his back, giving him a seductive smile.

His eyes warmed with fire before crinkling with regret.

"What?"

"It's Saturday, right?

"Yeah, I think so." I cringed, trying to remember why this weekend was important.

"I'm out tonight. Damn, I forgot. It'll be a really late one, too." He sat away from me, rubbing a large hand over his beautiful face and pinching his nose.

"The charity dinner." It was hard to keep the disappointment from my voice.

"Yeah." He winced. "Travis said it'll be good promo for the show."

"Lisa told me." I pulled the sheet back over me and propped myself up on one elbow, frowning as the day's events flashed through my mind. I'd no doubt be collecting a tux and shining shoes.

"Who's going again?" I rubbed my temple.

"Travis and his wife, and I'm pretty sure Quinn and Trudy are going. Con and his girlfriend." He shook his head. "I can't remember who else. Maybe Isabella and Dean?"

"So partners were invited then?" I asked casually enough, picking at the bed sheet as I did it. When I'd asked Lisa a few weeks ago, she'd said she was pretty sure it was just cast going.

Sean's breath caught in his throat, and I looked up to catch his blue gaze.

"You know I'd love to take you, baby, but that's not an option right now."

I spun the promise ring on my finger, reminding myself not to get into this again. No matter how hard I tried, this discussion seemed to pop up time and again. Sean's quiet persuasion always shut me up. His logic was sound...I just wished it didn't hurt so much.

His lips skimmed my shoulder as he went into persuasion mode.

"We gotta get up," I murmured, trying to ignore his tongue, which was blazing a trail up my neck.

He nibbled my earlobe. "You know if we showered together, we'd save time."

I smirked.

"I'm just tryin' be practical, baby. That's all."

With a chuckle, I pushed him off me and slid out of bed, throwing a demure look over my shoulder before beckoning him toward the bathroom. He jumped up and reached me before I was at the bathroom door, slathering kisses over my shoulders while running his hands between my legs.

My knees turned to jelly as I flicked on the shower, gripping the wall to give me support as Sean worked his magic, making the world turn fuzzy. Waves of pleasure rolled through my body as the small shower box filled with my cries of ecstasy.

When my limbs were a shaking mess, he spun me around and plastered me against the wall, diving inside me as the water rained over us.

It was easy to forget my malaise when I had the world's sexiest man sending me over the edge like this. I gripped the back of his neck, closing my eyes against the hot spray and trying to focus solely on the pleasure coursing through my body. But my mind was a cruel trickster, and in spite of my current state, I couldn't completely switch off my disappointment.

Sean was going to an event as a bachelor; at least, that's what the world would think. Only those closest to us knew the truth, and for some reason, that didn't feel like enough. The secrecy thing was getting old. Damn Travis and his stupid demands.

Yes, it was good that Sean and I were sharing nights now, but he always parked around the corner, and the longer he spent here, the further away he parked. At least his family knew I existed, but they were under strict instructions never to mention my name in public.

My brain skittered as Sean's rhythm increased, my muscles clenching tight as a shudder ran through his body. He pressed me hard against the wall, panting against my skin before pulling back and smiling at me with those electric eyes that made me forget.

His soft fingers caressing my face and the beam in his smile reminded me why I loved him so much.

I matched his expression and earned myself a tender kiss before we disentangled our limbs and finished showering.

We dressed in silence, scurrying around each other. Thanks to our interlude, we had no time for breakfast and were soon standing at my door.

Sean placed his hand over mine, stopping me from swinging the door open and charging outside.

"I am sorry I can't take you tonight. Rhonda

thinks it will be best to keep you in the shadows at least until the end of the season. I don't even know if the show will get picked up again. There may not be a second season of *Superstar*."

I tried not to roll my eyes. Of course there'd be a second season. The show was a total hit and what then? Even if I quit, Rhonda would convince Sean to keep me invisible. She'd come up with some warning he'd buy into. I'd tried to challenge him on it a couple of times, but he got pretty defensive, pretty fast.

Rhonda didn't know everything, and it bugged me that Sean seemed to do anything she told him to. Since New Year's hit, she'd had him at so many parties, he was basically running on empty before filming resumed, but if Rhonda told him to do it, then that's what he did.

I didn't get to go to any of those, either. Rhonda had accompanied him to three of them and Ashlee Johnston had gone to a couple more. I didn't want to be paranoid, but I couldn't help feeling like Rhonda was pushing Ashlee and Sean together. She kept harping on about how it was just for show, but my gut told me something was brewing, and I was scared Sean wouldn't know when to take a stand and say, "Enough's enough."

I ran my hand up Sean's chest and pecked him on the lips.

"I get it." I didn't really, but we were already running late for work, and I didn't think I could stomach the backlash from Travis. "I'm sure you'll have a great time tonight."

His hand landed on my hip, running across my lower back and pulling me to him.

"I'll tell you all about it tomorrow. Promise."

I let him kiss me, let him melt away my fears with his magic tongue. I wanted to trust him, I really did, but people could let you down in the blink of an eye...even the ones you trusted the most.

EIGHTEEN

SEAN

Ashlee's petite hand in mine was irritating. I wanted to let it go, but Travis had asked for a show and that was what we were giving the cameras. The bulbs flashed without mercy, stars spotting my eyes as I wrestled with the intense hype.

This charity dinner was a much bigger event than I realized. Typical Rhonda. She always kept the information vague when she thought it was something I wouldn't enjoy. I tried to quell my annoyance and pasted on a smile, finally finding the chance to let Ashlee's hand go. I put my arm around her shoulders and pulled her toward me so the camera could get the shot they wanted—Harley and Sasha in the flesh.

Travis gave me a winning smile. If only people knew. Most loved him, but I found him a little hard to stomach now. I didn't think I'd ever get over our little conversation in the storage closet. It bugged me that because of him, I'd never be able to bring Morgan to one of these events. Even if he did approve of us being together, I still wouldn't bring her. Why should she have to put up with his bullshit? She got enough of it during the day.

I missed her, though.

I wanted her sleek body standing next to me. In heels, she was my height. Her face would be next to mine, my arm around her waist. Those luscious curves of hers fitted perfectly against my side.

Forcing my smile even wider, I waved to the camera and moved toward Trudy and Quinn for a *Superstar* group photo.

I tried to find a good place to put my hand on Trudy for the shot. There was more skin showing on that woman than dress. I lightly placed my fingers on her lower back, trying not to imagine what Morgan would wear to an event like this. My insides stirred with longing as I grinned at the camera. I really had to put her out of my mind, but it was damn impossible. She was Aphrodite.

And the things she was going to do to me.

Damn, tomorrow couldn't come fast enough.

I glanced at Travis with his arm tucked around his wife. He was conducting a short interview while we milled around behind him. My gaze traveled to Trudy's hand, which was resting inside Quinn's. They were open about their budding relationship and the media loved it.

"Hey, Sean and Ashlee, a kiss for the cameras!" someone shouted.

Ashlee jumped to her toes and pecked my cheek, kicking her leg up in the air. I laughed at her playfulness, holding my arm around her waist to keep her steady.

"You are such a fool." I looked down at her.

"Just putting on a show." She winked. "You know how they lap this shit up. Smile for the camera, Seany."

She grabbed my chin and pulled a face, making me laugh. Thank God she was here. This night would have been unbearable without her.

It took forever to make it in the door and once we were inside, more cameras were there clicking. The charity dinner was more of a charity ball. The big dance floor in the middle told me that.

"Let me guess, we're doing a number later, right?" I pulled out Ashlee's chair.

"I thought you knew," she said over her shoulder as I pushed it into place.

I sat down beside her and shook my head. "Rhonda probably told me," I muttered.

"Yeah, I notice you've been extra tired at work since Christmas. Did you have an energetic break, Mr. Jaxon?" Her eyebrows wiggled and I cringed.

Morgan was usually the only one who called me Mr. Jaxon in that flirty tone...and I kind of wanted to keep it that way.

I gave her a half-smile and she giggled.

"I thought so." She poked my side. "Who is she?"

Clearing my throat, I looked away and shook my head.

"Oh, come on." Leaning toward me, she pressed her lips close to my ear. "I won't tell a soul, I swear."

I gave her a sideways glare. "Like I'd trust you with that information."

"You know you can."

"Nah, she's too precious." I gave Ashlee an earnest smile, and her expression softened to marshmallow.

"That is so beautiful." She touched her chest. "Oh my gosh, Sean, you're totally in love."

My smile grew.

Ashlee touched my arm and gave it a gentle squeeze, and then she didn't say another word.

Cameras clicked throughout the night. I was pretty much over it within the first hour. My cheeks were hurting from smiling so much and after all the champagne toasts, I was feeling a little buzzed. All I wanted to do was drive to Morgan's place, pull her against my body, and fall into a blissful sleep. No such luck for me though; the band was kicking in, and it was time for yet another performance.

I held out my hand to Ashlee. She took it with a grin, and I led her onto the dance floor where we performed a couple of numbers from the episodes that had already aired. Something inside me shifted as I spun Ashlee around the floor. The crowd loved it, enraptured by our performance; you could feel the frisson as Ashlee and I moved together. She was no Morgan Pritchett, but she was great to dance with, her moves confident and sharp. As my body lost itself to the power of the music, I was reminded once again why I loved my job so much.

I got to dance, party, and act for a living. It was pretty freaking amazing. As a kid, I never thought I'd catch a break like this.

I held Ashlee for our final pose and the music thumped to a finish. Thunderous applause filled the room as we separated and took a bow. Ashlee was lapping it up; she loved the limelight, and I couldn't deny that the thrill was pretty kick-ass.

On the way back to our table, I was stopped by numerous donors, telling me how wonderful I was and how much they enjoyed the show. A marker was placed in my hand at some point and the evening was whittled away signing autographs and laughing with strangers.

At around three in the morning, the limo dropped me off at my pad. Part of me wanted to head to Morgan's right then, but I was too buzzed to drive, and after a day of running around doing last-minute prep for Travis, she needed as much sleep as she could get. Stumbling into my apartment, I shrugged off my jacket and threw it over the armchair in the corner of my room. Slipping off my shoes, I fell onto the bed with a grin.

Damn, my job was cool.

NINETEEN

MORGAN

Reynold's pub was busy, as usual. Ella was working the bar with Cole. I sat on a stool at the end, chatting to her when she had a few minutes to spare. The two waitresses bustled back and forth from the kitchen carrying trays of gluten-free food. I still couldn't believe they'd pulled it off. Provided a menu that was ninety percent gluten-free, just like Cole promised he would. I grinned as I scanned the tables. The non-typical bar food obviously didn't bother any of the patrons. The waitresses looked rushed off their feet as they moved from table to table while a solo artist in the corner calmed everything down with her acoustic guitar.

I sipped my coffee with a quiet smile, soaking in the atmosphere. These two had done an amazing job, turned the place into an LA version of Quigg's. The Chicago bar, owned by Cole's foster parents, was a place Brad and I had frequented. I wished Sean was here with me, but he didn't like going out to such a public venue. He always joked that he wouldn't have been able to keep his hands off me. Someone was always watching and we didn't want to get caught.

Frankly, I no longer cared who was watching or if we got caught, but I *did* care about Sean and so I'd keep relishing the private moments we had together.

Ella smiled at a patron while he swiped his card to pay. In her usual style, she kept a sweet banter going with the man and passed him his receipt. No wonder people loved coming here. I caught Cole glide past her, gently squeezing her waist and kissing her forehead before grabbing a glass and deftly pulling a beer.

They worked around each other as if they were doing some kind of dance. I'd been watching them for the past hour and not once had they collided or unintentionally touched. They seemed to work in sync, a quiet repartee flowing between them, punctured only by laughter and the odd kiss. Their open displays of affection sent a knife of envy shooting through my middle. I sat up straight and rubbed my stomach.

Ella slapped her hands on the countertop beside me. "Sorry about this, I should have warned you how busy Sunday lunchtime gets."

"That's okay." I rubbed her hand. "I love that you guys are so busy."

She looked over her shoulder and took in the bustle, turning back to me with a beaming smile.

Cole approached her from behind, his hands

nestling on her hips. "Hey, why don't you go take a quick break? I'll hold the fort so you can two can chat."

"Are you sure?" Ella gazed up at him.

"Of course." He nipped her nose with his lips and patted her butt before returning his attention to the bar.

"Come on." Ella beckoned me with her hand, lifting up the bar so I could duck underneath. We wove past the steaming kitchen and up the narrow staircase.

Ella opened the door and fell straight onto their threadbare two-seater, her arms flopping onto the cushions.

I sat down next to her. "You look exhausted."

"I am." She turned her head and gave me a tired smile. "Things are going so well since we opened...and I may be tired, but I do love it."

"It must be nice working with Cole."

"It is." Her eyes sparkled. "But you know that already, you get to work with Sean."

"Hardly." I didn't usually let myself pout, but this was Ella, and I could be whomever I wanted around this girl and she'd love me regardless. "I'm so busy and he's busy. We don't get to see each other as much as you might think. Plus, with having to hide it all the time..."

Ella squeezed my knee. "That part must suck."

"Yeah, it's..." I shifted on the couch, leaning forward and resting my elbows on my knees. "I get why we have to do things this way. He wants to protect me, but sometimes it doesn't feel like that. I wish he wasn't so put off by that one threat from Travis. I mean, *Superstar* is huge, and the audience would be livid if Travis wrote Harley off the show. The guy might be an asshole, but he's not stupid."

"So why do you think Sean's hesitating?"

"Because of his stupid manager!" I shot from my

seat, the unexpected burst of anger surprising me. I took in a breath to lower my voice. "Ella, he does everything she says and again, I get why, but her influence over him really bothers me sometimes. I feel like she has this clandestine plan for his future that not even he knows about! Like he's her little puppet or something." I huffed, rubbing my temples. "I just really hope that all her advice is in *his* best interest and not only hers. She gets a pretty damn big cut of every deal she secures for him. The bigger his name, the bigger *her* paycheck."

Ella listened in empathetic silence like she always did. I glanced at her, knowing I could rabbit on for the rest of her break if I wanted to.

With a heavy sigh, I slumped back onto the couch. "I know she doesn't like me. I know she wants me out of the picture. It's pissing her off to no end that I'm still around."

"Why do you say that?"

I threw Ella a sad smile, letting out a heavy sigh before launching into my pre-Christmas natter with the lovely Rhonda Dickens.

"Oh my gosh!" Ella's mouth dropped open when I'd finished. "When did that happen?"

"A few days before Christmas." I spun the ring on my finger, rubbing my thumb over the sapphires.

"Well, did you tell him?"

"I tried." I flicked my hands in the air. "But he brushed it off as nothing. I mean, he did call and follow it up, but apparently I misunderstood her." I put on a snarky voice. Crossing my arms with yet another huff, I threw my head back on the couch. "I didn't want to argue with him over the holiday break. Everything was perfect, and I just wanted to forget the outside world existed."

"Since when has Morgan Pritchett ever shied away from a fight?"

"Since it could mean destroying my lover's career and possibly losing him in the process."

Ella's smile was soft. "He's different, isn't he? You really love him."

"Yeah. Sometimes I wish I didn't, but then..." I shrugged. "The idea of him not being around kills me, like I can't live without him."

Ella shuffled along the couch, wrapping her arms around me and squeezing tight. I rested my cheek against the top of her head, and she gave me one more hard squeeze.

"Okay, I get it. I love you, too." I squeezed her back and let go, holding her at arm's length and smiling.

She didn't smile back and my gut clenched.

"What?"

Ella pressed her lips together and stood, walking over to the little table parked against the wall and lifting her laptop screen.

The photos hit me first; they were bright and vivid and made my insides want to fall out my backside.

I lurched up and stumbled toward the screen, taking a seat at the table and soaking in the images of Ashlee and Sean. It was a full-page spread, and in every single photo they were touching. If she wasn't kissing his cheek, she had her arm around his waist. There were two images of them dancing together and then a series of three. They were sitting at a table and she was whispering in his ear. Then he was smiling at her and she was touching her chest and giving him a mushy smile.

I slammed the lid closed, feeling sick.

"It's probably nothing."

"Ella, the headline says, '*Superstar's* next hot couple.'"

"Yeah, but it's all for show, right? I mean, you're smart enough to know that."

I cleared my throat and gave a firm nod, trying to convince myself it was true. Crossing my arms, I held them tight to my chest and stood, needing to pace.

Ella nibbled her lip. "I wasn't sure whether to tell you or not, but after what you just told me about Rhonda... I don't know, do you think she's trying to manipulate this somehow?"

I scraped my nails through my hair and closed my eyes. "I don't know! Maybe!" I spun around and pointed at the laptop. "Damn it, she's probably right. They look amazing together."

"Don't say that. You look way better with him than she does. Anybody can see how into each other you are."

"Anybody?" I scoffed.

"Anybody close to you guys. You know what I mean," Ella muttered.

I slumped onto the couch, squeezing my eyes shut. "I wish you hadn't shown me."

"I'm sorry." She nestled down beside me and rested her head on my shoulder. "I just felt like you needed to know, so you could talk to Sean and hear his side. It's most likely nothing. Headlines are crap anyway, right?"

"Yep." I nodded, clipping the word short.

"Morgan, I know you don't want to fight with Sean, but this whole secrecy thing is obviously getting you down. Maybe you need to try telling Sean again, about Rhonda."

"He doesn't want to hear it."

"It's doesn't matter. He needs to." Ella kissed my cheek and then glanced at her watch. "Sorry, babe, I gotta get back down and help Cole. You're welcome to stay."

"No, that's okay. I should probably swing past Dad's anyway. Make sure he's taking care of himself."

Ella's smile was soft and kind. "You're really good at doing that, you know."

"Doing what."

"Looking after everybody."

I shrugged. "I guess it's what I do best."

"Just as long as you look after yourself, too."

My laughter was dry and hollow. "That's what boyfriends are for."

A sad anguish crested over Ella's face. I turned away from her, snatching the keys out of my jacket pocket and standing from the couch.

"Don't work too hard." I brushed past her and headed down the stairs first, trying to outrun her sorrowful gaze.

TWENTY

SEAN

Morgan bailed on me. She didn't say why, just said she'd see me at work on Monday. To say I was disappointed was an understatement; I was looking forward to telling her all about my night. Well, I was, until I ended up at Helena's house and she started teasing me about Miss Ashlee Johnston.

"What are you talking about?"

She slapped down the entertainment section and wiggled her eyebrows.

I read the headline. "Aw, shit." Then glanced at the photos. "You've gotta be fucking kidding me."

"Watch your mouth." Helena clipped the back of my head. "My babies are in the next room."

Kip chuckled, shoving an entire chocolate chip

171

cookie in his mouth and brushing the crumbs off on his jeans.

"The trials of fame, lil' brother." Residue cookie popped out of his mouth as he laughed, a fine dust sprinkling the counter.

I wrinkled my nose and shifted away from it.

"Wonder what Morgan's gonna say." He guffawed.

I pulled out my phone and spent the next hour trying to reach her, before calling Rhonda.

"Don't worry about it, honey. I think this is great."

"Ashlee's not my girlfriend, this isn't great."

"Calm down. Andrew and I have already talked; we're doing a spin on it, saying how well the cast of *Superstar* gets along. It's really no big deal. You know better than to read headlines; that's my job."

"Yeah, yeah, I know. I just..."

"You're worried about Morgan's reaction, aren't you?"

She took my sigh as a yes.

"Don't be. She's a smart girl. She knows there's nothing going on between you and Ashlee. It would be irrational for her to think otherwise."

"I should have taken her. Travis said we could bring partners."

"Not her! That never would have flown with him and you know it. How many times do we have to talk about this, Sean? You want to protect her, remember? Last night would have opened her up to all kinds of exposure. She's not ready for that. You're keeping her safe by keeping this a secret. You're protecting her from the likes of Travis and all the other media. You're doing her a favor."

"Yeah, I guess." I pinched the bridge of my nose. "I can't get in touch with her."

"You know what I think would be best? Let her

cool off. She's a sensible woman, but she is a still a woman. If she *has* seen the paper, she might just need a little time and space to process it. Come tomorrow, she'll be dying to see you again. I know what you two lovebirds are like."

Rhonda's chuckle made me grin.

"Thanks. You're a great manager."

"Hey, I'm only doing what's best for you."

I hung up feeling better. Rhonda was probably right; Morgan could get pretty fired up, and she probably needed some time to cool off. She would have seen my calls and heard my messages. She would know I wanted to talk to her. Now I just had to be patient and let her come to me.

*****

"Hey." My face lit with a grin as she slipped into my dressing room and shut the door.

"Hey."

Just seeing her made my insides stir. I didn't care that we were at work; stepping around my chair, I gathered her into my arms and placed a sweet kiss on her glossy lips.

She reciprocated, but her usual passion was amiss.

I pulled back. "You okay, baby?"

Her head tipped to the side, giving me a cynical smirk.

"Hey, I wanted to clear this up yesterday, but you wouldn't return my calls."

"I got caught up at my dad's place. It was mess. There was laundry and dishes and he's been eating such crap food, so I had to go shopping and cook him some meals and clean the bathroom and..." She poked out her tongue. "I didn't really have the time or the energy to deal with you and Ashlee being a hot new couple." She rolled her eyes.

I gave her waist a light squeeze. "You know that's not true."

"Yeah." She sighed. "It's still not very fun seeing it though."

"I can't control what the papers write. Ashlee and I are friends; that's it."

"I know." She held up her hands and backed away from me. "I'm glad you guys had a good night."

"No, you're not." I grinned.

She made a face and flipped me off. I clasped her finger and pulled her toward me, kissing the tip of it before running my finger over the promise ring.

I gave her my smile, the one that turned her brown gaze into bedroom eyes. "I don't care what the papers say. You're my girl, Morgan."

She gently wriggled her hand free, her bedroom eyes nowhere to be seen. "Nobody else knows that, Sean."

My jaw worked to the side as I tried to think of an intelligent reply that didn't involve the same words I'd been spouting off for weeks.

"I know you're doing this to protect me. I know you want to keep me safe, but I told you I wasn't afraid. If anything, it feels like *you're* afraid...afraid to let the world know you've fallen in love again. Afraid of what they might think of us together. Afraid of how it might hurt your career."

"It's not that. It's Travis..."

"It can't just be Travis. He's not going to write you out of the show. Harley is too important."

I had no reply. Rhonda told me to keep it quiet and I agreed, because I was protecting the girl I loved. Morgan said she got that, but she didn't seem to. Maybe I hadn't been clear on how much the Abigail thing nearly destroyed me...or how powerful Travis really was. I couldn't jeopardize my career again.

Her phone saved my ass. She cleared the message and huffed, shoving it back into her pocket.

"I gotta go."

I wanted to hold her one more time, promise that everything would be okay, but instead, I let her walk out the door.

"You coming?" Isabella paused in my doorway, giving me an odd look before indicating with her thumb that we had work to do.

I rubbed my hand over my lips and nodded, whipping off my shirt and changing for dance rehearsal.

Three hours later, I was a sweaty mess. I had forty minutes to get showered and down to makeup. I only had a short scene to shoot today and I was grateful. This whole Morgan thing was making me restless. All I wanted to do was get her back to her place and show her how much I cared about her.

"Hey, sweaty man." I looked up at the sound of Rhonda's voice. Her warm smile made it impossible not to reciprocate.

"Hey, how's it going?"

"Good, I was driving past and thought I'd drop off those cologne posters for signing. I collected them this morning and they look fantastic. I popped them in your dressing room, so if you can find a minute to scrawl your name on those today, that'd be great."

"Yeah, yeah, sure." I wiped the towel over my face.

"Oh, and Andrew and I have pulled a few strings. There's going to be an article in the next *Entertainment Weekly* about the show. Travis is on board and a few people will be flitting around set taking photos and such, and I wanted to assure you that we'll make sure we go for that cast-is-close type spin."

"Thanks, I appre—"

"You didn't ask for blue, you specifically said gold, because you wanted it to match the color themes of the show." I recognized Morgan's terse tone immediately.

I frowned, pausing outside the office door to make sure she was okay.

Travis snatched the sheet she was holding and slowly ripped it in half.

She tutted, pulling her neck straight and lifting her chin as the pieces of paper floated to the floor.

"You dumb piece of shit. Can you not do anything right?"

Morgan's shoulders shuddered as if the dormant volcano in her belly was finally being unleashed. She made two fists and then let them go, throwing her face to the sky.

"You know what, that's it! If I'm so stupid and useless, why the hell don't you fire my sorry ass!"

Travis stepped back from her venom, a smirk resting on his lips. Slowly crossing his arms, he gave her a goading smile before quietly asking, "Why don't you just quit?"

"I wouldn't want to give you the satisfaction, you sadist."

Travis guffawed. "Good, because your pain is my pleasure." He leaned toward her, his beady gaze making her recoil. "So please, keep coming to work. You're the best form of stress relief I have ever had, and I wouldn't want to lose you."

He ran his knuckle gently down her cheek. She slapped his hand away, making him snort with laughter. I flinched, my insides scorched hot with rage. That was it. He just crossed a line. I went to step into the room, ready to introduce Travis to my own very effective form of stress relief. My fist rounded into a tight ball as I moved, but Rhonda pinched my arm, her long nails sinking into my skin.

"Stop," she whispered between clenched teeth.

I glanced over my shoulder as she pulled me down the hall. "I can't let him treat her like that."

"If you go in there now, he's gonna know, and what do you think he'll do to her then? What do you think he'll do to you?"

"Oh come on."

"Listen to me, Sean." Rhonda's sharp tone made it impossible not to. "He's the bigwig, and he's psycho enough not to care that you're the cash cow for this show. He'd write you out of this just for fun; then where will you be?"

"He's not going to fire me."

"How do you know? If he's sick enough to keep her around for stress relief, don't you think his brain's warped enough to make your life hell?" Rhonda's eyebrows rose as she dipped her head forward and gave me that *get what I'm telling you* look. "Don't throw it all away. You love your job; this is a great chance for you. You deserve this, Sean."

"Morgan des—"

"Morgan is a tough chick, that's one of the things you love most about her."

How could I argue with the truth?

"She'll get over this. She's strong and you'll be there to comfort her at the end of the day. She doesn't need you to fight her battles, and if she thought it would jeopardize your career, there's no way she'd ask you to do it." Rhonda shook her head. "If she loves you like she says she does, she'd never let you put your job at risk."

I pressed my lips together, hating Rhonda's words but knowing they were right. A flash of movement from the office caught my eye, and I glanced up to see Morgan stride out of the room.

She saw me and jerked to a stop.

I gave her a sympathetic smile, letting her know I'd heard it all and I was there for her. No one else but Rhonda was in the hallway, so as she walked toward me I reached out my hand.

Her gaze narrowed as she approached, her arms remaining locked at her side. She gave my manager a sharp look before her cold glare landed on me.

"Thanks for your help," she choked out before brushing past me.

I knew I'd let her down. I should have barreled in there; I should have stood up for my woman.

"Just give her time to cool off, Sean. It'll be okay." Rhonda patted my arm. "Don't go chasing her down while she's fiery-hot like that. You'll just get in a fight and then everyone will find out and all your work at keeping things quiet will go down the pooper. You're doing this because you love her. Just remember that."

I nodded, licking my lower lip and heading for the shower. I felt like the piece of dog shit you scrape off someone's sneaker.

I didn't want to lose my job or Morgan. I didn't want to lose favor with Travis. I hated that work was hard for Morgan, but wouldn't it be even worse if it was hard for both of us? I didn't want to open my girl up to further humiliation.

All I could hope was that Rhonda was right, because seeing that look of betrayal on Morgan's face about killed me.

TWENTY-ONE

MORGAN

I slammed the car door shut and started the engine. My nerves were frayed to fine threads, barely holding me together. To say work sucked was the understatement of the century. My outburst seemed to ignite some sick pleasure in Travis, his dark side finally having a chance to unleash.

"Stress relief," I muttered as I reversed out of my spot and spun the car in the right direction. Slamming down the gas, I screeched out of the parking lot, barely pausing for the barrier to lift. I wanted to smash straight through the damn thing. Now *that* would be stress relief.

I looked at the clock on the dash and cringed.

10:23. I had hoped to do my weekly check-in with Jody today but felt like it was too late to hassle her now. What if she was asleep already? I could tell by the tired way she constantly answered the phone that school was taking its toll. I had heard that performing arts courses were taxing, but I didn't realize to this extent. It probably didn't help that she'd turned into a partying maniac. I knew she was tough enough to take it, but that didn't stop me worrying about her.

I really wanted to talk to her, though. I needed the distraction.

Worrying about someone else's problems was so much easier than focusing on my own. Sean had finished earlier than me. I'd seen him loitering on the sidelines, no doubt trying to catch me in secret before he left. I stayed as busy as I possibly could, sticking to the most crowded areas on set. He must have given up, because when I went to leave, his car wasn't in the lot. I should have probably called him, sorted this out, but I honestly didn't have the energy to get into it.

How could he just stand there and listen to Travis treat me that way?

If there was a line, my boss had freaking pole-vaulted over it, and my boyfriend had done jack-all. I wanted to blame Rhonda; she had been standing right there, no doubt trying to stop him.

I gripped the wheel, anger surging through me like a tidal wave.

I wished I didn't need this stupid job. I wished there was something better out there for me.

"I wish, I wish, I wish. Shut the hell up, Morgan! Stop feeling so damn sorry for yourself."

I bit down on my lip, relishing the pain. It was a habit I'd picked up as a teen. I never went as far as cutting, but during those really bad months I used to dig my nails into the soft flesh of my arm, anything to stop the tears from falling. When I didn't have any free hands my teeth went for my lip.

My eyes stung as I drew to a stop at the red light. I was two minutes from home, and it was the last place I wanted to go. Putting on my blinker, I decided a late-night drive wouldn't kill me. I needed to unwind or I'd never get to sleep.

Collecting my phone, I unlocked it to look for some music and noticed I was still on my contacts list. Jody's name was highlighted on the screen; that was as far as I'd gotten throughout my hectic day. I pressed the number and slid the phone into my hands-free unit. I didn't care what the time was; I wanted to check up on my sister.

"Hey, sis, what's up?"

Her sweet voice was like a soothing balm. "Oh, good, I'm glad you're up. I didn't want to wake you."

"Nope. Awake."

"You sound tired, though."

"I'm always tired."

"Me too." I chuckled. "Work can be a real bitch that way."

"Yeah, tell me about it." She still sounded flat.

How could I get her voice to sparkle again?

"So, how is work?" Jody cleared her throat.

"Oh, it's okay, I guess." I shrugged as if she could see me. "I mean, my boss is still a total asshole, but you know, a job's a job."

"Yeah, true. Plus you get to work with your boyfriend all day."

"Hmm, not as much as you think. This whole secret relationship thing...I don't know, it's hard to catch those moments sometimes."

"I thought you loved it...being pulled into some dark closet to make out with Mr. Hollywood."

I forced a chuckle. "Yeah, that only happened

once and didn't end so well."

"But he still comes over after work, right?"

"Yeah." I cleared my throat.

"Let me guess, it's not happening anymore." There was a bitter twang to her tone, which concerned me. I was opening my mouth to ask about her fella, fish for information, but she got in first. "I saw the paper, Morgan. I'm guessing it's bullshit, just the media spinning a story, but is that all it is?"

"Yeah, definitely." There was no way I wanted to dive into that conversation; I'd finally managed to put it out of my head. "Sean told me not to worry...and I'm not. Really."

"You don't sound convinced."

"I am. I trust Sean. I know he cares about me."

"Then why do you sound so down? Why the hell are you calling me at like ten-thirty at night when you should be in bed with your man right now?"

I sighed, figuring I might as well tell her the truth. I needed to talk to someone about my day, and as much as I didn't want to burden her, she had asked.

"I had a really crap day, Travis went off at me and was totally cruel, and Sean didn't do anything to stop it. I guess I felt kind of let-down."

There was a long pause. I could picture Jody licking her lips, giving the receiver a sad smile. I was waiting for her sigh of sympathy, her words of comfort. I was definitely not expecting what she dished out.

"Why are you doing this again?" she snapped.

"Excuse me?"

"You let your boss treat you that way and you didn't walk out the door? You let Sean listen to that bullshit, do absolutely nothing about it, and you didn't slap him in the face?"

My face scrunched with a frown. I looked at my phone screen in horror. Jody had never spoken to me like that before. She didn't yell when she got angry—she sulked. And she certainly never made people feel bad.

"You always do this, Morgan. End up in these shitty situations that you just refuse to walk away from, even though you totally can!"

"What...where...where the hell is this coming from?"

"When was the last time you were single? When have you ever gone more than like a week without having some lousy date or scoring some loser boyfriend?"

"Sean is not a loser."

"This isn't even about Sean anymore! I'm talking about the fact that you seem capable of looking after everyone but yourself. You feel needed so you stay, you stick around and you let these people take total advantage of you."

"That is not true! I'm not like that at all. I am a strong, confident woman. People do not push me around." I flicked my hand in the air. It landed back on the horn, setting it off with a loud honk.

I flinched at the sound, but unfortunately it wasn't enough to stop Jody's diatribe.

"Your boss treats you like a maggot, and your boyfriend isn't doing anything about it...oh yeah, and he's hiding you in the shadows, which you hate and he knows...but he's not doing anything about it."

"What the hell is your problem?"

"My problem is that you are better than this. You don't belong in the shadows, Morgan. You are amazing and talented and you're selling yourself short, because you're too afraid to just take a leap! And the thing that pisses me off the most is that you can, you can do and be whatever the fuck you want; nothing is holding you back except you!"

And with that she hung up.

"Jody?" I glanced at my phone and tried to redial her, but it went straight to voicemail. Her sweet, chirpy message was damn irritating after the bitch-fest I'd just endured.

I looked back to the road and slammed on my brakes, the car screeching to a halt seconds before I almost plowed into the back of a mini-van. I pulled in a breath through my nose, leaning my head against the steering wheel until the car behind me honked.

Lightly pressing the gas, I made it through the intersection in one piece, despite my shaking hands. Glancing at the street sign, I realized I was unwittingly heading to Reynold's Pub, so I figured I might as well keep going.

I increased my speed, hoping I'd make it there before closing.

Fifteen minutes later, I parked the car and hustled down the road. The lights were still on.

"Thank God," I whispered, flinging back the door and having to quickly jump out the way.

The man stumbled past me, collecting himself before landing face-first on the pavement.

"And you're not welcome back." Cole pointed at him.

The man gave him the finger, swearing loudly as he stumbled off down the street. My eyebrows rose in question. Cole rolled his eyes and ushered me inside, locking the doors firmly behind us.

"So, what just happened?"

Ella shook her head, gently collecting up the pieces of shattered glass on the floor. "Some mouthy guy was accusing me of robbing him." She stood and placed the pieces on the table, looking at Cole with an apologetic frown. "I swear I gave him the right change."

"I don't care if you gave him the wrong change; no one talks to my girl that way."

He looked pissed, in a righteous kind of way. Cole was a good-looking guy, but as a knight in shining armor he was damn sexy. Ella was a lucky lady...and she knew it.

Her sweet smile said it all.

"C'mere." Cole pulled her into his strong arms, kissing the top of her head before resting his chin there.

"Thank you." At least I thought that's what she'd said. Either that, or I love you. The words were muffled by his shirt.

He pulled back from her, tenderly touching her face. I turned away from their little moment, my eyes burning as I imagined what Sean might look like in his armor. I had a sinking feeling I'd never know.

"So, Morgan, sorry for that welcome. Do you want a drink?"

I spun to face Cole's question.

"Sure." I nodded, moving to the bar and parking it. "Something strong, please."

Cole's eyes darted to Ella's. I ignored the look passing between them and sat up straighter as Ella perched herself down beside me. "What's up?"

I drew in a breath, figuring I'd go for a downplayed version of events, but as the air came out of my lungs, the words just tumbled free, a quick torrent that recapped my nightmarish day in all its glory.

Both Ella's and Cole's mouths were hanging open by the time I got to my phone call with Jody. Once that recap was done, their chins were basically on the floor.

"What is up with her at the moment, anyway!" I snatched the shot glass and downed it, not even knowing what the liquid was that burned my throat.

"Yeah, we're worried about her too. She's seemed really distant lately." Ella gently took the glass and passed it to Cole.

"Well, she's told me jack-all. I have no idea what the fuck is going on in Tucson and part of me doesn't even want to care."

"But you will...because you're Morgan." Ella's smile was tender.

"And according to Jody, that's half the problem!" I threw my hands in the air. It felt good to raise my voice and shout a little.

Ella's voice was in calm contrast to my ranting. "Can I be one hundred percent honest?"

I wanted to yell NO, right in her face, but this was Ella, the sweetest human being on the earth, and so I shrugged and mumbled, "Of course."

She drew in a breath, smiling at me as she collected up my hand. "You've spent half your life looking after other people...you were forced into that position way too young, and I think you've tried to compensate by dating all these other guys, desperate for someone to look after you...but then you don't get out of the way to let them do it. You've always needed control to keep yourself sane."

"Great, so now I'm a control freak?" I snatched my hand back.

"You already know you are."

"So you're saying it's *my* fault that no one will step up to fight for me."

"Maybe...no one knows you need them to. You're so strong and sure of yourself."

"I've told Sean. I made it very clear that I don't want to hide anymore, and he keeps on spouting off about protecting me, but it's wearing pretty thin. Dammit, Ella, I would have done anything to have him put Travis in his place today. But he didn't say a word. He just stood there, too afraid of losing his job to do anything." My voice quivered. I sucked in a breath, blinking fast. Crying wouldn't solve anything.

"You deserve a guy who will stand up for you." Ella's voice was so quiet, I barely heard it.

I pinched my nose and drew in a sharp breath. "But I love Sean. I mean, it's the first time I've ever felt this way...you know, to this magnitude." My jaw clenched tight.

"Then tell him what you need and give him the chance to do it."

A cold fear crept through me. "And if he doesn't?"

Ella's mouth turned down, her expression filling with such a deep sympathy I could barely stand to look at it. "Then maybe he's not the one," she whispered.

And as much as I wanted to deny it, I knew she was right.

TWENTY-TWO

MORGAN

I tried not to let Ella's words burn, but they did. They simmered inside of me all week. Sean was waiting for me when I got home that night, and he took away the sting with his soft kisses and gentle hands. I let him. We didn't talk about it, just made love and fell asleep against one another.

I'd forgotten to set the alarm, so we both woke late and scrambled to get out the door on time. The issue went undiscussed for yet another day and by Wednesday, I felt like it was old news, and I didn't even want to raise it. That was so unlike me. Usually I dealt with stuff head-on, but work was exhausting, and Sean's hands, lips, mere presence, was the only comfort I had at the end of a day. He slept at my place every night that week, but that didn't seem to stop the chasm growing between us.

It was like the words had run from our relationship, hidden themselves away, and even though Sean could set off fireworks throughout my entire body, something had shifted.

I paused outside the studio door, knowing Travis would yell at me for being late, but not caring. This week had been hell. My disintegrating love life, my evil boss, and a sister who refused to return my calls were sending me over the edge. Since my outburst with Travis, his stress relief had taken on a whole new form of cruelty. Although I told him I wouldn't give him the satisfaction of quitting, I didn't know how much more I could withstand.

And then there was the scene before me.

I knew it was just acting, but my heart felt crushed under the weight of watching my lover wrap his arms around Ashlee. Their slow dance routine was seductive, sensual...and reminded me of the night Sean and I made love on this very floor.

"Burn" by Usher played as the couple practiced their farewell scene for next week. Sasha and Harley were still going through the motions, wanting to be together but fighting their love at every turn. Sasha, starting to realize she'd never get what she wanted, was pulling away from Harley.

Sean's hand slid down Ashlee's arm, grabbing her fingers and pulling her back to his side. Her leg came over his hip, his hand gliding up her thigh as he dipped her.

Isabella's choreography for this number captured everything. The emotion in the room was electrifying. She caught my eye and gave me her excited smile. I grinned back, not wanting her to know how much this killed me.

"They look good together, don't they?"

I flinched, recognizing Rhonda's voice immediately. I threw her a sidelong glare and turned back to watch the couple.

"Almost as if they're made for each other," Rhonda continued softly.

I hated that she was right.

"You know, there are actually rumors circulating that these two have something going on off-set. It's creating quite the buzz. I think people really want them together."

A dull static rang in my ears, my throat constricting as I tried to press the brakes on my heartbeat.

"You know that's not true." I clenched my jaw, refusing to look at her.

"Nobody else does." I saw her smirk out of the corner of my eye. "Face it, Small Time, if he really loved you, he wouldn't be keeping you a secret. Why don't you step aside now and avoid the hurt while you can. It'll only get worse if you stay. If it were me, I certainly wouldn't want to be with a guy who let my boss treat me like that. Work is more important to him than you are."

I swallowed. Unable to resist, I looked down at the woman. She pushed her glasses up her nose before scratching her right eyebrow with a beautifully manicured nail and smiling at me...with sympathy.

I wanted to punch her.

"I know you don't want to hear that, Morgan, but it's the truth. You'll never come first, and if that's not what you want, you may as well leave."

I didn't know what she was trying to pull, but it was working. I stood frozen beside her, downtrodden and buying into every syllable coming out of her mouth. My eyes stung as I fought the tears that wanted to break free. As if I'd give this bitch the satisfaction of crying.

With as much dignity as I could muster, I lifted my chin and pushed myself off the doorframe, forcing one more polite smile before brushing past her and pretending there wasn't a machete protruding from my heart.

When I got back to the office, Travis was sitting at his desk. His beady eyes traveled the length of my body, his leering smile enough to make me throw up.

I couldn't do this anymore.

Throwing the clipboard onto his desk, I straightened to my full height.

"I've done everything except collect your dry cleaning, but I'm sorry, I have to leave." I rubbed my temple, the onset of a thunderous headache actually quite real. "I'm not feeling very well."

"I don't care how you're feeling. You're not leaving 'til you get me that dry cleaning."

Snatching my bag, I hefted it onto my shoulder and crossed my arms. "No, I'm going home to lie down. If you have a problem with that, then fire me."

I looked him straight in the eye, daring him to do it. For some unfathomable reason, he didn't. Instead, he gave me a silent glare that was more than unnerving.

With a sharp nod, I spun on my heel and left the room, dreading what tomorrow held for me. I hustled out to my car, unlocking it with shaking hands and slamming myself inside. I started the engine and reached for the steering wheel, my actions slowing as I looked at the ring Sean gave me. I rubbed my thumb over the sapphires, trying to remind myself of the promise, but I couldn't hear it anymore.

Squeezing my eyes shut, I drew in a quick breath and, desperate for home, accelerated out of the lot. All I wanted was a hot shower and bed. I wanted to close my eyes and forget the world existed. I needed oblivion.

I needed...

My lips parted as I pulled up to my apartment. Sitting on my doorstep was the last person I expected to see. Her chin was resting on her knees, her blonde curls splayed over her shoulders, her blue-green eyes bright from crying.

Jumping out of the car, I raced up the path toward her.

"Jody, what are you doing here?"

"Hey, sis." Her smile was glum as fresh tears lined her lashes.

I crouched down beside her, brushing away the lock of hair stuck to her wet face.

"I just wanted to apologize for being such a bitch the other night." Her voice shook, her lower lip trembling before she caught it with her teeth. "You kind of caught me at a really bad time..." She sucked in a breath.

"Jody, what's going on?"

Her face folded, new tears spilling free as she pressed her lips together. She brushed them off her face and sniffed before finally squeaking, "I'm pregnant."

TWENTY-THREE

MORGAN

My world stopped. Literally. Everything around me went silent, my vision blurring as my kid sister's words sunk in. I had no response; I couldn't even think straight. Closing my eyes, I dropped my head and forced my mind to shift from numb to active. Jody needed me.

My head snapped up, and I pushed a gentle smile over my lips.

"Come on, let's get you inside."

She let me help her up. I collected her bag and wrapped my other arm around her, giving her shoulders a gentle squeeze. She rested her head against me, a sob breaking free. As quickly as I could, I ushered her inside and sat her on the couch, running to the sink to get her a glass of water before sitting down beside her.

I kept my movements slow and deliberate, rubbing circles over her back as she hiccuped and heaved.

Eventually her agony quieted to a murmur, and I was able to speak.

"How far along are you?"

"Four months," she whispered.

My eyes rounded.

"I was worried I might be when I was home for Thanksgiving. I didn't know for sure, I just...something was off and my period hadn't come. I was freaking out."

"But you got totally drunk."

"I think that was actually the onset of morning sickness. I'd just been drinking water all night."

I gaped at her. "I thought it was vodka! Why didn't you tell me?"

"How? I couldn't!" She slapped her legs, rising from the sofa and pacing away from me. "I get this great opportunity to go to this amazing school and follow my dreams. What do I do? I fall in love with my dance teacher, who knocks me up and then says he can't handle it, because teachers and students aren't supposed to be fraternizing, and if anyone found out, he could lose his job!"

My eyes narrowed. Part of me wanted to rip into her for being such a fool.

"He pursued you?"

"We pursued each other." She flicked her hand. "There was chemistry there, right from the second we met. We were...in love."

"But not in love enough to stick around when you need him." It was impossible to keep the snark from my tone. What an asshole! Putting his job before his girl. I wanted to throttle him.

"I was so scared to tell him, but he noticed. He

said my dancing was getting sloppy, and he was worried that I looked tired and wasn't feeling well. He wanted to make sure I was okay." She sniffed, wrapping her arms around herself. The baggy T-shirt she was wearing pressed into her body and I saw it. The small curve of her belly. It was subtle; most would just think she'd gained weight, but...

I closed my eyes, pinching the bridge of my nose.

"He asked me to get an abortion. Told me I was giving up everything if I didn't, and I thought about it, I really did." Her voice cracked. "But then, you know, I just started thinking..." She rested her hand on her belly. "Mom told me once that she nearly aborted you. Her and Dad weren't ready. They weren't even married."

I swallowed, remembering the story.

"And she said she was always so grateful that she didn't, because then she would have denied the world a Morgan Pritchett, and that would have been a tragedy." Jody's voice squeaked, and she ran a finger under her nose to catch the drips.

I jumped up and snatched a Kleenex from the side of my bed. She took it with mumbled thanks and sank back down onto the couch. I studied her for a minute before grabbing the entire box of tissues and perching down beside her.

"The school's asked me to leave. There'll be a spot open in August next year if I want it, but I can't stay and perform in my current state."

"So, I guess you'll move back home?"

Her blue eyes were huge as she spun to face me. "I can't tell Dad. Morgan, you know I can't tell him."

"Jody, you have to. It's not like you're gonna be able to hide this."

"Yes, I can. I'll stay here. I'll be a hermit; no one will even see me leave the house."

I frowned. "And what are you going to do after the baby's born?"

"Adopt it out to some loving family who can take care of it. Then I can go back to school and no one will know the truth. No one, but you and Stefan," she ended woodenly.

That's right, Stefan. The dance teacher I wanted to murder.

I ran my hand down her arm, squeezing her fingers. "I'm sorry. I'm sorry he broke your heart."

"I really did love him. I thought..." She punched out a breathy laugh. "For one second, I thought he might pull a Dad and marry me."

I swallowed.

"This is probably better, you know. Mom and Dad didn't last. I wouldn't want to do that to my kids, just walk out on them." She blinked. "This is better. I'll adopt this little one out, and then it can have a good and normal life, and I can go back to chasing my dreams." Her giggle was breathy and lifeless.

"Have you seen a doctor yet?"

She shook her head.

"Okay, so that's the first thing we need to arrange." Grabbing my purse, I pulled out a note pad and pen, flipping it open and starting a list. "You can stay here tonight, of course, but I can't agree to you not telling Dad. I just—"

"No! Please, Morgan! He'll be so...disgusted with me. I can't. I can't handle him looking at me like that. He'll be so disappointed."

"Jody, we can't hide this from him."

"Yes, we can!" Her hopeful yelling would not win me over, but I could see her hysteria quickly building. Her chest began to heave once more and I raised my hand.

"It's okay. Just calm down. Everything will be okay. We'll work it out." I snatched up the list and added *contact adoption agency.*

I felt sick writing it. Lists usually filled me with a sense of purpose; this one filled me with dread. How could this happen? Jody, the most talented person I knew, had gotten herself pregnant and kicked out of school.

My head spun, the ache searing through my brain. On top of everything else, I wasn't sure I could handle this. Panic skittered inside of me, but I swallowed it back. Jody didn't need to see me fall apart. I had to be strong for her...like I always had.

"Can we at least tell Ella?"

Jody's head bobbed, and I reached for the phone before she could stop me.

Forty minutes later, Ella burst through the door. Her face was pale, her large eyes rounder than usual. They filled with tears the second she saw Jody. Without a word, she wrapped her in a hug, and they clung together for what seemed an age.

I wrapped my arms around myself as I watched them, the weight of my future a heavy burden. Could I do it? Could I honestly take this on?

I had to. What choice did I have?

Jody needed me. There was no Mom. There was just me.

*****

I answered my phone after three rings, ducking outside as I noticed the number.

"Hey, you okay?" Sean's deep voice was soft and husky.

"Yeah, I just had a headache."

"I didn't see you leave."

"You were in rehearsal, and Rhonda was waiting to speak with you. I thought it'd be best to leave." I tried to keep my voice light. I had no idea if it was working.

"Travis was pretty pissed you left."

"Travis is always pissed."

Sean chuckled. "Well, I just wanted to check in. Things aren't going great here today, so I'll probably be late. Don't wait up for me."

"Actually, do you mind sleeping at yours tonight? My headache is really bad, and I kind of want to be on my own."

"I can come over and look after you."

"I'll be asleep by the time you get here anyway, so there's really no point, Sean. You go home and I'll see you at work tomorrow."

"Are you sure you're okay?"

I closed my eyes, wanting to spill it all, but what was the point? Like he could help me with this nightmare.

"I'm fine. I'll see you tomorrow."

"Okay. Love you, baby."

I swallowed, wondering how much he meant it. "Love you too," I croaked and hung up.

Easing back into the apartment, I clicked the door shut quietly and looked across at my bed. Jody was asleep, finally at peace after her harrowing day of tears.

Ella sat on the edge of the couch, looking up at me as I stepped toward her.

"Everything okay?"

"Yeah, just Sean checking in."

"Did you tell him about Jody?"

"Not yet." I sighed. "He...I don't even know if I want to."

"But this is huge. You have to tell him."

"I know." I rubbed my forehead. "Ella, I don't know if I can do this." My voice hitched as I looked across the dimly lit room at my baby sister...my pregnant baby sister.

Ella's tiny hand landed on my arm and gave it a

gentle squeeze. "You have to."

"I can't..." I swallowed. "I don't know if I can handle everything...work, Sean, now Jody. It's too much."

"What happened today? You're usually stronger than this. You look like you're ready to fall apart."

My chuckle was dry and brittle. "Everything around me is falling apart, I can barely keep myself together...and now I have to play mother again."

"You can do this, Morgan." Ella's quiet voice was firm. "But maybe it's a case of prioritizing. If you can't handle it all, then something needs to give." She pursed her lips and looked over her shoulder at my bed. "And we both know that thing can't be Jody."

I slumped back onto the couch, wanting to scream. Instead, I bit my bottom lip and stared at the ceiling until I could find my voice again.

"Rhonda told me today that people want Sean and Ashlee together. She took such delight in telling me. I wanted to punch her."

"You have to tell Sean."

"What difference will it make? He's not going to do anything. He's not gonna fight for me."

"Then it's time to start fighting for yourself. If Sean's not going to do it, then you shouldn't be with him."

I looked across at her, anguish swirling inside me like a tornado.

"You don't want to end up like I did." Her face scrunched with sadness. "In a relationship that was slowly killing me. If I hadn't met Cole..." She shook her head.

"But I love him."

Ella smiled. "Sean loves you too; he just needs a really big wake-up call. You deserve someone who is going to lay everything on the line for you, and if he's not willing to do that, then there's someone out there who will."

"What if there never is?" Fear clutched at me, restricting my airways.

"Then you're gonna be fine on your own. You're bulletproof, remember?"

I shook my head with a scoffing laugh.

"Yes, you are." She shuffled toward me and squeezed my arm again. "You are gonna walk in there tomorrow, and you are gonna tell Sean that unless he's willing to fight for you, you can't stay together, and then you're gonna go to your boss and you're gonna look him in the eye and say..."

"Say what...?"

"I'm bulletproof," Ella sang in a whisper, her voice traveling over the chorus of "Titanium." The words rained over me. I knew Ella was singing them to make me feel strong, like I could take on anything, but I didn't feel it.

"And when you're done saying that..." Ella licked her lip. "You're gonna...you're gonna give him the finger and say, 'I deserve respect and since you seem incapable of giving that to me, I quit.' And then flip him the bird one more time as you walk out the door."

I chuckled, but the laughter faded quickly. "And then what am I going to do? I'll be single and jobless."

"Yeah, I know...it's a whole new world full of possibilities." Ella's smile was sweet and full of hope.

I grabbed her hand and squeezed it back, like it was somehow a lifeline.

Was she right? Could I do this?

Once again, I glanced over at my sleeping sister.

Yes, I could. I had to.

TWENTY-FOUR

SEAN

I slept badly. I couldn't stop tossing and turning, invisible demons haunting my sleep. Work had been a killer the day before, but in the end we'd nailed the scene and all left on a high. I wanted to head to Morgan's place and share my elation, but I didn't want to wake her.

She had me worried. She hadn't been herself this week, and her voice on the phone was near lifeless, none of the cheeky spark I loved.

Pulling my car into the lot, I was pleased to see hers parked in its usual space. I raced into the building, hoping to steal her into a quiet corner for a quick kiss. It felt wrong starting my day without one.

Heading to my dressing room, I kept my eyes out for her, but she wasn't around. I opened the door and my sigh morphed into a smile when I spotted her perched on the edge of the armchair.

"Hey, baby."

My smile faded.

She looked tired, frazzled. What the hell had Travis done to her now?

I held out my hand, ready to pull her into a hug, but she didn't take it. My stomach curdled, disquiet shimmering down my spine. Her pale brown eyes wouldn't meet mine, and I somehow knew what was coming.

My defenses kicked in before I could stop them, my jaw clenching tight as I stepped back from her.

"What's up?"

"Jody's pregnant." She ran tight fingers through her hair, which was never down at work. "She was sitting on my doorstep yesterday, sobbing her heart out. She's been kicked out of school until after the baby's born."

I crouched down in front of her, my heart aching as I took in her wooden voice. Gently touching her face, I tried to get her to look at me. Eventually our eyes connected, and the sadness swimming in her gaze hurt. There were no tears, just a deep sorrow and tired resignation.

"I'm sorry."

"She's staying with me, doesn't want to tell Dad. I don't know...I..." She sighed. "I don't know if I've got the energy to look after her."

"You can do it."

"Yeah." Morgan sat back. "That's what everyone keeps telling me. 'You're strong, Morgan. You're so good at looking after people. You can do it. You can do it, Morgan. Nothing beats you!'" She spat out the last few words.

I was waiting for her back to go straight, for that

ping in her shoulders, but she stayed slumped in the chair, and all I could think to do was caress her face with my thumb.

"I can't do it, Sean. I can't look after her and put up with Travis. I can't keep giving out everything to everyone." She sniffed. "When's it my turn to be taken care of? When's someone going to look after me?"

"I'm looking after you, baby."

"Are you?" Her eyes snapped toward me. "Because it doesn't always feel like it."

I frowned, dropping my hands from her face.

"Work's still hell for me, Sean. Are you ever going to stand up and say anything?"

"You know I can't. I could lose my job."

"But it's okay for me to lose mine?" She shot out of the seat, nearly pushing me to the floor.

I caught myself and slowly stood. "Come on, Morgan. It's different and you know it. This could ruin my entire career."

She flicked her hand at me. "That asshole cannot ruin your career. I don't care how much power he has in this industry. You have power, too." She clicked her tongue and then mumbled, "You're just afraid to use it."

I shook my head, ignoring her statement. She was wrong. I might be Sean Jaxon, but compared to Travis McKinnon, I was a nobody.

"Look, I hate that he's doing this to you. Just quit, get another a job."

"Yeah, because that's so easy!" She scoffed.

I crossed my arms, hating her venom. "Well, what do you want me to do?"

"I need you to fight for me, Sean. I need my boyfriend to stand up to the asshole who is treating me like total shit and tell him to back the fuck off." She huffed.

"You're asking me to put everything on the line.

I can't risk—"

"Yes, you can. You just won't." She pointed her long finger at me.

"I'm not just doing this for me. He said he'd make your life hell."

"He's already making my life hell!" Her voice pitched high. "I am so sick of looking after everybody else. Fighting to make sure everyone is okay and *no one* will fight for me. When's it my turn?"

"Come on, Morgan, you're overreacting."

"Am I?" Her face washed with something I didn't understand. She pinched her chin and sucked in a ragged breath. "I don't think I can do this anymore."

"So, you'll quit?" I hated that idea, but if it was what she needed, then I'd support her. Sure, I wouldn't get to see her as much, but as long as she was happy.

She tsked, her jaw working to the side. "Yeah, I'll quit."

I stepped toward her, my arms outstretched for a hug. As soon as I had her in my arms, I'd tell her we could walk down together. I'd be waiting in the wings to comfort her as soon as she'd told Travis.

But I stopped.

Morgan gently slid off the ring I'd given her and held it out to me.

"If I walk out that door, I'm not just walking away from the job," she whispered. "This ring means nothing if you're not willing to stand up for me."

"What are you doing?" I frowned, refusing to reach out for it. "Don't do this."

She remained firm, her stance unyielding. "I never wanted to be the kind of girl to give a guy an ultimatum. I always thought that was weak and manipulative, but..." She shrugged. "It doesn't seem to matter how much I love you. This can't work. Until you're ready to stand up for me, I can't be with you. I know you love me, Sean, but I need you to prove it, and you're not willing to do that right now."

I couldn't help a surge of anger. She was just walking away from us? She was willing to give up on everything, because I wouldn't throw away my career? That was insane and totally unreasonable.

My arms remained firmly crossed against my chest. With a heavy sigh, she placed the ring on the table.

"Goodbye, Sean," she whispered, her body gently brushing past me as she walked out the door.

I didn't turn to watch her leave. My eyes were locked on the wall in front of me, my body frozen by a mix of anger, disbelief, and heartache.

TWENTY-FIVE

MORGAN

My feet were filled with concrete, but I forced them to walk away from Sean. I could actually feel chunks of my heart crumbling away. My lips trembled as I swallowed back the sob that yearned to break free. I wouldn't let it. I couldn't. Crying never achieved anything.

Strains of Ashlee's singing reached me from one of the studios. She was belting out "Break Free" by Ariana Grande. How appropriate.

Straightening my back, I turned into the office.

"Where the fuck have you been?" Travis flicked his hand at me and then started rattling off a list of things he needed done two hours ago.

Pressing my lips together, I waited until there

was a break in his stream of demands.

"I quit."

He froze, mid arm wave, and slowly turned to face me. "Excuse me?"

I shrugged. "You won. I can't do this anymore; you're killing me. I've never had to deal with such a jackass before, and I thought I was strong enough to do it, but I'm obviously not."

Snatching my bag from the little nook it lived in, I rested it on my shoulder and looked at him one final time...and felt nothing. There was nothing left to feel. I was numb. I had to be.

I pulled his wretched phone from my pocket and tossed it to him before marching out the door, leaving a symphony of cusses in my wake. He barked Lisa's name a few times, but I switched off to the sound, keeping my eyes to the floor.

I didn't feel free or relieved; I felt like someone had tied a ball and chain around my ankles and thrown me into a river.

Tears burned my eye sockets, but I wouldn't let them fall. I kept my stance straight, my body rigid all the way to my car. I couldn't fall apart. There was too much to do. I had Jody to think about now.

With a sharp sniff, I revved the engine and screamed out of the lot, forcing my mind to focus on my kid sister and not the guy who'd just let me walk out of his dressing room.

"Red" by Taylor Swift was on the radio, torturing me the whole way home. I didn't have the heart to change stations. Instead I let the words sink into me while I tried to convince myself that I had done the right thing. My knuckles were white, my fingers cramping by the time I pulled into my street.

Turning off the engine, I leaned my head against the wheel.

"You can do this, Morgan. You have to. There's

no other choice. Jody needs you right now."

I kept whispering the words to myself, pulling on all the strength and determination I'd had to employ eight years ago. I couldn't fall apart then; I couldn't now.

My phone tinkled loudly. I wanted to ignore it but felt guilted into at least checking the caller ID.

Isabella.

My thumb hovered over the *accept call* sign for three rings before I let out a sigh and pushed it.

"Hi."

"Oh my gosh, what just happened? Travis went psycho after you left. Threw a coffee mug against the wall and nearly hit me in the head. I just happened to be walking past his little tantrum."

I rubbed my eyes, wanting to apologize, but also not. It wasn't my fault he had a temper.

"Why'd you quit?"

"Really?"

"Yeah, good point." Isabella snickered. "Aw, man. I'm gonna miss you!"

I smiled. It was weak, but there. I was going to miss her too.

"You and Sean will still come out with Dean and me though, right?"

"Actually, Sean and I are on break now too."

"What?"

I bit my lip against her shock, needing that stinging pain to stop myself from crying.

"It's just what I need right now. I have a lot going on, and I'm struggling to cope. I really need to leave *Superstar* behind me, you know?"

She gasped. "That doesn't include me, does it?"

A breathy chuckle rattled out of my mouth. "As long as you promise never to talk about Sean or Travis...or actually anything to do with the show."

"Huh, that might be a little challenging. The show is basically my life."

"I know how all-consuming it can be...and my demands are unfair, so let's just not talk about Sean," my voice wavered, "and we'll be cool."

My comment was met with a beat of silent sympathy that I could almost feel through the phone.

"I don't know all the details, but I can guess why you're doing this and you know what? It just makes me admire you more. You're the strongest woman I know, Morgan. Stand your ground, sweetie...and I'm here in whatever capacity you need."

"Thanks," I whispered.

"I'll call you again soon, okay?"

"Yeah." Hanging up, I drew in a quick breath, trying to pull myself together.

Slowly releasing the air in my lungs, I shouldered my door open and ran into the house, pasting on a smile as I walked in.

Jody was sitting cross-legged on my bed, playing something on the iPad. She looked pale and tired, her eyes still puffy from all the crying she'd done the night before.

"Hey." My voice sounded deep and hollow. I cleared my throat and threw my purse onto the kitchen counter. "Okay, so that's done."

With a gentle smile, Jody quit out of her game and made a move toward me.

I stepped back, raising my hands and shaking my head. She paused on the edge of the bed, trying to read me. I lifted my chin and crossed my arms.

That was when her face folded, creasing with a sympathy that could have snapped my heart in two.

My head shake was short and sharp. I locked my jaw and looked away from her, busying myself by grabbing a pen and my notebook out of my bag.

"Okay, let's get you organized."

"Morgan."

I ignored her soft tone.

"I'll call and make a doctor's appointment in just a minute. We also need to look into the whole adoption thing. I don't know anything about that, but I'm sure there's some stuff online that will lead us in the right direction." I avoided her gaze. "You also need to ring Arizona and arrange to have your stuff sent back here. I know they've said you can come back in the fall, but I doubt they're gonna store your stuff. We may as well have it here." I tapped my pen against the pad and steeled myself for what was about to come. "And, um...oh yeah, we need to tell Dad."

Jody gasped, all sympathy for me flying out the window. "No! I thought we'd discussed that."

"No, we hadn't. You just told me that you want to hide this. I think that's the wrong decision."

"I can't. Morgan, I can't!" Her voice wobbled, tears popping onto her lashes. "He'll be so...I'm his little princess. I'm his sunshine. I don't do this kind of stuff. I don't screw up this bad."

I sighed. "But you did, Jody, and now you have to live with the consequences of that. He loves you. He's not going to kick your butt."

"I know, but he'll be disappointed and that's almost worse."

I clicked my tongue. The pen in my hand sounded like gunfire as I tapped it over the pad. My body wanted to move in fast-forward. It always did this when I was stressed. I usually went out and released all the tension with a heated one-night stand, but the thought of doing that now made me want to throw up. I couldn't even imagine anyone else's hands roaming my body. A pain rocketed through my chest as if my heart was actually weeping. I pressed my fingers into my sternum and reached for the phone to make Jody a doctor's appointment. I just had to keep moving, that was the only way I'd survive this.

TWENTY-SIX

MORGAN

"I can't believe I have to do this every month." Jody fingered the Band-Aid on the inside of her elbow.

"They need to make sure your blood work is good. It's for the baby. You may not be keeping it, but you want it to be healthy, don't you?"

"Yeah, yeah, of course." Jody's lips pressed into a thin line.

She'd been eerily quiet at the doctor's office. I'd basically had to do all the talking for her, unless I didn't know the answer. All her replies were soft mumbles that were nearly impossible to hear. I wanted to scream and slap her face at one point, but thankfully the doctor's gentle coaxing finally wooed her. She opened up a little near the end.

I glanced at her in the passenger seat. She looked pale.

Biting my lips together, I reminded myself that she needed my support, not judgment.

So she'd made a mistake; we all did. I hadn't exactly set the best example for her. I'd been sleeping around, well, ever since the year after Mom left. It was a miracle she'd made it to college with her virginity still intact. It killed me that this had happened to her.

Indicating left, I waited for traffic and turned into the road that led to our Pasadena home. Jody gripped the handle, her feet pushing into the floor the closer we got.

"What did you tell him again?" she snapped.

"Just that I was coming over for dinner."

I pulled into our driveway and cut the engine. Unbuckling my seatbelt, I turned to her and kept my voice as soft and soothing as possible.

"It's gonna be okay, Jo-Jo."

She nodded and unbuckled, sliding out of the car without a word.

I placed my hand on her back as we ascended the stairs and let ourselves in.

"Dad?"

"In the kitchen!"

Jody swallowed and wound her way through the living room pausing in the archway between the kitchen and dining room. Dad was at the counter, hacking up some carrots. I cringed, wondering how he'd survived this long without me.

He peeked over his shoulder to give me a smile and did a double-take when he saw his beloved little girl.

"Sunshine!" He gathered her into his arms for a tight squeeze.

I noticed the way Jody's fingers dug into his sweater as if she wanted to cling to him forever, but then he let her go, kissing her cheek with a loud smack.

"What are you coming to surprise me for?"

A shaky smile quivered over her lips and she swallowed.

"What's the matter?"

Her blue gaze shot to mine, terror running over her expression.

"Why don't we sit." I swiveled back into the dining room and pulled out the closest chair. As I slid into place, my mind flashed with the worst memory of my life. It was at this very table. A bombshell that destroyed my world.

The laughter was rich and hearty. Jody was regaling us with one of her school stories. Her blonde pigtails swished as she re-enacted the playground drama with her usual flair. Dad was completely enamored as he watched her, laughing at the silly voice she was using.

I caught his eye and poked out my tongue, causing his shoulders to shake even more.

Mom stepped into the room, placing a suitcase at her feet. Her gaze was sad and my belly pinched. It was like some kind of premonition. I didn't know why I had it, but the second before the words slipped out of her mouth, Jody's words turned to fuzz, and the only sound I could hear with crystal clarity was Mom's voice.

"I'm leaving."

Jody's giggle was cut by an invisible pair of scissors. Dad's took a second longer to die, his face wrinkling with confusion.

"Where are you off to, sweetness?" He grinned.

"I can't do this anymore." She gripped the back of her chair. "I'm sorry. I know it's going to hurt you, but I have to go."

"Go where?" I frowned.

"Vegas."

"Vegas?" All mirth had left Dad's tone. It turned hard, a note of recognition running through it.

"You know it's what I want."

"I told you, we can go at Christmas."

"I don't want to go there for a holiday, Marshall. I don't know how many different ways I can say this to you." Her voice hitched. "This life is killing me, and I need out."

Jody looked at me, her blue eyes vibrant as they shone with tears. She knew what her mother was saying. She might have only been ten, but the message was clear.

"I've given fourteen years of my life to this. I've sacrificed everything, and now it's my turn."

"You can't abandon your family." Dad's whisper was harsh.

"You'll be okay." She straightened, gazing at me with an agonized smile. "Morgan will take care of you. She's amazing and capable. You three have each other, you don't need me anymore."

"Yes we do!" Jody shot out of her chair. "Please, Mommy, don't go!" Racing around the table, she wrapped her arms around Mom's waist, squeezing tight. The tears glistening in Mom's eyes finally broke free, streaming down her face as she kissed Jody's head and pulled her arms free.

"I have to go." She stepped back from her youngest daughter then looked straight at me. "I'm sorry."

And with that she turned and left. Jody started screaming then, trying to chase after her, but Dad grabbed her into his arms and held her tight against him. I couldn't do anything. I was frozen by shock, the weight of responsibility landing on me like a ten-ton truck.

"I'm sorry." Jody's wobbling voice pulled me out of the memory with a sharp snap.

"Sorry for what?" Dad leaned across the table, gathering up Jody's fingers as she bent her head forward and started crying. "What's going on?" He glanced at me, his soft gaze hardening at the edges.

I knew it was fear.

Since that fateful dinner eight years ago, Dad didn't take bad news well.

Clearing my throat, I straightened up. "Jody's pregnant. She's seventeen weeks along. We had that confirmed at the doctor's today."

I ignored Dad's shell-shocked expression and barreled through.

"Because of her situation, the school has asked her to leave for the rest of this academic year, but they will consider taking her again in August, so Jody's decided that she wants to see the pregnancy through and then give the baby up for adoption."

Dad's jaw went slack, his forehead crinkling with what I could only describe as despair. Jody's wailing sobs crescendoed into the silence, making me want to roll my eyes. Her inner drama queen always shone around Dad.

Letting go of his little princess, he leaned back in his chair, disappointment cresting over his expression.

"I'm sorry, Daddy. I know it was stupid, and I wish I could change it."

"Geez, Jody." Dad ran a hand over his thinning hair. "Have you never heard of protection before?"

"It was the first time I'd ever had sex, okay." Her face flushed pink.

Yeah, not exactly the conversation you wanted to have with your old man.

"I didn't even think you could get pregnant your first time!"

"Oh give me a break. You are not that naive," he snapped.

"It was just this spontaneous, passion—" Her voice died off as she caught Dad's sickened gaze. She swallowed. "I couldn't stop myself, all right?"

She slumped back in her chair and mumbled, "We were safe every time after that."

"Yeah, well, it was a little too late by then, wasn't it?" Dad slammed the table. "Who the hell is this guy, anyway? And why isn't he sitting here beside you right now?"

Jody's face crumpled, fresh tears running down her face. She drew in a shaky breath. "He's my dance teacher."

"Your teacher? Oh, good Lord, Jody!" He squeezed his eyes shut. "How old is he?"

"I don't know, thirty maybe."

Dad let out a noise of disgust.

"We were in love."

"Obviously! Which is why he's...where?"

Jody swallowed, swiping at her tears. "His job's important to him, Dad. He'd get in so much trouble if this came out."

"Well, he should, damn it! He's sleeping with one of his students...who's a decade younger than he is." Dad rose from his chair and paced away from us.

"It's not that big an age gap," Jody mumbled.

"It's big, okay!" Dad rounded on her. "You're nineteen! You're an innocent freshman." He cringed. "You've only been at the school five months, which means he must have gotten into those tights of yours pretty damn quickly!"

"Dad," I warned.

"I'm calling the school."

"No!" Jody jumped from her seat. "Don't you dare. This is my decision! I can do this without him."

"You shouldn't have to. He's the father." Dad pointed at her belly, his voice softening. "He has a responsibility for you and that baby."

Jody touched her belly, the fabric pulling tight so we could all see the soft curve. "Well, he doesn't want it, and he's too good a teacher to get fired over this."

"Jody, this is your life we're talking about. Why should his career be more important than yours?" Dad ended on a whisper, his expression broken as he looked to the floor.

We all knew he was thinking of Mom, how much she'd sacrificed so he could start up his little business. As soon as it was really thriving, she left...and he'd never gotten over it.

"I'm not giving up my career. I'm just putting it on hold for a little while."

Dad nodded, his bottom lip sticking out as he stared at the wall.

"Please, Daddy, I'm sorry, okay."

His jaw clenched tight and he wouldn't budge, even when she rested her head on his shoulder, something that always got a smile out of him.

I crossed my arms over my chest, squeezing tight to keep it all in. I wanted to shatter, fall into a million pieces and forget this life even existed.

Dad's stony silence was unnerving. Jody turned to look at me, desperate panic washing over her face. I shrugged, not sure what she wanted me to do. With a gasping sob, she covered her mouth and raced from the room.

I expelled a heavy sigh and rose from the table. "Don't shut her out, Dad, please. She needs us right now."

"How the hell did this happen, Morgan?" His round face sagged with sorrow.

"She made a mistake." I shrugged.

"But this was her chance. It's everything she's been working for." He gripped the top of his head. "I want to kill that guy."

"Get in line." I leaned my butt against the table and gave Dad a sad smile.

He scoffed, his laughter sounding more like a

cry.

"Look, I know it hurts, but we can't get emotional about this. Jody just needs to get through the next five months, have this baby and then...she can get on with her life again."

"You really think it's that easy?" Dad stepped toward me, gripping the back of his chair. "That was our plan, you know. You were a very unexpected surprise and your mom was set on giving you up. I wasn't sure, but I loved her," he whispered. "I would've done anything she wanted me to."

I hated talking about Mom. I hated the way Dad's voice softened whenever he referred to that selfish bitch.

"But then you were born and we took one look at your face." A gentle smile crested over his lips. "I asked her to marry me right then and she said yes. She was only twenty." Dad's voice broke and he pressed his fingers into his eyes, denying the tears.

I wrapped my arms around him before I could stop myself. He shouldn't have been crying over her, but I knew his heart would never fully mend. Now his beloved daughter was in the same position, and I could only imagine how sick with worry he must have felt.

"Jody's not Mom," I whispered.

"She's exactly like your mother." He squeezed me.

"She doesn't have to be." I squeezed back, refusing to buy into that lie. Jody was not a self-centered, egotistical cow. She would do what was right for her and that baby. I was sure of it.

I stepped out of Dad's arms but kept hold of his shoulders.

"We're here to help her, Dad. She's gonna be okay. We just have to focus on taking care of her and making sure she stays healthy through all of this."

"Yeah." Dad nodded. "Yeah, I know."

"Her original plan was to keep this all a secret and stay with me, but my place is too small. She won't be comfortable there." I looked to the floor.

"Fine. She can stay here."

"She's worried that your disappointment will be too much to bear."

"What does she expect me to be?"

"I don't know, Dad." I threw my hands in the air. "Supportive."

"I can do that."

"Without judging?"

He glared at me.

"Maybe I should move back, too." I had to choke out the words. It was the last thing I wanted to do, but it was for the best. I was now jobless, so the ability to pay rent would soon become a problem. Besides, Jody needed my support, and if she was going to stay healthy, I sure as hell couldn't leave her with Dad's cooking skills.

As much as I hated to admit it, I knew they'd fall apart without me.

It was time to once again shelve my dreams and put my family first. I'd done it once; I could do it again.

TWENTY-SEVEN

SEAN

I sang into the mic, but my voice sounded dead. I'd been in the recording studio for just on three hours. I was tired and over it, but I couldn't leave until I got it right.

I hit the high note with a cringe, my voice cracking.

"Shit, sorry. I just..."

"That's okay, Sean. Let's uh, take a break." I glanced up at the speaker and squinted at the glass before nodding. Pulling off the headphones, I dumped them on the chair behind me and stepped out of the room.

The last thing I wanted to do was walk around to the sound desk to find out everything I'd been doing wrong, so instead I slumped onto the couch against the wall, resting my head back and closing my eyes with a heavy sigh.

"Tough day?" Ashlee's sweet voice made my eyes pop open.

"Hey." I grinned, shuffling over so she could sit beside me.

"Don't worry about it." She slapped my leg. "It's a difficult song."

I grimaced. It wasn't the melody that was killing me, although after my performance today, you'd think it would be. It was the words.

"Now You're Gone" by Basshunter. Who the hell chose that song? The writers were obviously out to get me. I nearly died when I got handed the latest script. Sasha, unable to stand Harley's back and forth commitment, has taken a job. She wasn't going to. She was going to stay at the school and keep training, but Harley won't give her what she needs, so she's splitting. Franklyn Performing Arts School without her is a lonely, torturous place.

Damn, it was way too close to the bone for my liking.

Morgan had walked out my door two months ago and yes, I'd done absolutely nothing about it. My anger had kept me silent at first, made me bubble and brew with righteous annoyance. Rhonda had talked me through it, telling me it was for the best. But with each passing week, the anger ebbed, replaced with a deep sadness I couldn't shake.

I missed my girl.

"You're not loving Harley and Sasha's story at the moment, are you?"

I shook my head.

"I know it's not my business, but you've been really out of sorts lately. Like, angry and sad and just not yourself. Do you need to, I don't know, talk about it?"

"Probably." I scoffed, shaking my head.

"It's about that girl you were in love with, right?"

I clenched my jaw. "She dumped me."

"Ouch." Ashlee rubbed my shoulder. "I'm sorry."

"It was probably my fault," I mumbled.

"How? You're like the nicest guy I know."

A sidelong glance at her cute expression made me grin. I licked my bottom lip and turned to face her. "She wants me to do something that could put my career at risk."

Ashlee's eyebrows rose. "Why?"

I shrugged. "She says that if I can't fight for her, then I obviously don't want her. The thing is I do. I want her..." I pinched my nose, "but I want this job too."

"Why can't you have both?"

"Because Travis is an asshole," I whispered.

Ashlee snickered. "He can be, but his vision for this show is amazing and look how well we're doing."

"Yeah."

"I love working with you, and this show is just...I don't know, the dancing, the singing...I love it all."

"Me too." I patted her knee. "It's awesome."

"You shouldn't have to give that up. She shouldn't be asking that of you."

I made a popping sound with my lips as Ashlee came back to the same argument I always did. Rhonda had reminded me of this again the week before.

This show meant the world to me, and I really didn't want to give it up. Ashlee and I were the stars. This was everything I'd been working toward...and although Morgan didn't buy into

Travis's threat anymore, it still hung over me like a storm cloud.

Morgan shouldn't have asked me to risk it all. It wasn't fair.

"I guess at the end of the day, if she really cared about you, she wouldn't expect you to throw it all away. I think it's kind of selfish."

Ashlee's soft words fueled my anger, making me feel justified once more. If only they could take away the sadness that had taken root inside of me too.

TWENTY-EIGHT

MORGAN

I'd found a job. Well, actually Dad had found it for me. Derek was a friend of a friend and owned a small accounting firm in Pasadena. His receptionist was on maternity leave and he was desperate for a temp. I took it. What choice did I have? With three mouths back in the Pritchett house, we needed the extra cash flow. Jody was now six months pregnant and filling her days with part-time work at a grocery store in Santa Monica. I tried to convince her to find work closer to home, but she didn't want to bump into anyone she knew. So instead she got up ridiculously early to get there on time and came home exhausted each night. She didn't want to go out and do anything, so she hung around the house in a quiet stupor.

To say it was painful was an understatement.

I glanced into Grandma Deb's living room to check on my little sister. She was sitting on the edge of the couch, her feet tucked up beneath her butt, her round belly resting against her knees. She looked beautiful. Her long, blonde curls resting on her ample breasts. She said she was starting to feel fat and clumsy, but I'd bet if she had a supportive guy sitting next to her right now, she'd be glowing. Jody's sunshine had been reduced to a dim ray that was only just visible. It was like looking at her through a thick fog.

It didn't help that Dad was sitting on the other edge of the couch, stiff-necked. He was trying really hard to be supportive, but every time his eyes skimmed her belly you could see a flash of disappointed sickness spear him.

I wished I could fix it, but I'd run out of words.

"So, tell me about work." Grandma Deb pulled me back into the kitchen, handing me a knife and two Lebanese cucumbers. Of all the people on this earth, she understood me the best. I could tell by the twinkle in her eye that she was forcing me out of my disheartening situation by making me busy. She reminded me a little of Gloria Jackson. My heart squeezed as I pictured Sean's mom bustling around the kitchen, her nonstop chatter filling the air. Would I ever get to see her again?

"Morgan, honey?"

I looked up from the chopping board.

"How's work?"

"It's okay." I sliced the ends off the cucumbers and shrugged. "I'm the receptionist so I answer the phone a lot and you know, do receptionist stuff."

"And you're enjoying it?"

"I guess. My boss is really nice, warm, friendly...happy, so that helps." I snickered.

"You deserve a good boss after that nutcase. I can't believe you lasted for as long as you did."

"It wasn't him keeping me there, Grandma."

Her head tipped to the side, her smile taking on a loving quality that I couldn't look at.

I kept my eyes on the cucumbers, trying to slice them slowly and carefully. I usually chopped as quickly and efficiently as I could, but not today. I needed to keep my hands busy or I'd go insane.

"Things going okay at home?"

"Do you really need to ask?"

She chuckled. "You'll survive this. You always do." She patted my arm with her soft hands and turned back to the sink.

Thankfully she didn't say more after that, and we got busy preparing lunch for the family. It was her sixty-eighth birthday today. I knew she always missed Grandpa the most on special occasions. They'd been two peas in a pod their whole married life. When he'd died of cancer three years ago, I didn't think she was going to make it, but Grandma Deb pulled one out of the hat and refused to give in to her despair. After a few months, it was like she rose from the ashes and came out strong, volunteering for anything she could get her hands on.

"Giving out gets you through, Morgan." She chirped that at me the first Christmas she had to survive without him. I'd found the comment inspiring and tried to live by it as much as I could. Taking care of others did make life richer...most of the time.

I dumped the cucumber into the salad bowl, tossing it through the lettuce and cherry tomatoes. Grandma scraped the feta cheese and olives from her board and went to wash her hands. I joined her at the sink, taking the dishtowel off her when she was done.

"Right, supper's ready!" she called into the living room.

I carried the homemade pizza into the dining room and laid it on the table. Grandma followed with the fresh salad and homemade dressing. Jody held her belly as she slid into her seat and was rewarded with a loving smile from her grandmother. She reciprocated, reaching for her hand as we all bowed our heads for grace.

Dinner actually turned out to be a delight. Grandma Deb regaled us with stories from her past, including some hilarious anecdotes about Dad as a child. We laughed and whooped, forgetting all our angst. Jody's smile was delicious as she giggled at the stories. With her belly hidden beneath the table, it was easy to pretend life was normal. Even Dad managed a few chuckles.

By the time Grandma had blown out the candles on the cake I'd made her and we'd sung "Happy Birthday," everyone was on a high. We ate the chocolate cake in silence, and it wasn't until Grandma started offering coffees around that the balloon popped.

"I can't drink coffee," Jody whispered.

"I know that, dear." Grandma patted her hand, but it didn't erase the frown this time. Jody stifled a yawn as she stood from the table.

"Marshall, I think it's time you take Jody home."

"No, that's okay. We should help you clean up." Jody started for the kitchen.

"You know that won't be necessary. Morgan will stay and help me."

Jody's face dropped, her eyes growing wide at the prospect of being alone in the car with Dad.

"That's okay; I can take Jody home then come back."

"Don't be ridiculous." Grandma waved her hand at me. "Jody, you will be fine. You need to go home and rest. Marshall, you're looking a mite tired yourself. You're not working too hard now, are you?"

He grinned. "You know me, Mom."

She chuckled and walked around the table to give them both a hug. In spite of Jody's reluctance, Grandma Deb shuffled them out the door. I felt a little bad. I should be taking Jody home. I'd driven her here and Dad had met us after work. He didn't usually work on a Sunday, but it'd been an emergency call.

I waved goodbye and forced a smile, trying to encourage Jody to relax. She returned my pleasantries with a deep frown. I dropped my hand with a sigh.

"Don't you worry about her. It's you who needs the break right now."

"I'm fine." I squeezed Grandma's shoulder and closed the door behind her, heading into the kitchen to start cleaning up. I couldn't believe she still didn't have a dishwasher. We'd been trying to persuade her for years, but she wouldn't budge.

"A few dishes never hurt anybody," she always said.

"Put those pots down, Morgan. Let's have a coffee first." With a shrug, I lowered them back onto the stovetop and moved to the kettle, filling the jug while Grandma sorted out the mugs.

"So, now that we're alone, you can tell me how you're really doing."

I took the mugs from her. "What do you mean?"

"Morgan, I see your pain. You try to keep hiding it and stay strong for everybody, but you can't live like this for the rest of your life."

I opened my mouth.

"And don't tell me everything will be fine after the baby is born, because I know that's not the issue. Your agony has nothing to do with Jody."

"I'm not..." I frowned. "I'm not in agony."

"You're unhappy. You're going through some kind of pain."

I swallowed, keeping my eyes on the boiling kettle.

"It's Sean, isn't it? You still miss him." Her hand gently patted my back, and I wanted to step out of her reach.

The kettle whistled, and I poured hot water over the coffee granules.

"I'm fine. That's over. He couldn't do what I needed. I thought he might call, try to win me back somehow, but he didn't. That's life. There are more guys out there. There's... You suck it up and you move on. You stay bulletproof and nothing can hurt you." I slammed the kettle back down.

Grandma cleared her throat and gave me a dry look as I snatched the milk off her. "You know what your problem is?"

The milk slopped out of my cup. I huffed, pinching the dishcloth next to the sink and cleaning up my mess. Without replying, I handed Grandma her coffee.

Her strong gaze remained on me, her expression unflinching. There was no getting out of this. I brushed past her, taking my coffee into the dining room and sitting down with a straight back. I held the steaming cup in my hands, the hot ceramic burning my fingertips.

"Okay, what? What is my problem?"

She slid into her place, blowing on her drink before taking a sip. Lowering her mug, she looked at me across the leftover pizza. "You harp on all the time about being bulletproof, but you're not."

My chuckle was dry. "I'm tough. I think I've proved that. There's no way I could have survived if I wasn't."

"Sweetie, being tough and being bulletproof are

not the same thing."

I pressed my fingers into the mug, my jaw working to the side as I looked at the only woman in my life who'd never let me down.

"Honey, it comes from in here." She pointed at her chest, pressing her index finger just below the locket Grandpa gave her four Christmases ago. "When you can find that place of total peace... it's a place that's birthed from love and acceptance...and forgiveness. When you find that, it's like you're titanium. Because no matter what is thrown at you or who rejects you or treats you unfairly.... All those horrible bullets that get fired your way, they just bounce straight off, because you're okay. In here." She tapped her chest.

I swallowed at the lump rising in my throat. I would not cry.

Grandma's smile was soft, her eyes beaming as she pointed at me. "When you can get to that place of inner peace." She shook her head with a grin. "You can give without feeling exhausted, and you can love without expecting anything in return."

I took a sip of my coffee, not knowing what to say.

"And you know the best part about that?" She raised her eyebrows and I shook my head. "When someone does give back...when someone loves back...it's like the fudge sauce on your sundae."

I couldn't even imagine it. Someone loving me back seemed like an impossibility at the moment. I thought Sean had finally been the one—the guy who would wipe away my string of bad choices before him.

But he hadn't.

And unlike all the rest, I couldn't seem to move past him. I'd never been single for two months before. It was horrible! I couldn't imagine sleeping with anyone else. I wanted Sean...but he didn't want me, not enough to fight for me anyway.

Tears burned my eyes and I quickly blinked them away, sniffing sharply and lifting my chin.

"I don't have time to find inner peace, Grandma. I don't even know where to start. Jody needs me; it's not like I can go on some retreat to discover myself!"

"Be careful there, Morgan."

"What?"

"With Jody."

I frowned.

"Don't try to step in and take charge of this situation just to fill the gap. You'll rob her of the chance to become the woman she was meant to be. And it'll do nothing to help your heart."

I closed my eyes, hating her words. Jody needed me, damn it! I needed her too...at least until the pain went away.

Just hearing myself think those words was like a revelation of its own. I huffed out a sigh, pressing my elbows into the table and catching my head with my hands. "It's not just a gap I'm filling. It feels like a black vortex. If I don't put something in there, I'll get sucked into oblivion."

"Oh, Morgan."

"How do you find that peace? It feels so out of reach." I stretched my hand across the table and clutched at thin air. "What do you do?"

"I talk to God." She shrugged. "He's my constant. He sustains me."

"And He's enough?"

"He's enough for me." She tipped her head, her smile soft and peaceful. "When your Grandpa died, I thought my soul would be shattered forever." Picking up the locket, she squeezed it between her thumb and forefinger. "I had to find something to keep me going, or I never would have made it out of bed. So I got myself busy. I filled my days until I was so exhausted, I could barely see straight. I nearly drove myself into the ground, you remember, don't you?"

I winced, remembering that terrible phone call. I'd been in Chicago, listening to Jody's tears as she told me they were on the way to the hospital. Grandma had collapsed, and they had no idea what was wrong with her.

It'd been a harrowing few days as we waited out test results. Turned out she hadn't been taking very good care of herself. I'd nearly moved back home, but she'd kept me in Chicago with her soft commands, telling me I owed it to myself to stay.

"I had to let go, really look inside myself and figure out what I needed." She shrugged. "Being on bed rest for a couple of weeks really gives you time to think. It's funny how those crisis moments help define us, make us shake hands with our demons." Blowing on her coffee, she took another sip. "I had to stop in order to find my way. I wonder what you're gonna have to do?"

"Great, so there's still a crisis coming?"

"I hope so."

I scoffed and looked to the ceiling. "Thanks a lot. I already feel like I'm living in one big crisis."

"Then maybe you should take this time to stop and figure out what you really need."

Sean.

I said his name in my head until I was shouting it, but I knew it wasn't the answer Grandma was looking for.

"Morgan, honey, you're bound by things you haven't dealt with yet. You've buried them deep and let them fester."

My teeth ground together, my breathing shortening to a bare whisper.

"You need to root those out, like a weed." She snapped her fingers. "If you can do that, you'll find your happiness, you'll find that peace. You'll be bulletproof." She pointed at me and winked. "Like I said, if you can learn to be happy on your own, just think what a bonus it will be when the right man comes along."

"The right man *did* come along, and I walked away from him." I slammed the table.

"But you're not ready. Honey, if you don't shake hands with those demons of yours and tell them they are no longer welcome in your life, you'll never be ready for anything, especially a relationship."

I hated this conversation. I wanted to shoot out of my chair and make a beeline for the car, but Grandma's steady gaze had me locked in place.

"You need to forgive her," she whispered.

Snatching my coffee, I took a sip, my entire body resisting those words.

She left us. She turned me into a mother at the age of fourteen! How the hell was I supposed to forgive her! I hadn't spoken to my mother since I slammed the phone in her ear on my fifteenth birthday. Like she even had a right to call!

"Don't let her do this to you anymore. Take back control of your life and fight for the woman you were meant to be. She's in there. I see glimmers of it all the time."

"I don't know how," I mumbled.

"I just told you how! Now go and do it!"

"I don't—" I rose from my chair, pushing it back into place. "I don't have time for this." Desperate to avoid her gaze, I shot back into the kitchen and busied myself with dishes. Grandma remained mercifully quiet, calmly working beside my ridiculous flurry of movements.

Forty minutes later, I was kissing her goodbye.

"I love you, Morgan. I wouldn't challenge you if I didn't."

I forced a smile. "I love you too."

Raising my hand, I raced down the path, shutting myself into the safety of my car. Revving the engine, I flicked on the radio and turned up the volume until it thumped through my car, carrying me home and forcing the rattling conversation with Grandma Deb out of my brain.

TWENTY-NINE

SEAN

"Sean! Sean!"

Isabella raced up behind me, pulling me to a stop with her tiny fingers.

"I need to see you before you leave today. I've come up with some great moves for your solo next week and I want to go over them."

I inwardly cringed. I'd been trying to avoid our choreographer all day, knowing she had the moves set for me. I did need to get onto it, otherwise I wouldn't know the part in time for filming. I just really didn't want to dance that song.

"Yeah," I sighed. "Yeah, of course."

"Are you free now? I've got an hour."

"Uh-huh." I didn't want to be free; I wanted to

go and hide out in my room until Con needed me back on set, but Isabella had me now, and there was no way I could get out of it.

I forced a smile and followed her up to the rehearsal room.

"Okay." She stretched her arms wide. "So this piece is pretty awesome. You don't often get a complete solo, so I'm happy for you, and I love the way it's going to flash to Sasha as you're singing. I can picture it all really clearly. So let me show you what I've got, and then we can go from there."

I nodded, pinching my lower lip between my fingers.

"I Wish You Were Here" by Cody Simpson filled the room. My stomach curdled, his voice instantly reminding me of the night Morgan and I had made love in this dance studio. My gaze left Isabella's body and landed on the spot Morgan had lain, naked and glorious in the pale light, her long legs wrapping around me as I buried myself inside her.

"Hey, are you watching?" Isabella clapped her hands, grabbing my attention.

"Huh?" I glanced at her, going for innocent, but she saw straight through it.

Her hip popped out to the side, her hand finding a quick home there.

"Dude, you have it bad."

"What?"

"When are you going to do something about it? You've been a freaking basket case." She held up three fingers. "Three months, Sean. You idiot!"

I frowned, my head jerking back. "I don't even know what you're talking about."

"You know exactly what I'm talking about." Her little body pinged straight and she marched toward me. Her head only came up to my shoulders, but the little small fry could be intimidating when she wanted to be. I took a step back. "Morgan told me, okay. I can't believe you just let her walk out the door!"

"It's not that simple. You don't even know—"

"I *do* know! I talk to her all the time!"

"You do?" My arms dropped to my sides, the air in my lungs evaporating.

"Yes, we're friends."

"Is she...? How is she?"

"Oh, you know, working some receptionist job with a company she doesn't care about." Isabella's eyebrow quirked. "Why don't you call her and find out?"

"Because—" I threw my hands in the air. "Because I can't, okay! I can't give her what she wants!"

"All she was asking you to do was fight for her, Sean."

"No." I waved my finger. "She was asking me to choose between her and my career."

"I think you're being a little dramatic."

"Am I?" I punched the air. "What do you think Travis is gonna say if I go down there and tell him he's an asshole and if he ever talks to my woman that way again, I'm gonna smash his face in?"

"You wouldn't say that to him."

"I want to!"

Isabella sighed. "Sean, I don't think she wanted you to do that. She just wanted you to claim her."

"I was *trying* to protect her. Besides, claiming her could jeopardize my entire future as an actor."

"Who is feeding you this horseshit?" Isabella scowled. "Is it Rhonda?"

"Hey, she's been good to me."

"Yeah, I'm sure she has *your* best interests at heart."

"She does!"

Isabella raised her hands, stepping away from

my accusing finger. "I don't doubt that she has your career very firmly taken care of, but is that all your life is about?"

"You don't know how hard I've worked to get here." I shook my head, gripping the back of my neck.

"Yes, I do. I know how hard this business is."

"If I cross Travis, he could destroy me. I don't want to go back to being some poor nobody. I spent my entire life that way."

Stepping toward me with a huff, the little dancer punched me in the arm. "You're more talented than you think you are. Audiences love you, Sean. They loved you as Mr. Bulletproof; they adore you as Harley. You've got more power than you think you do."

"No, I don't." I gritted my teeth. "I'm too late anyway, Bells. I've left it too long. She'll have moved on and found someone to take care of her...give her everything she deserves. I just have to focus on my career and make the best of it."

"Nothing's ever too late when it comes to love." Her gaze was so intense, begging me to reconsider.

I didn't know how to respond.

She opened her mouth to say more, but I cut her off before she could.

"Let's get on with this." Marching toward the stereo, I collected the iPod and found the song, nodding at her to show me the moves.

The song washed over us as she stood there in reluctant silence, but I wouldn't budge.

Eventually she sighed her way to my side and took her stance. "Start the song again."

I selected the song and carefully watched her as she went through the moves once more, joining in for the repetitive steps. I blocked out the lyrics, trying to forget the fact I'd have to record them next week. Singing about missing my girl and wishing her by my side was a real killer. Harley's story line sucked ass, and I couldn't wait for the damn season to be over. After this, only one more episode to go. All I could hope was that the writers had a decent conclusion, because I didn't know how much longer I could keep acting a role that mirrored my life.

THIRTY

MORGAN

I covered my yawn and looked at my watch. Thirty-three minutes left to go. Blinking, I sat up straight and tried to wake myself up. I needed another coffee. Rising from my receptionist post, I went to get myself a refill and poured one for my boss at the same time.

"Thanks so much, Morgan. You're amazing." His broad smile was hard not to mirror. The guy was so full of compliments—a refreshing change from Mr. Hardass, to say the least.

"You're welcome. Is there anything else you need before I go?"

He glanced up at the clock on the wall and cringed as he handed me some paperwork.

"Actually, I was wondering if you could punch in these final figures for me. I want to work on them tonight. I've already told the wife I'll be late for dinner." He winked.

I swallowed, forcing a cheery smile as I reached for it.

"Sorry if it means you have to stay late. I'll pay you overtime...or let you leave early tomorrow if you like."

"Sure." My smile turned genuine. He really was a nice guy. I may have found the job boring as hell, but at least I worked for a man who respected me. He was friendly, warm, and easy to be around. I wasn't going to complain.

Slumping into my chair, I spun to face the computer and got to work, opening up the database and punching in numbers I didn't want to take the time to understand. This job was a filler, something to tide me over until I could get my life figured out.

That familiar weight of depression fell into my belly as the big question loomed. What did I want from my life?

Sean was always the first word that popped into my head, but I batted it away. He hadn't even tried to call me once. It didn't matter that I'd changed my number and moved. He'd picked me up from my house in Pasadena once; it didn't take a genius to know where I would have gone.

Besides, he saw Isabella almost every day, and I was still in contact with her. She'd become a good friend, and although it was stupidly hard, I made a concerted effort never to ask how he was doing. I didn't want to hear that he'd moved on.

The phone on my desk buzzed. I collected it up and grinned. I always found it funny when you were thinking of someone and they actually called.

"Hey, how's it going?"

"Good. Tired." Isabella groaned. "These dance rehearsals are killing me."

"Not many more to go." I tried to keep my voice light.

"Totally. I've only got two more dances to choreograph, and then I'm taking a month off. Hubs has made me promise I will."

I grinned. I loved the way she called Dean "Hubs". It was cute.

"How are you going to cope with time off? You thrive on being busy."

She chuckled. "I know, but I have some plans."

I didn't have the energy to find out what they were. I didn't want to know about her awesome plans. I wasn't trying to be bitchy, but life was all about survival for me at the moment, and I didn't need to hear that other people were moving on and up, while I was stuck treading water in my scummy pond.

"So, what can I do for you?" I pressed the phone against my ear and kept typing in numbers.

"I just wanted to see how you were doing? I had a really great rehearsal today with Sean and—"

"Hey, you know the rules. No work talk. I don't need to know."

"Yeah, I just..." She sighed. "You're right. It's not my place. How's your work going?"

"Oh you know; same old, same old." I glanced at Derek's office door and hunched over my phone, whispering, "It's so boring here, I think my brain falls into a coma the second I walk in the door."

She giggled.

"But then I get home and it's electrocuted into functioning again, because I have to face Jody and Dad."

"Are they still at each other?"

"Not so much *at*, just unable to be around each other. Every time Dad sees Jody's belly, he cringes.

It's like he can't help himself. If Jody ever sees it, she gets all defensive and starts going off about how his disappointment is killing her." I roll my eyes. "She's such a drama queen, and the amount of tears. I mean, I know she's hormonal and the situation sucks for her, but part of me wants to slap her and tell her to toughen up. Life sucks; get used to it." I winced at my bitter tone.

Thankfully Isabella let it slide. "Has she decided if she wants to keep the baby or not?"

I groaned. "She says she doesn't want to, but every time I bring out the paperwork from the adoption agency she changes the subject or says she doesn't have time. I really have no idea what is going through her brain. It's so exhausting, Isabella. And don't even get me started on our first Lamaze last week." I groaned.

Isabella chuckled. "I know it must be horrible. Hey, why don't we hang out tonight? Go dancing or something."

I licked my bottom lip. She'd been asking for weeks to catch up face-to-face, but I kept putting her off. Seeing her would remind me of everything I was missing, and I couldn't dance. I'd barely been able to listen to music lately. It was too painful.

"I have to work late tonight."

"Aw, man. I had something really cool I wanted to show you."

"What?" I stopped typing and pressed the phone to my ear.

"No way, I'm not telling you over the phone; it's a surprise."

I grinned. "I'm sorry, but I really can't tonight. Maybe tomorrow?"

"I'm holding you to that."

"Okay." I cringed. What had I just done?

"Trust me, it's good. You'll like it."

"Yeah, I'm sure I will." I couldn't sound upbeat,

because I didn't believe her. There was nothing to like about my life at the moment. I was lonely, frustrated, bored, exhausted.

I was lonely. My stomach pinched.

"Well, chica, I better fly. I'll *see* you tomorrow night!"

"Ciao." I pulled the phone away from my ear and gazed at the screen.

Without meaning to, I flicked to my contacts list and scanned the numbers. I saw Brad's name flash by, and my thumb hovered over it for a minute.

What was I thinking?

Seriously? Brad?

He didn't even live in LA! And I seriously should not have his number on my phone anymore.

But the thought of hooking up with an ex-boyfriend was kind of nice. Go out for a drink, have some fun. Life had been about nothing but work and Jody lately. I needed to let loose.

I flicked my thumb up the screen and watched it travel through the rest of the numbers. I was lonely. I needed someone to fill that space again. Not like a relationship or anything, just... Would a one-night stand really be that bad? I couldn't stomach the idea of going home to Jody and Dad's tension. I couldn't stomach the idea of dancing...but getting tipsy and screwing some nameless face— that somehow had appeal.

Oblivion.

Ecstasy.

Losing my body to that mind-numbing pleasure. It had always been my best release.

The names on the screen turned fuzzy as my eyes lost focus, my conversation with Grandma Deb rearing over me again. It had been doing that a lot lately. I wanted to forget we'd ever had it.

As if forgiving my mother would give me inner

peace.

I'd vowed never to speak to her again. I didn't want to open that door. No, my best option was to move on and forget. I'd find peace some other way...in some guy's arms. That had always worked before.

Suddenly motivated, I popped my phone beside me and hurried through the rest of the data entry. As soon as it was done, I was gonna hit the town, find a busy bar, and get me some liquor. This was probably why I hadn't been able to push out of my depression. I'd been moping around missing Sean when I should have been throwing myself back into the dating pool. It wasn't so bad, and at least I could forget my troubles with a good night out.

I was tempted to call Isabella back and see if she did want to go dancing, but I wrinkled my nose. I didn't want to dance tonight, at least not that kind of dancing. I needed to go out on my own.

"You nearly done?" Derek walked out from his office, making me jump. "Sorry." He grinned.

"Nearly." I smiled back. "One page to go."

"Great, just pop into my office before you leave." His eyes lingered on me for a minute.

"Sure." I nodded, turning back to the screen.

Thirty minutes later, I had finished. Saving the files, I popped them into DropBox for Derek and turned off the computer. I collected my things and double-checked the area, deciding to file the paperwork in the morning.

With a quick knock on Derek's door, I stepped inside.

"All done."

"Great." He stood and walked around his desk. He was actually a really handsome guy. My guess was mid-forties, but I'd never actually asked. I knew he had two kids—three and five—and a wife named Mandy.

"Well, I guess I'll see you in the morning then." I lifted the bag onto my shoulder and stepped toward him.

Whatever cologne he was wearing smelled really good. It laced up my nostrils, making my belly quiver.

"Thank you for staying late." He took a step closer until he was standing right beside me. "I can't tell you how grateful I am to have you working here. You're efficient, intelligent, kind, thoughtful. It makes me wonder how I coped before you came along."

I grinned. "Thank you, Derek."

His eyes lingered on my face, a warm smile touching his lips. "So, what have you got planned tonight?"

I shrugged. "Not sure exactly." Like I could tell him what I really wanted to do.

"You have seemed a little antsy the last few weeks; it'll probably be good for you to go and blow off some steam."

It was an effort to hide my surprise. I didn't realize the pressure building inside me was starting to show.

Derek reached for my hand and gave it a little squeeze. "Sometimes all you need is a night out, so you can forget your troubles, right? Something to release that pressure."

My lips parted. I was working for a telepathist, and I didn't even know it.

He dropped my hand, his fingers skimming up my arm and nestling on my shoulder. A wave of warning spiked through me, but I stood my ground. It felt good to be touched gently, to be told that I was thinking and doing the right things for a change.

It was refreshing not be put down, dismissed, ignored...for my needs to be acknowledged and agreed with.

"Yeah," my voice was husky.

Derek stepped into my space, his body brushing against mine. "I might not know exactly what you're going through right now, but I do know that life can suck and sometimes we just need to be impulsive, spontaneous...let ourselves go. For the sake of our sanity."

He leaned toward me, his lips aiming for mine. I knew I should have turned away, but I didn't. I gave back, letting his tongue slide into my mouth. The bag dropped from my shoulder before I reached up and wrapped my arms around his neck. His hands swarmed my body, gliding over my curves. A moan of pleasure swelled in his throat as we deepened the kiss.

It felt good.

I switched off my brain, smashing away the warning bells. I needed this. I needed to forget.

My hands scrambled for his shirt, tugging it out of his pants as his lips roamed my neck. My fingers skimmed over his firm torso and a smile tugged at my lips. Not bad.

Nothing on Sean's six-pack, but...

Sean.

I swallowed, closing my eyes against the sound of his name.

Warnings continued to lash at me, beating against the force field I was trying to construct. I didn't want to know.

I needed to forget!

We stumbled toward Derek's desk, my butt pressing into the edge as he lifted my knee and perched my foot against the chair behind him.

Derek's fingers trailed up my leg, pushing my skirt out of the way. He squeezed my inner thigh before hooking his thumb into my panties. The pads of his fingers pressed into me and I softly moaned. I hadn't been touched for three months...which for me, was a really long time.

It felt good.

Another warning slapped against my brain, but the force field remained intact as I lost myself to the tingles firing down my legs, clinging to this man as if he was my full-time lover.

Derek pressed himself against me. I could feel him, ready to go, and flashed forward to where we might do this. Would he throw me to the floor? Sweep everything off his desk and lift me onto it?

My limbs were turning to putty as his fingers continued to work me over, slipping inside me and bringing me to that sweet edge, where I could tumble into oblivion. The world didn't exist in that place. There was no right or wrong, just the movement of two bodies tangled around each other and rushing for that mindless liberty.

I was nearly there, nearly ready to let a guttural scream rip from my throat before scrambling for the zipper on his pants, but that's when a shock of awareness slapped me.

His ring. I felt it skim against my back as he lifted my shirt free and pressed his cool hand into my skin.

My eyes popped open, my force field disintegrating. Every warning trying to break through hit me in a rush so strong, it actually hurt.

I pushed him away from me, dropping my foot to the floor.

"What's the matter?" he puffed, trying to pull me back.

I stepped out of his reach, adjusting my panties and pushing my skirt back into place. "You're married." I spat the words. "What the hell am I doing?"

"It's no big deal, Morgan. No one needs to know. It's just one night, so we can forget."

"I can't." I snatched my purse off the floor, pushing past him. I felt like a newborn giraffe, my limbs shaking and awkward as I stumbled to the door. "I won't be that woman. Your wife deserves your loyalty."

"And what do you deserve?"

I could think of a few things, and none of them were good. What the hell was wrong with me? I was turning into a marriage-breaking whore now?

I yanked the door open.

"Morgan, wait. I'm sorry. I was out of line."

"I quit."

Again.

What was that, two jobs in four months? Good going, Morgan.

Before he could say another word, I ran out the door, tripping over my heels as I raced for the car. I somehow managed to unlock it and climb in, slamming the door behind me.

Heaving breaths burst out of my mouth, like dry sobs. I clutched the wheel and rested my head against it. Hating myself.

I was seriously fucked-up.

The phone in my purse buzzed with a text alert. Worried it might be Jody, I snatched it out of my bag.

A relieved sigh left my lips. "Ella."

Hey, how's it going? We're kind of quiet here tonight, so I'm heading over to yours to watch a movie with Jody. Are you gonna be there? What should I bring?

My fingers trembled as they hovered over the screen.

I didn't want to see her. The second Ella caught sight of my face, she'd know. She'd ask me all the right questions, and the truth would spill out of me. I might not have slept with a married man, but I let him touch me. Bile surged up my throat. I swallowed it back down.

Can't make it. Have to work really late. I'll catch you on the weekend. Take care of Jo-Jo for me.

I knew she would. It was in her nature.

Throwing the phone back into my bag, I glanced at the office building. Derek's light flicked off and my heart seized. Scrambling for the key, I turned the ignition and fired out of the parking lot. I had no idea where I was going; I just knew I couldn't be there.

Tearing down the road, I drove aimlessly through the streets, sticking with green lights and not caring where they took me. Eventually I slowed to a stop at a big intersection, the red light forcing me to take a break. I was second in the queue, my fingers gripping the wheel as I waited. I felt jittery, antsy, wanting to hit a bar but loathing the idea of someone else touching me tonight.

So where the hell was I going to go then?

My eyes darted from street to street and then settled on the big sign above me. There was a cross of arrows all leading to different places, but only one caught my eye.

LAS VEGAS - 260 Miles

My knuckles turned white.

Las-fucking-Vegas.

She'd be there. Singing into some microphone, lapping up the applause while she forgot about the family she'd abandoned. The daughter she'd completely screwed over! The one who'd given up her first true love—dancing—in order to play mother to a scared little ten-year-old. The one who'd run from one guy to the next, trying to fix it, to fill that gaping wound just so the pain might stop for a second.

How many guys had I slept with?

I didn't even want to count.

How many guys had used me for a good time

and I'd let it slide, not caring because I was in control. I was the one taking charge, not them. They were fulfilling my needs. They were helping me forget.

How many guys had I fallen in love with? Let them take a piece of my heart with them and told myself I didn't mind. I was bulletproof; their rejection couldn't hurt me.

My chest restricted, making it hard to breathe.

I'd never felt so peppered with holes. Machine gun fire rattled through my head as I pictured my body jerking with each hit, yet I couldn't fall. I kept standing, a mesh-like mess that couldn't move forward or backward.

The light turned green and I pressed the gas, my fingers hovering over the indicator.

It was her fault. If she hadn't left, I would have stayed young and innocent. I would have danced my high school years away and who knows where I would have ended up. Certainly not at some dead-end job with a boss who played nice but secretly wanted to cheat on his wife.

A horn blasted behind me. I jerked, flicking the indicator and heading toward the I-15 North and Sin City before thought could stop me.

THIRTY-ONE

SEAN

I wriggled in my seat. I hadn't been still since my rehearsal with Isabella that afternoon. Our conversation haunted me, her final words eating at me until I couldn't think clearly.

"So, you're gonna need to take someone." Rhonda tapped her long fingernail on the table. "This is a big event. It'll be televised, and the paparazzi will be out in full force. Giovanni Saito is a big name in this town, and the fact he's invited you to the first festival he's created is... Sean, this is huge. There are gonna be a ton of A-listers there, not to mention all the big-wigs in the music industry. There'll be more Emmy, Oscar and Grammy winners there than fans will know what to do with. Saito is pulling out all the stops to get this thing off the ground and he'll succeed. The man's a genius when it comes to the entertainment industry."

I nodded.

"So have a think about who you want to accompany you, and I'll make all the arrangements." She pressed her elbows onto her desktop and grinned at me. "You know, Ashlee might be a good choice. You'd look great together and the crowd will love it."

She raised her eyebrows expectantly. I knew I had to answer with something, and because I couldn't deal with the drama today, *no* wasn't exactly an option.

"I'll think about it." I slumped back in my chair.

"You okay?"

My bottom lip stuck out for a second and I forced a nod. "Just tired."

I didn't want to get into it with her. Every time I mentioned Morgan's name, she'd go into her speech about how it was for the best. I couldn't stomach it tonight.

Morgan was the best, and I'd let her walk away.

Was it too late to get her back, or was Isabella right?

I pictured my tall girl, her long legs and killer-watt smile lighting up the room. I wondered what she was doing at this moment. All I could hope was that she was happy and safe.

But I didn't want to just hope.

I wanted to see her, feel her, know for real that she was okay.

Rhonda moved on to the next item on the agenda while I tugged out my phone. Morgan had changed her number, but I could hunt her down if I wanted to. I had Cole's number. The guy who owned Reynold's. He'd given it to me the night of the dance party, back in November. He'd for sure know where Morgan was.

I pulled up my contact list, gazing at his name.

But what would I say? When I *did* reach Morgan, what would I tell her? After this long, it couldn't be some lame-ass small talk. It needed to be something real.

I could tell her I loved her, that I missed her like crazy, and she'd probably just reply with a, "Prove it then."

"And they want you to re-sign for Season Two."

Rhonda's words snatched me out of my reverie.

I sat forward in my chair, reaching for the contract.

"The show's a huge hit, mostly because of you and Ashlee. Travis is going to move forward with a second season and he wants you in it."

My eyes skimmed the small, black text, flicking over the page and gazing at the blank space near the bottom.

"It's all standard stuff, Sean, so you just need to sign it. I figured it was a no-brainer for you." She twisted her pen and passed it to me.

I looked at it, perched in her fingers, and couldn't move.

"What's the matter?"

"I gotta go."

"What? We haven't finished."

I shook my head, ignoring her sharp tone.

"Sean."

Snatching my keys off the table, I shoved my phone into my back pocket and walked to the door.

"Hey!"

I closed the door on Rhonda's yelling and walked to my car in a daze. I'd left the contract on the table.

What the hell did I do now?

What did I do?

I slid into my car and glanced at my watch.

7:08 p.m.

I should have gone home for some much-needed sleep, but I didn't want to. Flicking on the ignition, I headed out to the street and drove on autopilot until I found my car outside the small wooden house I'd been raised in.

With a sigh, I gazed through the dim light at the small structure. How the hell seven of us had lived there for so long still baffled me. I grimaced, remembering us squished together in those tiny rooms, living in each other's pockets. I'd hated it as a kid, always envious of the rich kids at school. Until I'd won my first paid acting gig, I had never owned any new clothes. Everything was a hand-me-down. Every shirt, every toy...everything.

I'd wanted new, fresh, shiny and I'd gotten it.

With a sigh, I ran my fingers over the wheel and jumped out of the car.

I'd hated counting pennies, I'd loathed the hand-me-downs, but at the end of the day, I loved my parents. I loved my brothers and sisters, and that was what kept me coming home.

Walking up the steps, I knocked once on the door and let myself in.

"Mama? Pop. You home?"

"Sean, baby?" Mom came around the corner, her face crinkling, her white teeth bright inside her dark skin. "My boy." She snatched me down into a tight hug. I squeezed her back and let her kiss my cheek.

Finally she let go and I straightened up.

"Let me look at you." She held my arms out the way she always did, making me feel like I visited once a century rather than every week...or every month lately.

"Come on, Mama." I claimed my arms back and followed her into the living room, flopping onto the couch like I always did.

She crossed her arms and looked down at me, her eyes narrowing at the corners. Every time I'd stopped by lately, her eyes had done the same thing. It was damn unnerving. Thankfully I'd been surrounded by family and taken off before she could corner me.

I looked over my shoulder, wondering why the house was so quiet.

Damn, I was a fool to have come here.

Squirming in my seat, I trained my eyes on the worn carpet.

"So, how's Morgan doing? You don't bring her around no more."

I couldn't hide my wince. That woman knew how to get straight to the point.

Last time she'd asked, I fudged some excuse about my girl working too hard. Tonight, I didn't think I could fudge anything, so with a heavy sigh, I let the confession slip free.

"We broke up about three months ago, Mama."

Her eyebrows shot north, making her forehead wrinkle. "You what? What the hell is wrong witchyou?" Her long fingers skimmed the air. I knew if I'd been standing there, she would have cuffed me.

I moved forward in my seat and rested my elbows on my knees. "She broke up with me."

"Why, Sean?"

Glancing up, I noticed Mama now had her arms crossed, her mouth forming that *don't you mess with me* expression. I ran a hand over my head, the urge to cry suddenly coming over me. I squeezed my eyes shut and willed the emotion away.

"Sean Phillip Morris Jackson, you better start talking to me."

"She was asking me to put my entire career on the line, and I couldn't do that."

Mama's head bobbed back, her chin doubling up for a moment before she stepped toward me and nudged my shoulder.

"Move your butt over, I am sittin' down now. You tell me everything, boy."

With yet another sigh, I let it all spill. Travis, Rhonda, the job...the ultimatum Morgan had given me before she walked out my door. The fiery anger that had kept me inactive for so long had dimmed a little, only sparking as I recaptured that moment in my dressing room.

I swallowed. "She said she'd spent her entire life looking after people, and for once she wanted someone to look after her. I watched her walk out that door, Mama, and I wanted to follow her so bad, but I couldn't. I was mad at her for putting me in that position...and how can I possibly do what she wants me to?"

Mama didn't even wait a beat before giving me her opinion. "Boy, you a damn fool."

I rolled my eyes and dropped my head into my hands.

She gripped my arm, urging me to look at her. "You had a love worth fighting for."

"It's not just about love, Mama." I dropped my hands and turned to her.

The stern gaze I'd faced before fell away, her brown eyes softening with a smile.

"Sean, life is all about love. Loving God, loving each other. It's that simple, boy. We raised you that way; how can you forget so easily?"

"It's not simple, Mama." I gently flicked her hand off my arm. "I can't just sacrifice everything I've worked for. I like where I am. I love my job. I love my life."

Mama's lips dipped into a frown. "Which is why you sittin' here on my sofa looking like your dog just died. You know, 'cause you love your life."

I threaded my fingers together and squeezed until it hurt.

"You don't think I know what it's like to sacrifice for love?" Mama's voice was quiet. "Your daddy and I were a checkerboard couple in the 60s. Now, yes, it was the late sixties, but that don't mean it wasn't hard. Me in Alabama, your daddy in New Orleans. Prejudice was ripe, believe you me. Now, I know persecution. I lived it."

"Mama, this isn't about color."

"It doesn't matter what the fight is, baby. If it's love, you fight for it. The day your daddy chose me over his inheritance was the day he became a man. He wanted me, Sean, and he fought to have me. I fought to have him. I am grateful for that every day." Her fingers flicked in the air the way they always did when she got going like this. "I ain't sayin' life been easy every day of the week or nothin'. But we been happy. We had each other. Our life was built on a foundation of love, and we will never regret the choices we made."

My leg bobbed as I swallowed back a quick reply. I pushed my tongue over my bottom teeth and drew in a breath.

"But I've worked so hard to be where I am today. Standing up for her could... There's so many chances and opportunities coming my way right now. This has done wonders for me. They're asking me to re-sign for Season Two. *Superstar* is a major hit; I mean, there might be an Emmy in my future!"

"You wouldn't even be doing the show if you hadn't met her!" Mama clicked her tongue, waving her hand at me. "Your mysterious karaoke girl. She put you on this path. Now, I ain't sayin' I'm not proud of you, because baby, I am." She squeezed my arm again, but with a smile this time. "But who you gonna take to the Emmys, huh? You gonna walk your mama down the red carpet? Is that what you want? Or would you rather have some gorgeous blonde on your arm, legs the length of the Empire State Building, eyes brown like milk chocolate." She shook her head with a grin. "You know, it was your daddy's eyes that stole my heart. Eyes tell you everything, Sean. They fueled from the soul. All you need to know is in the eyes."

She turned to me then, gently grasping my face. "I will be forever grateful that you got your daddy's eyes. Bright blue and filled with all the possibilities in the world."

I softly squeezed her forearms, my expression lighting with a smile.

"But they been looking sad lately, boy, and no Oscar or Emmy or Golden Globe is gonna make them shine. Those things ain't important, and they certainly can't give you babies."

I twisted out of her grasp. "Come on, Mama. Don't you have enough grandkids already?"

"You don't think I'm serious? Sean, that girl was gold, and the way you talkin' you don't even deserve her. I can see you miss her, don't you be lyin' to me." She tapped the side of her head. "The eyes. They tell me everythin'."

Hers bulged wide as she stared at me, and I had to give in and admit it.

"Yeah, I miss her, Mama. I thought it'd get easier with time, but the feelings aren't going away."

Mama collected my hands with a soft sigh, rubbing her thumbs over my knuckles. "Baby, no matter what you choose to do, I will love you and I will be loyal, and proud of you forever. Winning an Emmy would certainly go over well with ladies at the bridge club, but I'll be more proud to tell 'em my boy's gettin' married...and so will your daddy."

I gave her a sidelong glance.

"Where is Pop?" I eased my fingers out of her grasp and looked behind me.

"He gone to collect the grandbabies. The little terrorists are spending the night. Lord, help me."

I chuckled. She could only be talking about Morris's kids, the Three Stooges, and the biggest troublemakers this world had ever seen.

"Well, good luck with that. I might split before I get caught in their tornado." I stood from the couch, straightening my shirt.

"Sean, please listen good now." Her voice and gaze were so earnest, I couldn't do anything but follow her command. "Your career could rise or fall any day. You in the entertainment business and there ain't no guarantees, but you fight for your woman, and she will be there for the rest of your life, no matter what job you have."

I swallowed, bereft of words as I gazed down at the woman who'd raised me, showered me with unconditional love, and coached me through life...was still coaching me through life. Her words rang with a truth that was impossible to ignore.

I thought back to the contract on Rhonda's desk, questions and arguments warring within me. My mind flashed with images of accepting an award on stage...and having no one to dedicate my speech to.

"Thanks, Mama." I bent down to kiss her cheek and skipped out before she could say any more.

I felt heavy, weighted down by life-changing decisions I didn't want to make.

If only there was a way I could have it all.

But I knew I couldn't. Sacrifices needed to be made, and now I had to decide which ones I was willing to live with.

THIRTY-TWO

MORGAN

It was nearing midnight by the time I pulled onto the Strip. I had no idea if my mother still worked at the Tropicana, but it was a starting point.

Glancing at the car clock, I cringed. Did I really have the energy to go hunting tonight? I was being held together by caffeine and terror. I knew sleep would be impossible, but if I wanted to function when I found her, I did need to rest.

Pulling into the Tropicana, I grabbed my purse and headed for the lobby. My fingers wouldn't stop trembling, and I'm sure the lady at check-in noticed, especially after she told me exactly which lounge Roxanne Rivera sang in. I couldn't believe she'd stayed in the same place for so long.

The receptionist put me up in one of the cheapest rooms. I didn't need much. As soon as I saw my mother and said my piece, I was out of here anyway.

Pushing the keycard into the door, I dumped on the round table the cheap Las Vegas T-shirt and yoga pants I'd just purchased, and walked to the window. The lights were bright and dazzling, the city alive no matter what the hour. I should have been out in it, walking the Strip and soaking in the atmosphere.

Wrapping my arms around myself, I let my mind wander back to Derek's office and his fingers touching me. Nausea swirled in my stomach, making me lurch for the bathroom. I clung to the bowl and let the endless cups of coffee spill out of me, filling the bowl with a brown stench that made me want to retch all over again. I clung to the porcelain, resting my head against it as those dry, heaving sobs punched out of my chest.

How had it come to this?

Sniffing, I pushed myself up, grabbing a glass of water and trying to swill the filth out of my mouth. Turning for the shower, I pushed the spray to scalding as I shakily wrenched off my work clothes. I knew I couldn't wash away my mistakes, but I wanted to. I wanted to scrub my skin until every finger and tongue that had every touched me was wiped away. I wanted to be clean, fresh, untainted...new.

*****

I didn't feel fresh or new as I sat in the lounge bar. My finger tapped my arm as I waited for the singer to come on stage. She was doing an afternoon shift, singing a little jazz to entertain the drinkers who were taking a break from whatever table they'd thrown their money onto.

I had barely slept. My eyes felt gritty and sore. My skin was still raw and pink from my burning shower. My frantic sudsing had done nothing to dispel the malaise roiling within me.

I felt so far from inner peace it was almost comical.

Trying to sound upbeat on the phone as I lied to Dad about my whereabouts was nearly impossible. I couldn't believe he bought it. As if Derek would ask me to do a business trip to San Diego. The guy barely had enough clients to stay afloat, but Dad didn't need to know that...and he certainly didn't need the truth, either.

He'd tried so hard never to criticize Mom in front of us, but I could see it. She'd cut him, butchered him, and he'd never recovered. It had been eight years, and I'd never seen him go on one date. The guy had dedicated himself to his work and us girls. That was the only thing that had gotten him through.

"Hello, everyone."

A tendon in my neck pinged tight at my mother's husky voice. She introduced herself and then began to sing "Come Away With Me" by Norah Jones, her sultry sound rising over the small audience. It was unfortunately beautiful. I wanted her to suck. I wanted the audience to be hissing at her, throwing rotten tomatoes, not smiling and nodding at the pure tone that stretched across the room and nestled inside me.

I closed my arms, pinching my biceps until they hurt.

That sound was so familiar. She used to sing me to sleep as a child, brushing the locks of hair off my face, her sad voice covering me.

She still looked the same as I remembered, maybe a touch older...and thinner. Definitely more glamorous. Her thick makeup was hiding her wrinkles, her fake lashes making her eyes large and bright. They were turquoise and vibrant, just like Jody's. The sequined dress she wore fit her perfectly, highlighting her curves in all the right places. She was obviously going for an elegant lady from the fifties. All she needed was a white dress and an air vent, and she'd be Marilyn Monroe.

She'd probably love it if she knew I was thinking that.

Air shot through my nose as the urge to run skittered down my legs. I dug my heels into the carpet and made myself stay.

It took thirty minutes for her to finish her set. I was a shaking wreck as I rose from the table and approached the stage. She didn't see me coming. Her back was to me as she chatted with the pianist.

"Roxanne."

She glanced over her shoulder, her body going still.

I held my breath as I waited for her to fully turn and face me. Eventually she spun, a soft smile growing on her lips. Holy crap, I was staring at an older version of Jody. It stole my breath for a second.

Her vibrant gaze traveled over me, her brow wrinkling at my Vegas sweats and high heels. I didn't have it in me to put my work clothes back on. They were currently shoved into a waste paper basket in my hotel room, never to be worn again.

My mom blinked at tears as she stepped down from the stage.

"Morgan." She reached out for me, her arms stretched wide.

I moved out of her way and folded my arms across my chest.

She bobbed her head and gave me an understanding smile.

"Do you want to sit?" She pointed to a table behind me.

"No, I'm not staying long."

"What are you doing here?"

"I needed to see you...to tell you—" I swallowed.

"Tell me what?" she asked after my pregnant pause.

I licked my bottom lip, my angry words sitting in my mouth and just not going anywhere. Why couldn't I unleash my fury? She deserved it! Tears stung my eyes, no doubt brought on by her gushy expression.

I frowned, ordering them away. Lifting my chin, I gazed down at my mother and opened my mouth.

"How could you do it? Just walk away like that; do you have no soul?"

Her face crumpled, her rosebud lips disappearing as she bit them together. Placing her arm gently on my elbow, she guided me to a corner of the room, behind the grand piano.

I flicked her off me and stared down at her, impatiently waiting for my explanation.

"I couldn't stay, Mister; it was killing me."

Mister. The only person in the world to ever call me that. My middle name was the same as hers, Roxanne, making my initials MR...mister. She'd thought it was a very smart and funny nickname; I had too, until she left and I banned anyone from ever calling me that again.

"I was going to bed at night and wishing I wouldn't wake up in the morning, because I didn't think I could live through another day." She wrung her hands. "And it wasn't you or Jody or your dad. I just..." She pointed at her chest. "I couldn't do it anymore. I'd given up my dream to mother you and I just...ran out of steam."

She shrugged as if her explanation was enough.

"Ran out of steam? You selfish bitch!" I wanted to slap her then, crack my palm right across her face, but heads turned our way, and I didn't want to be escorted out of here before she'd heard me out. "You turned me into a mother at the age of fourteen! Sacrifice? I had to give up everything to look after Jody and Dad while you swanned off here to make your dreams come true. You know what happened to my dreams?" My voice hitched. "They ended up in the gutter, and now I've just quit my second job this year, I have no life, no boyfriend, and I hate myself...and it's your fault. You turned me into this. You walked out on a family who needed you!"

"Hey, I waited, okay. I waited until I knew you could handle it, and it's not like I didn't tell you guys where I was. You could've come and gotten me, tried to win me back."

I scoffed, pressing my fingers into my forehead and wanting to scream.

"You were the adult. You were the one who was supposed to look after us! Don't put your shit on me. Win you back? Why would we? You left us!"

My final shout silenced the bar. I didn't care. I didn't care if every eye in the room was gazing across that piano. Shouldn't they know who was singing for them? She wasn't some sweet-faced angel with a voice like heaven. She was a turncoat traitor who had walked out on her husband and kids. Left them high and dry so she could sing in some sleazy bar.

"I know it was selfish," she said quietly. "I really have no good excuses for what I did. I just decided that it was time for me to start looking after myself." She nibbled on her lip. "You know, your dad was a really good man, but I don't think we would have married if we hadn't had you. I just saw your face and knew I needed to love you and feed you...until you could look after yourself."

"I was fourteen," I whispered brokenly.

"You've always been strong and confident, looking after those around you. You were a better mother than I could ever be. You remember what chaos our house used to be in. It used to drive you crazy."

"Yeah." I nodded. "Sometimes it did, but I would have taken chaos every day of the week over the silence, the emptiness that followed your departure. I tried to do a good job." I cleared my throat. "But I failed. I failed Jody...I failed myself."

"I'm sure you didn't." She gave me a kind smile.

I wanted to tell her that Jody was pregnant, that she was turning into her, but I couldn't do it. I wouldn't let that happen. Jody had me. That was the difference, and there was no way in hell I was abandoning her, no matter what she wanted to do with her baby.

Mom rubbed her arm, playing with the sequins on her dress sleeve as she smiled at me.

"You still dancing?"

My jaw clenched as I shook my head. "I gave that up when you left. There was no time to pursue it."

Her brows bunched together and she looked to the floor. "I was hoping you'd apply for that high school."

I shook my head.

"I used to love watching you, Mister. I lived for your performances; they were like a light in the darkness."

"Obviously not a very bright one."

She looked hurt by my sarcastic reply, and I didn't want to care, but it stung. My words, her expression. I turned away from it.

"You used to light up the stage. You know how there's always one dancer you can't take your eyes off. That was you." She pointed at me. "You were that girl." Her eyes grew distant as if reliving one of my recitals. "It was the only time you'd ever really let your emotions show. It's like you gifted a part of your soul to the audience when you danced. It always brought tears to my eyes."

My throat clogged, the lump too big to swallow.

"I don't expect you to ever forgive what I did to you. I know I don't deserve it." Her smile was sad. "But I hate the idea that my betrayal would stop you from doing something you loved. I know what it's like to try living a lie. It makes you do things you're not proud of." She blinked at tears. "Please, Morgan, don't give up your dreams. Don't let hurt and anger and bitterness hold you back anymore. You have to let go."

She reached for my hand, and for some bizarre reason, I let her take it.

"No matter what you become or where you end up in life, never stop dancing. It's who you are."

My hand felt limp within hers, but I forced my fingers to squeeze back. "I forgive you," I whispered. "I don't feel like it right this second, but you're right. I need to let go. I need to be free...of you. So I forgive you, and I'll keep saying it, every day, until I believe it. Because you cannot own me anymore."

Her expression held a mixture of pride and shame. As much as I didn't want her to be, she was my mother. Her genes inspired my dancing and Jody's singing. She'd given me this precious gift that in the past had given me so much joy. I'd let her steal it. I'd given her the power, and it was time to take it back.

"Goodbye, Mom." I leaned forward and kissed her cheek, walking away before she could say anything more.

As I stepped out of the darkness and into the sunlight, I felt it...a stirring in my soul. Like a quiet calm was meandering through my being, telling me it was going to be okay. It was a far cry from inner peace, but it was there, it was new...and I felt like it could grow.

THIRTY-THREE

MORGAN

Part of me wanted to call Grandma Deb and tell her I'd done it, but the bigger part of me wasn't ready to speak yet, so I wandered to my car and started the four-hour trek back to Pasadena. As much as I wanted to click my heels and mutter, "There's no place like home," the trip did me good. It gave me time to think, to breathe.

My knuckles remained white for most of the drive, but it was a different tension that ran through my body now. The future was still a massive question mark. I was once again jobless, single, and still living at home with my dad, but I didn't have to stay that way forever. I could move forward. I had to move forward, and this time I had to stop settling for something to fill the gap. I needed to hold out for what was right for me.

I flicked from one radio station to the next as I drove home, too agitated to listen to any one song. My mom's comments about dancing still lingered. I wanted them to make me angry, but they had somehow awoken a deep yearning inside of me. Maybe I should look at taking classes again, get fit and start doing a little choreography like I used to. My teacher used to always compliment what I'd come up with. I wondered what Ms. Finnermore was doing now?

Was it worth looking her up?

My phone started ringing, and I rummaged for it in my bag.

It was Isabella.

I answered on the fifth ring.

"Oh good, you're there." She sounded out of breath. "Where are you?"

"Just driving." I cleared my throat.

"Okay, cool, well I'm running a little behind, you know how it is, so can you meet me?"

Damn. I'd totally forgotten I was hanging out with her tonight. "I—I don't want to come to the studios."

"Oh no, you don't have to. I want you to meet me in Huntington Park."

I hesitated. "What's in Huntington Park?"

"An apartment I want you to check out."

I bit the inside of my cheek, keeping my eyes on the road. "What are you up to?"

"Nothing. It used to belong to my grandmother before she died, and I'm trying to decide what to do with it. I want your advice."

"I'm not an interior designer."

"I know, I just really value your opinion with this kind of stuff. Please, just meet me there."

I frowned, wanting to come up with some

excuse about being too tired. I was. I felt wrung-out and jaded.

"Please. For me?"

"Okay, fine."

"Sweet! There's a spare key under the green pot around by the back door. If I'm not there, just let yourself in, and I won't be far behind you." She rattled off the address, and I pulled to the side of the road, noting it into my GPS once she'd hung up.

I clicked my tongue and pulled back into the traffic, following the GPS instructions until I reached Malabar Street. I found the right number and parked outside what looked like an abandoned building.

In spite of my misgivings, I slid out of my car and headed for the back door, hunting around for a green pot. I found it easily and tipped it up, patting the concrete for a key. The glass door rattled as I unlocked it, but finally jiggled open.

It was dark in the stairwell, so I took care and grappled around for a light switch once I reached the top. I was expecting an apartment; what I got was a dance studio.

An old, dusty dance studio.

I sucked in my breath as I eyed the dirty ceiling-high mirrors and the barre attached to the walls.

Memories of a different dance studio flooded me, all good and filled with a warm fuzziness I wanted to swim in. Dropping my bag to the floor, I slowly stepped into the room, running my fingers along the dusty wood.

A stereo sat in the corner of the room, perched on a round table. I headed across to it, kicking off my heels and flicking them into the corner. I had no idea if it still worked, but I could see fingerprints in the dust, which meant someone must have used it recently. No doubt Isabella.

I leaned down to fiddle with the buttons and managed to turn on the CD. A steady beat pulsed out of the speakers attached to each ceiling corner. She must have been checking that they still worked.

I closed my eyes as the pulse of David Guetta's "Titanium" whispered through me. Then Sia started singing. I breathed in the words, tipping my head back as my foot tapped. I lifted my arm in a slow arc, raising it above my head and bending back as if dodging bullets that couldn't hurt me.

My body swung around, moving away from the table and dropping to the floor in a controlled spin. Sliding to the side, I stretched across the floor, slowing rising to the beat and letting the song take charge. It moved through me, my limbs and body dancing of their own accord as I let go.

A bubble rose in my chest, bursting with sound and light and freedom. It shot through me, electrifying my body with bliss. I didn't need oblivion when I felt like this.

My hunt was over.

I didn't need an edge. I needed to live and breathe every beat of this song.

I ran across the studio and fell to my knees, sliding across the old wooden floor, my body lost in the pleasure of the dance. I felt strong. In charge. In control.

I felt bulletproof.

Sia's voice stretched over the word *titanium*, and I arched my body to match, rising tall from the floor. The beat rose, slow and steady, building to a quick pace that had my body spinning in a frenzy until Sia's voice died away, and I was left in the silence.

I glanced to the mirror, taking in my final pose. My chest was heaving, breaths shooting out of my nose in rapid succession and then I noticed something.

My lips parted, my forehead wrinkling as I reached for my face.

Tears.

I licked at the dribble rolling past my mouth.

"Tears don't achieve anything," I whispered as my eyes swelled with more. I closed them, letting the water cascade down my cheeks. It wasn't a torrent; there were no heaving sobs, just a steady stream of tears that I had held at bay for probably far too long.

I brushed them off my face, sniffing and trying to pull myself together.

"That was amazing."

Isabella's soft voice made me spin. She was standing in the doorway, leaning against the frame, her arms folded across her chest and a soft smile playing on her lips.

"Hi." I swiped at my tears, pulling my body tall.

"You don't have to stop." She pushed off the frame with her shoulder and walked toward me. "It's a good release."

"The dancing or the crying?"

"Both." She grinned.

"I haven't done either in a really long time. I mean, I guess I've always danced, but..."

"Not like that." Isabella shook her head. "That was... you really let go. It was so...powerful." She touched her chest. "You moved me, chica."

I snorted out a soft laugh.

"Which is why I know I'm making the right decision."

"What do you mean?" I wiped my face for what I hoped was the last time. Tears seriously did not suit me. Maybe they were good for me, but I certainly didn't enjoy them.

Isabella stuck her hands in the pockets of her cargo pants and swung back on her sneakered feet.

"I want to offer you a job."

"A job?"

"Yeah." She looked around. "See, I used to come here every day as a kid. Mom worked so Grandma would bring me here and I'd watch her teach all these little kids and dream of the day when I'd choreograph my own dances. She made me who I am. I credit it all to her."

"I know. You must miss her all the time."

"I do." Isabella's face crested with pain. "And that's why I can't keep using my job as an excuse to ignore this." She raised her arms and pointed around the studio. "This place used to thrive, but then she got sick and I was away at college, dancing and carving out my future." She shrugged. "Then she died and there was no one to keep it going. I was too heartbroken to even think about coming in here. I couldn't believe she left it all to me." Isabella gazed around the old space, a nostalgic smile cresting over her lips. "But it's time. I guess I've just been waiting for the right person to help me."

"And you think I'm it?"

"I know you're it." She scratched the top of her head. "You're talented, passionate, organized, you have a degree in business that has gone to total waste. You're intelligent, confident and I think that you, and only you, can take this place and turn it into a great little school."

"You want me to run a dance school?"

She looked me straight in the eye, a little smirk playing on her lips. "You betchya."

"I'm—I've never done anything like that."

"Me neither, but you've got what it takes, Morgan. Come on, can you honestly say your current job is fulfilling?"

I pressed my lips together and looked to the floor.

"This could be amazing! We'll clean it up and get it ready to go. We can hire an extra teacher and just start with a few after-school jazz classes. There are two studios." She pointed across the hall. "And the performing arts schools are busting with students who want to teach and get more experience. We can totally get something going. We could have little concerts for the parents to attend. It'd be great. I've got all these ideas, but I just don't have the time or know-how to actually make them happen. I need you, Morgan. I need your help."

I looked across the space, scratching my arm and trying to think it through.

"Oh yeah, and there's a little apartment studio-type thing upstairs, so you could live here too, if you wanted. Free of charge."

My nose twitched as I stepped to the barre, running my fingers along it. "Would there be a wage?"

"Of course. Grandma left me a little nest egg to go with the studio, so there's enough to pay a small wage, and then as soon as this place is making a profit we can increase it. The place is freehold, so it's not like we have mortgage repayments to deal with."

"How long's it been sitting empty like this?"

"About five years. Mom's been trying to convince me to sell it, but I just can't do it. I need to keep Grandma's legacy going, you know?"

"Yeah, that's cool." I leaned against the barre, a quiver of excitement whistling through me. I could do this. I knew I could. It'd be hard, and I'd feel like I was drowning until I got my head around everything, but I could do it.

And the best part was...I actually wanted to.

"Okay." I nodded. "Okay, let's do this."

"Really?" Isabella jumped to her tiptoes and let out a squeal before running toward me for a hug.

"Thank you!" She stepped back, holding me at arm's length. "You are not going to regret this."

I grinned with her and nodded. "You know what, I don't think I am."

She let out another squeal, and I pulled her in for another hug.

It felt good.

Like I was doing something right for me.

The tendril of calm whispering through my soul pulsed a loud beat, reminding me that it was still there and ready to grow.

THIRTY-FOUR

SEAN

It had been four days since my chat with Mama, and I couldn't stop thinking about it. I rested my feet on the glass coffee table and pressed my head back into the black leather couch. When I first moved into my place, the silence was a gift. No screaming grandkids tearing around the furniture, no brothers debating whatever topic was hot, no sisters squabbling or squealing over their latest news. I'd relished the peace, the calm.

But now...

It was unnerving. After working such long hours, I would have thought a day at home on my own would refresh me, recharge my batteries, but it was just plain suffocating, and there was only so much screen time I could stomach.

Pop had rung me last night, to check in, but filming hadn't been going well and I couldn't chat. Since my big 'fess up, I knew they were both worried about me. I should have been popping down for lunch, but I couldn't move.

I was tired, down to my core. Good sleep was a thing of the past, my restless mind unable to switch off.

I gazed at the contract sitting on the glass near my feet. I still hadn't signed it. I hadn't even read the whole thing through; every time I started, the restlessness grew to an insane itch.

My eyes had skimmed the amount they were offering me, and it was near double what they'd paid me this season.

But was that enough to re-sign?

In the back of my head, I'd been assuming that I'd finish out the season and figure out what I really wanted to do. I could win Morgan back over the summer break and...then what?

The decisions were now on my doorstep, and I couldn't decide what to do. In my gut, I knew I had to go one way or the other and live with the fallout.

So it came down to the simple question...what could I live without?

The doorbell rang.

Part of me wanted to ignore it, but Lisa had told us our scripts would be arriving by courier today, and I needed to get on with learning my lines.

We would be starting rehearsals for the last episode soon.

Jumping up, I placed my beer down next to that wretched contract and vaulted over the couch.

A courier stood at the door, envelope in hand.

"Sign here."

I grabbed the pen and mangled my name over the screen. It was impossible to write on those things.

"Thanks." I nodded.

The courier gave me a shy, flirtatious smile, her cheeks blooming with color. I forced a grin before shutting the door.

Heading back to the living room, I tapped the envelope on my fingers, feeling a CD within it. That'd be the songs we had to learn. Ripping it open, I emptied it onto the dining room table, putting the CD on to play while I read over the script.

With the remote in one hand and the script in the other, I sat down and started reading.

Sasha was back, returning after her stint on the road. She and Harley meet up in the hallway at school, and the second he sees her, he knows...he can't live without her anymore.

I swallowed, the text on the page going blurry.

Blinking, I cleared my throat and forced myself to keep reading, pausing to play the songs. There was a pretty awesome all-cast number in the middle that I was sure Isabella would have fun choreographing.

I paused the CD and kept flicking through the pages, my face bunching into a frown as I neared the end of the script.

HARLEY: The truth is, Sash, I don't care what it costs me. I don't want to live without you anymore.

SASHA: You could lose everything. You love this job.

HARLEY: I love you more. This place without you is cold and lonely, and I'd rather not be here at all if I know you're with someone else. We should be together. You know it. I know it.

SASHA: But it'll be a fight.

HARLEY: It's love, baby. That's always worth fighting for.

Harley sings Fight For You.

With my heartbeat on hold, I pressed play and "Fight For You" by Jason Derulo began to play. I closed my eyes as the lyrics washed over me, soaking into my skin. I could imagine the kind of dance Isabella would have planned for us. The difference was, the only person I could picture in my arms was Morgan.

Squeezing my eyes tight, I gripped the script in my hand, the pages creasing before I threw them into the air.

They showered down around me, floating onto the furniture and over the floor.

Shit!

I was a fool.

I was a coward...and that stopped right now, because my karaoke girl was worth fighting for.

THIRTY-FIVE

MORGAN

I propped the mop against the wall and stood back to survey our progress. The floor was looking pretty damn good. I wanted it to shine more, but it would once Cole had brought back the wax.

I glanced at my watch, calculating how long it might take him. He should be back within the next 20 minutes, and I'd get to work on it right away. By tonight, this studio would be ready to go. I'd start on the next one tomorrow.

It had been a really long week, but the music had blasted the whole time, making cleaning up this place a pleasure.

I wanted it open-able by the end of the month. Isabella had already had a few sign-ups. We were starting out small, but with a little word of mouth, we'd grow.

She'd asked me to teach the first children's class that came in, which I nervously agreed to. As soon as *Superstar* finished filming in a couple of weeks, we would open up high school and adult classes. We were starting with jazz and hip hop, but hoping to branch into some of the old-school stuff eventually and offer up swing and ballroom dancing. I just had to track down some teachers. Our brainstorming session last week had been huge and totally inspiring. I had a feeling we'd be booming in no time.

I grinned.

Folding my arms, I watched my two minions cleaning the mirrors. It was a massive job. Ella was up on a chair, trying to reach the top. I'd have to get that later. She was such a shorty. I chuckled, walking over to help her.

Jody was down on her knees, her belly resting on her thighs as she sprayed and wiped. Brushing her hand over her forehead, she flicked some stray tendrils off her face.

She was looking tired today.

The baby was due in four weeks, and she was getting to that awkward waddling stage. She looked amazing if you asked me, but she would vehemently deny it when I called her beautiful.

Thankfully, she was healthy. The baby was growing fine, and the only thing Jody was really suffering from pregnancy-wise was heartburn.

She used the barre to lift herself up and pressed the side of her tummy with a frown.

"Baby kicking?" I asked.

"Baby freaking break dancing. The kid won't stop." She shook her head, but I noticed a small smile graze her lips. She wanted to be grumpy and bitter, but she actually had a light glow about her.

Not that I'd tell her that. When it came to her situation, it was better not to say anything.

I reached out to take the cloth off her but stopped when Ella squealed, "I love this song!"

She jumped down from her chair and slid over to the stereo, pumping up the volume and shimmering back over the floor as Beyoncé belted out "Single Ladies".

I threw my head back with a laugh and pulled Jody over to join her.

The three of us lined up in the mirror and copied Beyoncé's moves, singing along as we went. Jody, in spite of her shape, was awesome, dancing like the natural talent she was.

The music flowed over me, electrifying my muscles as I gave into it.

When the song came to a finish, we held our poses for a beat and then looked at each other in the mirror and all started laughing. I wrapped my arm around my bestie and kissed the top of her head, and then glanced over at Jody.

Her smile dropped away as her face bunched with a frown.

"You okay?" I moved around Ella and placed my hand on Jody's back as she bent forward and winced.

"Yeah, just pains."

Rubbing circles over her back, I murmured my sympathies.

"I'm gonna go lie down. My body is so not cut out for those types of moves anymore."

I stepped back with a smile. "It will be again. Not long to go now."

"You've seen my ass, right? It's the size of Mother Russia." She put on a Russian accent, flicking her hands in the air. "I can't ever imagine having a perky butt again, let alone dancing like some sexy young thing."

Ella and I both giggled.

"It *will* happen." Ella kissed her cheek and guided her toward the door. "Go lie down, Fatty." She winked.

Jody tried to throw her an evil glare but broke into a tired smile as she backed out of the room. I turned the music down and heard her clomping up the last few stairs. Cole had pulled a mattress up there for me a few nights ago. It was supposedly for me, but Jody had used it twice already.

I frowned.

"She's okay. She's just pregnant and tired." Ella gave me a sympathetic smile.

"Yeah, I know. I just hate that she's in this position."

"Me too, but she'll get through this."

"I hope she can make the right decision when the time comes."

"The adoption thing?"

I nodded. "We've managed to fill in most of the paperwork, but I haven't submitted it yet. I must get onto that." I made a mental note to call the agency and make sure I had everything in order before sending it all in.

"You're worried she'll regret giving it up?"

"No, I'm worried she'll keep it and then regret it...fourteen years later." I raised my eyebrows.

"She's not your mom and she has us. There's a big difference, Morgan. Your mom had no one, except your dad and a very judgmental mother-in-law."

I frowned.

"Come on, you have to admit that Grandma Deb has changed a lot over the years. She must have been a total battleaxe when your mom was first on the scene."

I had to give in with a small nod. It was true. Grandma Deb had grown in her old age, wisdom making her softer side bloom.

"Jody is surrounded by support. We're not going to let her down."

"No, we're not." I crossed my arms and straightened my back, more determined than ever to protect my kid sister. "I just wish I could have protected her from this."

Ella shrugged. "It was Jody's choice. You can't control what happens to her. Just like she can't control what that douche bag decided to do." Ella frowned. "Too worried about his career to fight for his kid? Seriously!"

That familiar wave of sadness washed over me as I thought of Sean's stance on his career. I dropped my gaze to the floor. Ella must have noticed, because I saw her grimace out of the corner of my eye.

"I'm sorry," she whispered. "I wish we could make people do what we want them to. Life would be so much easier."

"I guess." I shrugged. "But then it wouldn't mean anything, would it?"

Ella tipped her head, her eyes searching my face.

I flicked my hands in the air. "If the father of Jody's kid ever did man-up and arrive on her doorstep, she'd need to know it was because he really wanted to be there, not because she was making him."

It didn't take a genius to figure out that I was actually talking about Sean.

I recrossed my arms. "Sometimes people do things that hurt you, but you just have to let it go and move forward. You can't let other people's actions own you." I replayed the words in my head, vowing to say them with more confidence next time, to speak them until I believed them with my whole being.

"I don't know what it is about you." Ella's lips

tipped with a grin. "I thought at first it was this studio and the chance to do a job you'll no doubt love, but something else is going on. You were strong before. No, wait; you were tough, now you're strong. I don't know if I'm explaining that very well, but..." Her head tipped to the side, her eyes narrowing as she looked at me. "What happened to you last week? You know, before you quit your job."

A smile flashed across my face, but I quickly swallowed it down. "Maybe I'll tell you about it some time."

Ella's face crested with worry. "You're still my bulletproof lady though, right? Nothing's gonna beat you?"

My smile reappeared, the calm within me blossoming, reminding me it wasn't going anywhere. "Ella, by the time I work my way through all this, I'm gonna be freaking titanium."

I winked at her perplexed expression and then jumped as the music changed.

"Oh! I've been working on a dance for this. Thought it might be fun to do with the kids."

I ran into the center of the room and beckoned Ella to my side, holding my position until the beat kicked in.

Britt Nicole started singing "Ready or Not", and my limbs moved in quick, sharp moves that were crisp, clear, and strong. Ella copied me, grinning as the words pumped out of the speakers. I had kept the steps simple so the kids could pick it up quickly. I watched us move in the mirror, a smile pulling my cheeks wide. The song was all about shining a light, and that's how I felt as I spun and moved across the floor.

I was a beacon, and I wanted the young dancers to feel that way too. I wanted them to know that oblivion and darkness were not things to strive for.

They needed to shine and capture every moment.

The song had a quick finish, and we held our poses for a second, out of breath and grinning like monkeys.

A slow clap started in the doorway, and we spun to see Cole smiling at us, his blue eyes aimed at his girl. "I think that's about the sexiest thing I've seen all day."

Ella put her hands on her hips. "Sexier than me getting out of bed this morning? I am highly offended."

Her sweet giggle turned into a hearty laugh as he raced toward her and scooped her into a hug. She wrapped her legs around his middle and smiled at me over his shoulder. He spun her around and planted kisses on her neck, which just made her giggle more.

She pulled back and rested her arms on his shoulders, gazing down at him with a look that could only be described as pure love.

I told myself to turn away and let them have their private moment, but I couldn't. As their lips met for a kiss that said it all, a pain shot through my chest, an aching throb that continued to haunt me...no matter how far down the *forgive my mother* road I traveled.

Would I ever get what Ella and Cole had? A love to last the ages?

I instantly thought of Sean.

None of my other ex-boyfriends ever surfaced when I asked those questions. It was always him. He'd been different from the rest, captured me in a way no one else could.

Maybe that was why it was so hard to let him go.

Maybe that was why the fact he'd let me walk out that door killed me so bad.

THIRTY-SIX

SEAN

Rhonda was waiting for me after dance rehearsal. She stood outside my dressing room, tapping her long nails on the back of her phone.

"Hey." I rubbed the towel over my face and paused beside her. "I thought we were meeting later."

"I know. I was just driving by and wanted to pop in and talk to Ashlee, and I also came to pick up the contract, have you sign—"

"Wait." I raised my hand. "Why were you talking to Ashlee?"

"I wanted to ask her to accompany you to the Saito event. She said yes, so I'll find out what she's wearing and then get the tailor to whip you up something to match." She unlocked her iPad and tapped in a few details.

"I don't want to go with her."

She looked up at me and rolled her eyes with a sigh. "Well, you could have said something to me earlier."

"I didn't think you'd be arranging it for me."

"Oh please, I arrange everything for you. You know I'm in charge of your life."

I didn't smile at her cheeky grin, Isabella's words taunting me.

Who's feeding you this horseshit?

"So who do you want to go with then?" Rhonda ran a finger over her eyebrow and looked at me expectantly.

"Morgan." I swallowed. "I want to take Morgan with me."

"Oh Sean, please tell me you guys aren't back together. I thought we'd dealt with this already. That's over now. You have to let it go."

"No, I don't." I flicked the towel over my shoulder. "I don't have to let her go, because she was the best damn thing that ever happened to me, and I let her walk out the fucking door. I was too blind to even see it coming." I huffed.

She swallowed, her eyes skittering the walls as she cleared her throat.

I frowned. "Look at me."

Meeting my gaze, she raised her eyebrows, going for innocent, but I saw it...in her eyes.

Mama was right. They did tell you everything.

"You saw it coming," I whispered.

"Huh? What are you talking about?"

"You knew." I crossed my arms. "You knew it was brewing, and you didn't warn me."

"Oh come on, surely you knew it was brewing. She was making all those demands, asking you to risk your career. She was completely out of line...and she knew it too. I told her to watch it."

My eyebrows bunched together. "You what? Did you talk again...after that time you showed up at her house?"

Rhonda pursed her lips.

"I thought you were inviting me to those meetings. What the hell did you say to her?"

My manager flicked her head to the side, looking away from me. "I might have suggested that she think about what's best for you."

"What's best for me."

"Yes, she was getting in the way of your career, and I—"

"You told me she misunderstood what you were saying, but that was a lie, wasn't it?"

Rhonda's casual shrug said it all.

"I should have listened to her, but no, I stupidly stood up for you!"

She gave me a swift glare.

"My love life is none of your business."

"Your *whole* life is my business, Sean Jaxon. I took you from a fresh-faced, clueless wonder and made you the king of *Superstar*. I saved your reputation. You would have been in the gutter after Miss Tripoli was done with you. You'd be nowhere if it wasn't for me."

I stepped into her space, anger coursing through me as I pointed at her. "You didn't even want me to take this role. It wasn't until I met Morgan that I insisted on it."

Rhonda pulled back from me, lifting her chin. "Yes, and aren't you glad I went along with it and made it work for you."

I shook my head, breaths punching out of my chest as my fingers curled into a fist.

"Face it, Sean. She was holding you back. You want to be famous? You have to make sacrifices."

I clicked my tongue, my jaw clenching tight as I

rubbed a hand over my head.

"Who gives a shit about fame...and money." I kicked the wall beside me. "It feels worthless without her. She made me happy, Rhonda. She cared about me, she inspired me, and all she wanted in return was for me to stand up for her." My gaze was black as I looked across at my manager. "But you told me not to."

"Of course I told you not to. It was the right thing to do. Travis would have made your life hell. He could have written you out of the show in a heartbeat. She was not worth that."

"Says you." I shook my head.

"I did what was best for you. I'm your manager; that's my job."

"I can't believe I just kept taking your word for it, trusting you with everything, and you completely stabbed me in the back."

She rolled her eyes. "I think you're being a touch dramatic."

I opened my mouth to say more, but she held up her hand to stop me.

"Look, enough is enough. We can finish this conversation later; you're due for a read-through in twenty minutes, and I doubt you want to go smelling as you are." She held out her hand. "Now, can you please give me the contract so at least I can cross that off my list for the day."

I frowned, stepping away from her.

"Sean, please, not again. Tell me you've signed it."

"I'm not signing anything."

"What?"

"Rhonda, this is over. I can't trust your word anymore. It's time I started looking after myself."

"What the hell are saying to me right now?"

"I'm saying you're fired."

"You can't fire me. We have a contract." Her

words were like sharp nettles, but I rose to meet them, returning her steely gaze with one of my own.

"Contracts aren't bulletproof. You can check with my lawyer if you like. And by the way, my agent and publicist, they're gonna come directly to me now. I was gonna discuss this all with you tonight, but after what you've just told me I can't wait. You're gone, Rhonda."

Her eyebrows arched high, disappearing beneath her bangs. "That's really how you want to play this? Fine." She shoved the iPad back into her bag and flicked the strap up onto her shoulder. "Don't think for a second this will be easy, little boy. I have more connections than you know what to do with."

"I'm not expecting it to be easy. I just want it to be right."

Her mouth opened and shut for a few minutes, shock stealing her words. Finally she huffed and spun on her heel, stomping down the hallway and muttering a string of curses. I tipped my head back and rested it against the wall, fear skittering through me.

What the hell was I doing?

An image of Morgan floated through my head. Those soft brown eyes, that cute little smirk she used to give me. I grinned, a deep yearning pushing inside of me.

It felt good to know I was on the road to getting her back.

All I could pray was that she'd take me.

Snatching the un-signed contract from my bag, I ran out of my dressing room and down the corridor.

Travis was just stepping out of his office when I arrived.

"Travis!"

He stopped and turned to face me, impatiently checking his watch.

"Can this wait? I'm heading out the door."

"No, it can't. We need to talk." I held up the contract. "And we need to talk now."

THIRTY-SEVEN

MORGAN

The studios were now ready to go. I had a class starting on Saturday morning, and I was near giddy with excitement and terror. Isabella had been around the night before, and we'd gone over all the last checks. Ella had also put me in touch with the guy who helped them market Reynold's, and I had spent most of my day with him.

He was getting the website up and running, putting together some flyer options for us to choose, and he'd also given me a contact list for all the local schools. It looked like I'd be spending a day on the phone tomorrow.

I wrinkled my nose, hating that idea but knowing it needed to be done.

Placing my hands on my hips, I stretched high, rising to my toes and leaning into an arabesque. As soon as the marketing guy had left, I'd changed into my tights and run through my class for Saturday. I had eight seven-to-ten-year-olds to work with, and I wanted to make sure I knew exactly what I was doing. That way, I could spend my energy on group management rather than worrying about what to do next.

The forty-five minute session was full, and my only concern was fitting it all in rather than having dead time at the end.

Skipping over to the stereo, I flicked through my iPod, wondering if I should go through the class one last time. It was only ten p.m., and I could always sleep the night here if I wanted to…. But the idea of doing my own thing for an hour before locking up was too tempting, so I selected my own playlist and decided to just dance.

I had put this list together last week, ten softer songs I could unwind to. Rather than sharp, static movements, these songs brought out the flow in my muscles. I moved like water across the floor, letting the tune lap against me.

"Is It You" by Cassie swirled around me and I jumped over the notes, landing softly and kicking my leg back for a simple spin.

I was trying to let the words wash over me and focus only on the steps, but I couldn't. They haunted me, digging into my heart and making me ask.

Moving to the mirror, I grabbed hold of the barre, gripping the wood tightly and asking, "Is it him? Is he the one worth waiting for?"

I sucked in a breath, tears welling in my eyes. I let them fall. Since finally letting go on the night I'd labeled *my titanium moment*, I'd found that letting the tears out actually hurt a lot less than I thought it would.

Crying didn't make me weak; it made me open, and that in turn gave me a strength I never knew existed.

The song ended and I brushed the tears from my face, looking at my reflection in the mirror and gasping.

I spun around and drank in the figure leaning against the doorframe.

Oh man, he looked good.

His long legs were fitted with a pair of dark jeans, and a white tank was stretched over his buff torso. And then there was that black jacket of his. I loved that jacket.

My eyes traveled the length of him, until they crested over his chocolate face and my heart melted.

"Sean," I whispered, pushing off the barre and walking toward him. "What are you doing here?"

And how did I feel about it?

Did I want to run into his arms? YES.

Did I want to pretend that three months of radio silence never happened? YES.

Could I?

No.

I swallowed, stopping in the middle of the room to wait out his answer.

He pushed off the frame with his shoulder, his shoes echoing in the studio as he slowly moved toward me. "I just came to ask you a couple of questions and..." He pressed his lips together and clicked his fingers before running a hand over his head. "Depending on your answers, I'll stay...or leave you alone."

I wanted to shrug as if I didn't care either way, but my shoulders were too tense to move, so I stood like a Terracotta Warrior awaiting my fate.

"Man, I'd forgotten how beautiful you are." His

words breathed into the room, stealing the air from my lungs. A little grin pushed at his broad lips. "Well, I hadn't forgotten, but now that I'm seeing you again...damn, woman, you fine."

His white teeth appeared and I couldn't help a grin.

He thought I was fine?

I could barely breathe around this guy! And that was plain frustrating, because part of me felt like I should be really mad at him. Another part felt this huge weight of caution. Why was he back? Had he come to woo me and then just let me go again?

I'd never felt so confused before, and it pissed me off that above all those important questions, the only thing I wanted to do was wrap my arms around him and pretend we'd never been apart.

I brushed my hands down my thighs, resisting the urge to jump for him.

"So." I licked my bottom lip. "What do you want to ask me?"

The second his mouth opened, my phone started ringing. I glanced at it on the table, willing it to shut off, but it might have been Jody.

"Just a sec." I held up my finger to Sean and raced over to the table, picking up my phone with a slight frown. "Hey, Cole. What's up?"

"It's happening."

"What's happening?"

"She was here, complaining about a tummy ache and then she just doubled over like someone had punched her in the gut and then whoosh."

"Whoosh?"

"Yeah, her waters broke, all over the floor. Grossed out quite a few customers, if I'm honest."

"Wait a second, Jody's waters broke?"

"Yeah, Ella's taking her to the hospital now."

"She's having the baby now? She's not due until next month!"

"Well, from the way she was wailing when she left, the baby really doesn't care what her due date is. It's coming. Now."

"Holy shit! I gotta go. I gotta..."

"Take a breath, Morgan." Cole chuckled. "Ella will keep an eye out for you."

"Okay, I'm leaving right now."

"Drive safe."

I hung up, panic sizzling through my body as I went through the checklist.

"Is everything okay?"

I spun at Sean's question, blinking twice to remind myself he wasn't an apparition.

"I'm sorry. I have to go, Jody's having her baby early and she needs me."

"No, I get it. You go."

Snatching up my purse, I dug out the keys and threw my phone inside. "Okay, I guess I'll see you..." I pointed at him, wondering if I'd just lost my chance.

"I can drive you if you like?"

"No!" I surprised us both with my snappy answer, but a small part of me wasn't ready to hear what he had to say and I certainly wouldn't be able to absorb it while racing to the hospital. Jody needed all my attention, and I couldn't give that to her with Sean around.

I swallowed and mouthed an apology.

A smile spread over his lips. "It's okay. I'll wait here."

"Okay." I nodded stupidly.

"You go." He pointed for the door.

"Okay. I'll go."

"Okay." He chuckled. "Morgan, go."

"Right." I grabbed my slip-on shoes at the door and shoved them on my feet, hopping down the stairs and trying to push Sean out of my brain.

My sister was having a baby.

She needed me, and that was all I could focus on right now.

THIRTY-EIGHT

MORGAN

I heard Jody's wail before I saw her face. She was in room 317, Ella by her side, wiping a cool cloth on her face. I stepped into the room, dropping my bag on the chair and rushing to her side. Jody screamed my name, crying like a school kid as a contraction ripped through her. Grappling for my hand, she squeezed my fingers tight and whimpered.

"It hurts."

"I know, sweetie." I kissed her forehead. "But you can do this. Breathe through the pain, just like you practiced."

"But we're only halfway through the classes," she wailed. "This is like way early! I'm not ready.

I'm not ready, Morgan."

She started hyperventilating, panic scoring her features as another contraction rolled over her. She tipped her head back and groaned, tears streaming from the corners of her eyes.

"Good work, Jody, honey." The obstetrician patted her knee. "You're doing great. It's going to be time to push soon."

"Already?" I squeezed Jody's hand.

"Yep, this one is ready to say hello to the world." I could hear the grin in the doctor's voice and smiled.

"Wow." I looked across at Ella who had tears welling in her eyes, her face alight with wonder. "I can't believe how fast this is happening."

"I'm not ready," Jody cried again, fear stark on her face. I knew exactly what she was talking about. Crunch time was just around the corner: keep or adopt was looming large, and she still hadn't made up her mind.

"It's okay. You'll know." I patted my chest. "In here. Just listen to your heart."

She nodded, her face bunching as another contraction blindsided her. Her grip on my hand intensified to painful. I winced and breathed in through my nose. Finally she relaxed, and I wriggled my fingers to try to get the blood flowing again.

Jody was out of breath, already exhausted after only three hours of labor. Ella updated me in between contractions, and I soon had the full story. Cole had called once to let us know that Dad had gone down to collect Grandma Deb, and they would be here waiting as soon as the baby was born.

I looked at the clock. It was past midnight. Jody's baby was going to be born on May 12th...a date we would never forget no matter what her decision.

"Okay, Jody. It's time to start pushing, sweetie, so when that next contraction hits, I want you to bear down and go for it."

She pulled in a shaky breath, looking like a lost kid as she gazed up at me.

I smiled and gave her hand a light squeeze. "It's nearly over," I reassured her, before shooting Ella a nervous glance.

Her smile was soft and calm. She kissed Jody's cheek just as the next contraction came on. Helping her sit up, we repeated the doctor's words, coaching her through the first push.

By the tenth push, my arms were cooked spaghetti as we lowered her back down.

"I can't do this anymore," Jody whimpered.

"Yes you can, Jody." The doctor's voice was firm. "Only a few more to go. You're nearly there. Let's do it."

The contraction followed the doctor's words and Jody sat forward, a scream ripping out of her as she strained to set the baby free.

Ten minutes later a feeble cry whispered into the air, growing in fervor as a small, pink body was lifted away from Jody. Ella and I stared at each other, our lips parted in wonder as we listened to the sound.

Jody lay back, an exhausted mess, her chest heaving.

"Well done." I kissed her forehead, feeling more proud of her than I ever had.

She replied with a shaky smile, tears brimming on her lashes.

The doctor's voice was soft as she approached the bed. "She's all checked out and healthy, doesn't need the incubator and seems to be sucking fine."

I breathed a sigh of relief.

The doctor placed her hand on Jody's arm. "Do

you want to hold her, or should we take her straight to the nursery?"

Jody sucked her lower lip, her bright eyes searching mine.

"It's your choice." I nodded.

"A girl," she whispered.

I grinned at her awestruck whisper.

"I need to hold her." She hiccuped over the words, stretching out her arms as the nurse carried the bundle over. The little thing was still wailing pitifully as the nurse placed her in the crook of Jody's elbow.

Jody's fingers were shaking as she gently skimmed her daughter's face. "Oh you're beautiful," she breathed. "Like a little cherub."

The baby stopped crying as soon as she registered Jody's voice, looking straight up at her with dark-blue eyes.

Jody let out a laughing sob. "Hello, baby girl."

With that, the baby turned her head and started nuzzling, hunting for a new lifeline now that her umbilical cord was gone.

Without missing a beat, Jody arranged her top while the nurse moved Ella out of the way so she could help the baby latch on.

"I guess we're keeping her then, huh?" I gently rubbed Jody's shoulder as Ella stepped up beside me, squeezing my hand.

"I have to." Jody whispered. "I just feel like I'm instantly in love with her. How is that possible?"

"It's possible." Ella blushed.

"I don't know if I'm cut out for this, you guys. I don't know if I'll be a very good mother or not, but I have to try." Jody ran a knuckle down her baby's cheek. "I made my decision the second I slept with Stefan. This little girl's mine, and I have to choose her and live with whatever consequences that brings."

I swallowed the lump in my throat, squeezing her shoulder with a nod, knowing she'd be okay. She was biting the bullet and living with the fallout, something I needed to do.

I thought of Sean waiting for me in the studio and wondered what he had to say to me.

"So what are you going to name her?" Ella brushed the baby's arm, looking completely enamored.

Jody gazed down at the girl and murmured, "My little angel, what should I call you?"

"Angelia," Ella softly sung the Richard Marx song and giggled. "She is like an angel."

"I love it." Jody grinned. In spite of her pasty skin and slick hair, she looked radiant.

"You do?" Ella's eyes rounded and she bit her lower lip before breaking into a wide grin.

"Yes. Angelia Morgan Pritchett. That's your name, little one," she whispered, stealing the air from my lungs.

"Jody, you don't have to do that."

She glanced at me, perplexed. "Of course I do. You're my rock, Morgan, and my daughter's going to carry your name, because you'll no doubt be her rock, as well."

I smiled and leaned my head against Jody's. We gazed down at the little dot in her arms. For some reason she felt like mine, too, and I knew without a doubt I could love her with all my heart.

Aunt Morgan. I shook my head with a grin.

"I bet she'll be a dancer," Ella whispered.

"And I bet she'll be able to sing like an angel, too."

We softly chuckled together; The Terrible Trio had just become a foursome.

THIRTY-NINE

SEAN

It was nearly four o'clock in the morning. I had no idea how much longer I'd have to wait, but I refused to leave. Not until Morgan got back and I could say what I needed to.

I pulled my jacket around myself, leaning on my elbow as I tried to get comfortable on the floor and doze off for a few minutes. I was gonna die at work. Part of me wanted to call in sick, but that would never fly, especially after my last conversation with Travis.

I scrubbed a hand over my face and cringed. There was nothing I could do about it now. The truth was out there, and I wasn't taking back a word of it.

The door clicked downstairs and I flinched, rising to my feet as I listened to the sound of someone trudging up the stairs.

I stood in the doorway waiting. Morgan looked tired, still dressed in her tights and fitted tank top. Her hair was mussed, ragged waves of hair breaking free of their tie. She looked cute.

I squashed my grin as she reached the top stair and jerked to a stop, her lips parting.

"You stayed?"

"I have two questions." I shrugged. "I'm not leaving until I get to ask 'em."

"It's four o'clock in the morning."

I gave her a sheepish smile. "I'm not leavin'."

My words unnerved her. She drew in a shaky breath and brushed past me, setting my heart alight.

Heading for the stereo, she collected her wallet and put it in her bag.

So that's why she'd come back. Not because she thought I'd be here, but because she'd forgotten her wallet.

Her lack of faith in me hurt, but I guessed I deserved it.

Dumping her bag onto one of the chairs lining the wall, she rubbed her eye and then looked at me.

"Okay, go."

"Is Jody okay?"

"That's your question?" She smirked.

"No," I chuckled, stepping toward her.

Her expression softened to marshmallow, her teeth brushing her lower lip as she rubbed the back of her neck. "She's now the proud mama of a little baby girl, Angelia. She decided to keep her."

Morgan blinked at tears and sniffed. One escaped, running down her cheek. I've never seen her cry before. My heart spasmed as I fought the urge to brush it away with my thumb. Her stance was still guarded, and I needed to play this right.

"She'll be a good mother." Morgan sniffed.

"And she has you, so that'll help."

Her smile was both happy and sad. Watching the emotions scuttle over her face hurt. I needed to get rid of that sad.

"Sean." She looked pained, whispering my name. "Why are you here?"

"Okay." I raised my hands, nerves attacking me with a force I hadn't counted on. I cleared my throat and adjusted my jacket. "Question one..." Stepping into her space, I gently took her fingers, running my thumb over her knuckles. "There's a big charity event coming up next month."

Her forehead wrinkled. "Are you talking about the Saito Film and Music Festival? That's gonna be huge, right?"

"Yeah, and I got an invite."

She raised her brows, but I could see she was only partially impressed.

"I wanted to ask you to come with me."

Her eyebrows remained high, but her lips dropped open...and stayed that way when I lowered myself to one knee and pulled a box from my jacket pocket.

"And I want you to go as my wife."

She snatched her hand back and took a step away from me, ignoring the diamond I'd just revealed.

"You want me to go to a massive televised event as your wife?"

"Yeah." I nodded, suddenly feeling stupid. Had I taken it too far?

"Won't Rhonda have a conniption if you turn up with me?"

I snapped the box closed and rose to my feet. "She doesn't work for me anymore."

Morgan's brown gaze nearly knocked me off my

feet. "Start talking."

"I fired her. I decided it was time to take care of my own career."

"You fired your manager." Morgan's tone was doubtful.

"Yeah." I nodded. "And the same day, I told Travis McKinnon that I won't re-sign unless he sends you an apology and starts treating his staff with a little more respect."

"You're gonna try and make Travis McKinnon apologize to me?"

"He treated you like shit; it's the least he can do."

"But..." She rubbed her temple. "You didn't sign for Season Two? I thought that was a given."

"I won't." My lips bunched tight as I shook my head. "Not until he gives me what I want, and I've told him I'm not afraid to go straight to his daddy if he doesn't budge."

"You played the Mr. Bank Account card? He must be livid."

I grinned. "Yeah, he's pretty pissed."

"What exactly did you say to him?"

"That no one treats my woman that way and if he wants me to work for him, then he needs to make right what he did wrong."

"I'm surprised he didn't fire you on the spot."

I hissed in a breath. "Harley's pretty popular. I think I'm worth more to Polychrome than he'd like to admit."

"So, you're jobless? Or..."

"I'm not sure yet." I shrugged. "He said he'd think about it."

Morgan shook her head again, disbelief making her forehead wrinkle. "I can't..."

I gripped the box in my hand, slipping it back into my jacket pocket as I closed the gap between us.

"I can't believe you did that," she whispered. "Your career is everything to you."

"Not everything. I love acting, but that's not what makes me truly happy." I brushed my thumb across her cheek. "I don't care what I do, Morgan. I just know I want to come home to you at the end of my day, and I'll fight to make that happen."

Gently wrapping my arm around her waist, I pulled her against me and started singing "Fight for You", like Harley had the day before. Except this time, I was holding the right girl and actually meaning every word.

I slid my hand up her body, my thumb brushing the side of her breast as she gripped my jacket. She wanted to kiss me; I could feel it.

The restless agitation within me settled, replaced with a new anticipation which had been lying dormant for the last three months.

I leaned toward her, whispering softly. "So, do you have any answers for me?"

After a painful pause, she grinned. "Two."

"Okay. Go." I smiled back, my stomach exploding with nerves I didn't even know I had.

"Yes, to the first." She swallowed. "And as much as I want to say yes to the second, I'm not ready. I will be one day, but not yet." Her lashes skimmed her cheeks as she closed her eyes and drew in a breath. "I don't think either of us are."

"Hey, I'm not going anywhere."

"I don't doubt your love, but you are a Hollywood Superstar."

I watched her pink lips say the words and immediately shook my head. "So cynical."

She smirked. "Realistic."

"Beautiful."

She pulled a face and a rush whipped through me, speeding down my body as I kissed her nose.

"Gorgeous."

Her neck.

"Exquisite."

Her chin.

I stopped to gaze into her soft brown eyes.

"Mine."

I captured her smile against my mouth, her fingers gripping my jacket and pulling me against her until our bodies were melded together.

I closed my eyes, losing myself in the feeling of something so familiar and sweet. Something so incredibly right.

I had no idea what the future held for us, and I'd be a liar if I didn't admit that I was a little scared, but I had Morgan now and that meant more than anything.

That meant I could face it all and still come away a happy man.

EPILOGUE

MORGAN

Ella fluffed with my hair, pinning a few stray curls into place before stepping back and pursing her lips to the side. She then attacked me with a can of hairspray.

I coughed, waving my arms in front of me and poking out my tongue. "Enough."

"Well, I want it to hold for the whole evening."

She jittered around me, checking my makeup and adjusting the necklace around my throat.

"My gosh, you're more nervous than I am."

Laughter tinkled out of her mouth. "I'm sorry. I'm excited. I'm going to get to see my best friend on TV. This is huge."

"Yeah, let's just hope the fashion police don't

have a field day."

I stood up and smoothed down the tight dress. Thank God there was a split in the side or I wouldn't be able to move.

"No offense, but even though you look super-hot and you're going with Sean Jaxon, no one's gonna be interested in you."

I smirked and gave Ella a quick wink. "Suits me fine."

"Perfect," she chirped, holding out a pair of heels for me.

We'd measured them, and I would be a little taller than Sean if I wore these. I really hoped he didn't mind, but they matched the dress perfectly.

"I saw a limo pull up." Jody burst through the door, Angelia wrapped to her front.

The day before Jody and the baby came home, Grandma Deb and I worked our way through town spending up a ridiculous amount on all things baby. Jody's room now housed a crib, a fully-loaded change table, and enough pink clothing to cover the floor space of the entire house.

But the one thing, used more than any other, was the baby sling wrapped around Jody's middle and over her shoulder. Angelia basically lived in it and was probably the most contented five-week-old the world had ever known.

I breathed out my jitters and wriggled my toes, making sure the shoes fit comfortably. Wrapping Ella in a quick cuddle, I turned to kiss Jody and sneak a peek inside the sling.

"Good night, Angel. Sleep well for Mommy tonight, okay?"

She was dead to the world, her rosebud lips hanging open, blissfully unaware of the life going on around her.

Jody kissed my cheek as the doorbell rang. "Have fun." In spite of the tired bags under her eyes, her cheesy smile was back.

"Thanks, Jo-Jo." I gave her one more kiss and then headed downstairs.

Dad had opened the door for Sean, and as soon as my man caught sight of me, he sucked in a breath and gave me that appreciative smile of his. The one that turned my legs to Jell-O.

A spike shot through my core, and I was already looking forward to spending the night at his place.

"I'll see you guys tomorrow." I waved to everyone before slipping my hand into Sean's and trotting down the stairs.

The driver closed the door behind us, and as soon as the door clicked, Sean grabbed me into his arms, pressing his lips into my neck and moaning pleasantly.

"You smell so good," he breathed. "Let's skip tonight and go back to mine." His hand snaked up my thigh, curving over my butt before settling on my hip.

I snickered. "As much as I want to do that, you need to go to this thing."

He sat back with a groan. "I know."

"At least you don't have to work tomorrow."

His grin was delicious as he squeezed my knee. "Baby, I don't got to work for another five weeks, if I don't want to."

"I still can't believe Travis gave in." I leaned my head against his shoulder, chuckling as I relived the arrogant man's terse phone call.

Sean snorted. "I still can't believe you accepted his lame-ass apology."

"It was enough." I shrugged, smoothing down his lapel. "You look really handsome."

He grinned at me, puffing out his chest and putting on a face.

I laughed and lightly slapped him.

"I got nothin' on you, baby." He found the split

in my dress, his eyebrows wiggling as he snaked his fingers under the fabric.

His hands felt divine on my skin, and I was tempted to see if he wanted to swing by the dance studio on the way. We were turning making love on the dance floor into an art form.

I pressed my lips together, quelling the urge. With Sean not working and the dance studio still just taking off, we were seeing more of each other than I thought we would.

I knew that would change the second Season Two of *Superstar* started filming, so I was taking all I could get.

"Hey, before we get there..." Sean turned to me, his expression sweet and earnest. He ran his thumb over my lips and gently kissed them. "I know you're not ready to wear the engagement ring I bought you, but I was wondering if you'd put this one back on." Rummaging in his pocket, he pulled out the sapphire ring he'd given me in January.

Tears popped into my eyes before I could stop them and with a quivery smile, I nodded a yes. He slipped it on just as the limo turned toward the Los Angeles Music Center.

I squeezed his hand, nerves powering through me so hard and fast, I felt lightheaded.

"You ready for this?" His blue eyes caught me, holding me steady.

"I'm ready for anything."

His smile was broad, his teeth pearly-white. I kissed his lips quickly before the driver opened the door. Sean stepped out first, a loud crescendo of cheers and screams rising from the crowd. He raised his hand in greeting before reaching back into the limo for me.

No one knew who I was, but the crowd didn't seem to care, too enamored by the *Superstar* celebrity to even notice me.

I held Sean's hand like a lifeline as we slowly made our way down the red carpet. He paused to sign a few autographs and shake hands. I hung back, letting him do his thing. To say it was overwhelming was an understatement. I felt like a minnow in a river of piranhas.

I drew my body tall and raised my chin.

Sean shifted back to my side, taking my hand and leading me further into the fray. That was when we hit the paparazzi. The bulbs flashed so bright and fast, I wondered if I'd be able to see again.

"Sean! Over here!"

I dropped his hand and moved back, letting him take center stage, but he turned and pulled me to his side, wrapping his arm around me.

"Got to introduce my woman to the world." He looked at me.

"But don't they want photos of just you?"

"Maybe, but they're gonna get photos of me and my goddess instead."

I grinned.

"Smile, baby." He kissed my cheek, claiming me in front of everyone.

Questions were fired our way: curious reporters wanting the goods on Sean Jaxon's mystery date. He ignored the calls and kept grinning.

"That's all I have to do? Smile?"

"Yep, it's that easy." He squeezed my waist. "Look as though you're happy to be here, but think about the fact that later tonight I'm going to take all your clothes off."

I snickered. "Oh really, and what are we gonna do after that?" My lips pulled tight, my smile turning plastic as I kept it in place for the cameras.

"Baby, we're gonna do the Sean and Morgan dance."

"Nice." I chuckled. "I like the sound of that."

He turned to me, gazing into my eyes as if the world around us didn't exist. "The best dance in the world. It's a lifelong one, did you know that?"

I drank him in, loving the seriousness of his expression. "Maybe it is," I conceded.

"Oh baby, it definitely is." He winked and then pressed his lips against mine.

The cameras started snapping like crazy, a frantic moment of light and sound, but I didn't see any of it. As I touched Sean's face, the flashing lights faded to nothing. Sean and I were wrapped in our own little bubble, untouchable and completely bulletproof.

*****

Thank you so much for reading Bulletproof. If you've enjoyed it and would like to show me some support, please consider leaving a review on the site you purchased this book from.

*****

If you'd like to stay up to date with the SONGBIRD SERIES, please sign up for the newsletter, which will include cover reveals, teasers, and new release info for all the Songbird Novels.

http://eepurl.com/1cqdj

.

ACKNOWLEDGEMENTS

Working on a novel like this is pure joy for me. Part of what makes the experience so special is the awesome talent I get to work with.

Thank you so much to:

My critique readers: Cassie, Anna and Brenda. As always, your feedback and suggestions strengthened this story.

My editor: Laurie. You are such a great editor. I love your style.

My proofreaders: Kristin, Suzy, Lindsey and Karen. Thank you for spotting those last-minute mistakes.

My cover designer and photographer: Regina. Love your work, babe. You are such a talent, and it's an honor to have you as part of this project.

My publicity team: Mark My Words Publicity. Thank you!!!! Rachel and Ashley, you are so professional and amazing, plus two of the nicest people I've ever worked with. Love you girls so much.

My fellow writers: Inklings and Indie Inked. I love that I can come to you with every celebration and woe. You make this journey fantastic.

My readers: Love you guys! Thanks for your continued support.

My family: Thank you for understanding my passion and letting me rabbit on about it.

My savior: Thank you for being that constant peace inside of me. I know I can get through anything as long as you're there. You make me bulletproof and I love you.

OTHER BOOKS BY MELISSA PEARL

The Songbird Series

Fever

Coming in 2015:

Everything — Home — Lucky

The Fugitive Series

I Know Lucy — Set Me Free

Coming in 2015:

I'll Find You — I'm Not Lying

The Masks Series

True Colors — Two-Faced

Releasing Jan & Feb 2015:

Snake Eyes — Poker Face

The Time Spirit Trilogy

Golden Blood — Black Blood — Pure Blood

The Betwixt Series

Betwixt — Before — Beyond

The Elements Trilogy

Unknown — Unseen — Unleashed

The Mica & Lexy Series

Coming in 2015!

http://www.melissapearlauthor.com

ABOUT MELISSA PEARL

Melissa Pearl is a kiwi at heart, but currently lives in Suzhou, China with her husband and two sons. She trained as an elementary school teacher, but has always had a passion for writing and finally completed her first manuscript in 2003. She has been writing ever since and the more she learns, the more she loves it.

She writes young adult and new adult fiction in a variety of romance genres - paranormal, fantasy, suspense, and contemporary. Her goal as a writer is to give readers the pleasure of escaping their everyday lives for a while and losing themselves in a journey…one that will make them laugh, cry and swoon.

MELISSA PEARL ONLINE

Website:

melissapearlauthor.com

YouTube Channel:

youtube.com/user/melissapearlauthor

Facebook:

facebook.com/melissapearlauthor

Twitter:

twitter.com/MelissaPearlG

Pinterest:

pinterest.com/melissapearlg/

You can also subscribe to Melissa Pearl's Book Updates Newsletter. You will be the first to know about any book news, new releases and giveaways.

http://eepurl.com/p3g8v

CPSIA information can be obtained at www.ICGtesting.com
Printed in the USA
LVOW08s0418131016

508538LV00003BA/191/P